I0534630

SECOND ACT
Second Chances Series, Book 1

By Marsha R. West

Copyright

SECOND ACT, Second Chances Series, Book 1

© 2015 by Marsha R. West

Cover Art © by Charlotte Volnek

Editor Grace Kone of editsbyBFF

All rights reserved. No part of this book may be reproduced or transmitted in any form or by any means, electronic or mechanical, including photocopying, recording, or by any information storage and retrieval system, without permission in writing from the publisher.

The characters and events portrayed in this book are fictitious. Any similarity to real persons, living or dear, or events, is coincidental and not intended by the author.

Print and e-version published by MRW Press LLC and released March 2015.

ACKNOWLEDGMENTS

The number of people it takes to bring a book to publication still amazes me. The small and large tweaks that happen with the passing of each new gaze upon the pages continually shape the manuscript. Many writer friends over the years have looked at my writing and given me feedback. I'd like to recognize my first critique partners, who though they've not read this book, still influence my writing Jerrie Alexander and Jeannie Guzman. Thanks also to Melinda Smith for the original idea for the book.

Thanks to my editor Grace Kone of editsbyBFF, my cover artist Charlotte Volnek. I so could not manage without them. Special thanks to the followers of my blog who helped with the naming of this book and the series: Susan Bernhardt, Brenda Gayle, Rhianna Ulrich, Kate Wyland, Heather Frazier Brainard, Vicki Batman, Brenda Rumsley, Kenneth Hicks, Jerrie Alexander, Jo-Ann Carson, and JQ Rose.

While Margie Lawson hasn't looked at any of this book, her guidance with my first book led to publication and thus to my third book. Thanks, Margie.

None of this would be possible without the support of my wonderful husband Bob West, who shares his time so generously to edit my books and make suggestions to improve them, not to mention helping with the business end of things.

Any errors, however, are my own. I hope you enjoy the Second Chances Series, Book 1.

Table of Contents

CHAPTER ONE

Monday, September 24

"You promised this wouldn't happen again, Clay." Addison Greer glared at the man sitting across from her in her Cowtown Theatre office, the pitch of her voice higher than she intended. She hated confrontations, but those red numbers marching across the spreadsheets covering her desk made her stomach roil and her hands shake.

"Yeah, I know, Addison. I needed more wood than I'd anticipated. After we put the first set together, it didn't work out, and we had to start over. It wasn't my fault." His leg draped over the arm of the chair as if he had no worries, but his voice had taken on the whiny tone that sent Addie's blood pressure into the stratosphere.

Her fingers tightened around the marker she'd used to highlight the deficits. "No? Then whose? Going over budget isn't an option, Clay. The theatre can't survive this way, and since you can't change, you won't make it here either." Addison hated to put it that way, but damn, she'd been plenty patient with Clay Bennett, the theatre's artistic director.

"What do you mean, *I won't make it*. Are you threatening my job?" He set both feet solidly on the floor, jutted out his chin, and clenched his hands on the arms of the chair.

Good thing she wasn't alone in the building with him. She suspected he'd like to take a swing at her. The first show of the fall season closed last night, and crewmembers were working all over the place disassembling the set, cleaning the costumes, and evaluating make-up needs.

"That's exactly what I mean, Clay." The steel in her voice was unmistakable. She had to make him understand. "We had full houses during the run of the show, but we didn't make enough to pay for the production. You have failed consistently to bring in shows on or under budget. I won't let you continue to drown us in red ink."

She shoved the pages on her desk in his direction. He glanced at the sheets and broke into hysterical laughter. Chills scampered down her back like mice escaping a cat. The man was a creative genius and scary as hell right now, but Addie wouldn't cut him any slack on the financial issue. She'd given him enough second chances to last two careers.

"Being executive director doesn't give you the power to fire me, unless you get the support of a supermajority of the board." His lip curled into a sneer that matched his voice. "And you don't have that." He stood up and walked toward the door. His knuckles whitened on the knob before he yanked it open and turned to face her.

"Don't fuck with me, Addison. You'll lose." His whiny tone switched to a menacing one.

Her face warmed with the rush of blood at his language. She stood, met his gaze, and clenched her hands into such tight balls the nails cut into her palms. "You mess with this theatre, and I'll make you sorry, Clay Bennett."

"Everything okay?" Big, burly, redheaded Pete Talmadge stopped outside her office. Despite many years in Texas, his voice still held remnants of his New Jersey upbringing.

Their words had apparently traveled into the hallway. *Not particularly professional, Addie. Nor adult.*

"Everything is fine." She glanced at him then back at her AD. "Clay, I've been clear with you, and this meeting is over."

Clay pushed past the stage manager. His high-pitched laugh sent chills crawling up the back of Addie's head. Her temper, which she hadn't yet fully controlled, sparked. "Damn, damn, damn, damn." The words spewed from her gut. The pain in her middle doubled her over. Confrontations, regardless of how they turned out made her ill. When she lost her temper, she lost self-respect.

Pete stepped in and shut the door behind him. "So, are you auditioning for the part of Henry Higgins in some sort of reverse gender production of *My Fair Lady*? I suppose it might fly here in Fort Worth." He laughed at his joke.

Addie threw her pencil at him. He ducked, and it fell to the floor. "I guess everyone heard us. I hate to air the dirty linen in front of others."

"Yeah, well, don't let him get to you. He's a jackass, and many of us know that," he said in the gravelly voice of a long-time smoker.

"He's right though, Pete." Air rushed out on a long sigh, and she flopped into her swivel chair. "I can't fire him unless I can convince a majority of the board, plus one more, to support the action. He's got at least three members wrapped up in his hip pocket."

"Shannon DeWitt is one of them."

"I've never understood her support of him, so she's a prime target for me to change her mind. She's a smart woman. If I show her the financials from this production and the ones last spring, she'll get why I'm concerned. The numbers don't balance." Addie doodled with a red marker on one of the printouts.

"Who are his other champions?" Pete leaned against the wall, crossed his hands over his chest, and cocked one ankle over the other.

"James Duffy and Linda Alexander."

"Well, we know why he's got Linda in his court." He waggled his eyebrows and twirled an imaginary mustache.

"Pete." She dragged out his name in a scolding tone. "We don't *know* anything about that. It's just nasty speculation on the part of folks who ought to keep their opinions to themselves."

"You're too nice for your own good, Addie. Their relationship is a conflict of interest."

"Suspected relationship and I'm not the morals police. They're consenting adults. Sure makes the situation awkward, though." She rested her head on her hands for a minute before lifting her thick black hair off her neck.

"I'm not blind, and neither is the crew or cast." Pete walked behind her desk and kneaded the tension in her shoulders. "We know what you're dealing with, and most of us are behind you."

His words and touch comforted, but that was all. It would be nice if a spark or zing of some kind enveloped her. A good, strong man, he'd indicated an interest, but she'd been unable to reciprocate beyond an appreciation for his friendship. Maybe she'd never feel that excitement in the belly again. To experience a relationship, you have to trust. Addie wasn't sure she'd ever be able to do that after what her ex had done.

"Mmmm." She shrugged her shoulders into the pressure. Not as good as going in to see Mary Jane for a full body massage, but nice. "Thanks, Pete, and I appreciate having the staff support." Addie smiled up at him and patted his hand but then her lips drooped. "Who is in the other camp?" She hated to ask but needed to know.

Pete squeezed her shoulders once more and walked toward the door. "Clay snowed a couple of the younger, temporary ensemble members with his experience on Broadway. The permanent staff is with you." Pete leaned down and picked up the yellow pencil from where it had landed. He tossed it to her and touched his hand to his head in a mock salute. "You're welcome." He pushed through the door.

Addie fished in her pocket for her cell and searched for her important numbers. She placed the call to Shannon DeWitt.

◆ ◆ ◆

Wednesday, September 26

"I'm sorry I couldn't come in to see you earlier, Addie." Shannon spoke in low cultured tones. She didn't sound like she'd grown up in Fort Worth, but she had.

"That's all right. I appreciate you squeezing me into your schedule. Can I get you some coffee?" Addie moved to the credenza on the sidewall.

"Sure. Unusually early cold front out there." Shannon loosened her fur coat and sank into the chair in front of the desk while Addison set out the mugs.

"You take this black, don't you?" She poured the coffee.

"Yes, thanks." Shannon smoothed out unnoticeable wrinkles in her mid-calf-length wool skirt. It was the exact shade as her boots.

Addie settled herself in her desk chair, took a quick sip from her mug, savoring the caffeine zing before she leaned forward. "Shannon, you've always done a terrific job on our board. You ask good questions, and you come up with logical suggestions when addressing concerns."

"Thanks. I've enjoyed the work. It's one of my favorite boards to serve on."

"I asked you to stop by so I could go over some of our financial statements with you." Addie pushed up the sleeves of her sweater and laid a spreadsheet on the desk in front of the board member.

"This is about Clay, isn't it?" Using a red shiny nail, Shannon drew the paper closer.

Addie nodded. "He's gone over budget on the last three

shows and only broke even for the summer shows. I know you've been one of his supporters. No one can fault the man for the results. The shows have been well received by audiences and the press."

"But your job is to keep us financially solvent." Shannon drew her index finger across the figures before she met Addie's gaze.

"That's right." Addie folded her hands on top of the desk and leaned toward the woman she needed as an ally. "At this point, it won't matter how much we bring in on the fundraiser, we'll be swimming in red ink before the end of the year. I'm talking personally with you and two other board members to make sure you see the financial crises looming."

"At some point, you probably need to look at changing the bylaws, so it doesn't take more than a simple majority of the board to fire the artistic director." Shannon took a sip of the coffee. "Strong. I like it this way."

"In the meantime, all I can do is talk with you three and try to make sure everyone understands the numbers. If I can do that, then I should get the votes."

"Are you sure it's the only way? Can't you give him a second chance?"

"I talked with Clay after the shows last fall, and in the spring he went over budget again. I warned him then. We did better this summer, but now after this first show of the season we're in the red again. We can't have another year like the last one. He's had his share of second chances." Addie unclenched her hands before she gripped her cup and took a swallow of coffee. She had to convince this woman.

"Who approves his spending?"

"Roger Garland, our accountant." Addie set down the mug with care not to spill. "I've told him I want to see every bill before he pays them, but he hasn't always done that. Roger I can fire if he doesn't straighten up." She let out a rueful chuckle. "I don't need the board's approval."

"May I take these reports home and study them, Addie?"

"Of course. Those are your copies."

"I appreciate what we're trying to do here—affordable, high quality theatre." Shannon stood and slipped her arms into the sleeves of her coat. "I'll let you know my decision soon." She walked toward the closed door. "In the meantime, we have the fundraiser, and maybe that will get us over the crises. Thanks for the coffee. I'll be in touch."

Addison dropped her head in her hands.

And that was the board member she had the best chance to sway. Damn, the next two visits would really be tough. She stood and paced toward the windows and stared out at the parking lot with its smattering of cars and trucks. Cold air seemed to seep through. She shivered.

Since Shannon was iffy, she'd have to meet with the other two board members. Might as well go ahead and set up the next appointment. That'd be Linda Alexander, who had tons of money. Addie huffed out a long sigh. She wasn't looking forward to the meeting because she was relatively certain the rumors about Linda and Clay were correct. It just made everything so awkward. Straightening her shoulders, she walked back to the desk and punched in Linda's number.

"Hey, Linda, it's Addison Greer. I wondered if you have time to come in today or tomorrow. I'd like to talk with you."

"What's it about, Addison? I have tennis this afternoon, a massage in the morning, a facial later tomorrow." Linda's twangy Texas accent grated on Addie more than anyone else's did. "Couldn't we handle whatever it is on the phone?"

Not the kind of conversation Addie wanted to have on the phone. "How about the day after tomorrow. Any time then?"

"Not good either. What's this about?"

Addie gripped the cell so tight her fingers grew numb. "I want to talk with you about our budget." Linda's slight gasp made Addie grit her teeth while she waited for a response.

"Addison, if this concerns the rumors I've heard about of your efforts to fire Clay, then we don't need to talk in person. I won't support that action."

"But, Linda—"

"Don't mention it to me again. Goodbye." *Click.* The conversation was over.

Well, that was a total bomb. Addie leaned back in her chair, drained. She wasn't up to facing James Duffy right now, even over the phone. Besides, she had a meeting in thirty minutes with the planning committee for the fundraiser. They were holding the dinner in the large, glassed-in lobby, the auction in the theatre itself. For entertainment, the kids in their Children's Theatre and some of the adult ensemble players had prepared several numbers to present on stage.

In years past, they'd brought in a high profile performer and charged a lot for the tickets. As a community theatre and given the hard economic times, Addie had insisted they change in order to keep ticket prices lower and encourage more people to come. After initially balking, the board had gone along. Now it looked like the numbers were going to prove her right. They'd never sold so many tickets.

She set a fresh pot of coffee to perking and then pulled out the folders she needed for the planning committee. Even if this shindig were spectacular, the theatre would be financially hurting. As long as Clay held the position of artistic director, Cowtown Theatre remained at risk.

◆ ◆ ◆

Friday, September 28

"I'm always glad to make time for a board member. What can I do for you?" Clay asked the attractive woman sitting across from him. Shannon DeWitt had a lot of dough, so she could afford all the latest nips and tucks available to the very wealthy. He added cream to his coffee and stirred, waiting.

Shannon leaned against the booth in the rear of the coffee shop. "Why did you lie to me when I asked you about the financials?"

"I didn't lie to you." He sipped his coffee.

"Well, of course, you did, and you're doing it now. When I told you it looked like the last three big shows had lost money, you assured me that wasn't the case. Just a matter of the way the numbers were showing up, you said."

"Now, Shannon, take it easy. We may have lost a little, but we made money on the summer shows, so it's all good." He twisted the coffee cup in the saucer. Who did she think she was to question him?

"What's the matter with you? Do you think I'm stupid and not able to understand the statements? We broke even on the summer shows. That's not the same as making money." She raised one hand and rubbed her temple. "You're giving me a headache." With the fingers of the other hand, she massaged the area between her eyes. She heaved a sigh, dropped her hands, and straightened on the bench. "Listen, I want to be upfront with you, even if you haven't been with me."

He choked on a sip of coffee. What did the bitch mean?

"I won't continue to back you at board meetings. If Addison proposes firing you, I'll vote with her."

Clay's heart raced. Blood surged to his face. He struggled not to throw the rest of the coffee in her face.

"You've got tons of talent, Clay, but you have no self-discipline. You've got to follow the rules." She stood. "I'll pay for my coffee." She placed a five on the table. Without a backward glance, she stalked out, a woman sure of her power.

Clay drummed his fingers on the countertop. Fortunately, he had time to figure out his next steps. They'd just had a board meeting, so it'd be four more weeks before he had to make a reckoning on the books. Before then, they had the fundraiser, and with any luck that would bring in a chunk of dough. If not...well, he'd make Shannon sorry for threatening to pull her support. There'd be consequences.

♦ ♦ ♦

Thursday, October 4

Was the dress too much? Addie studied herself in the full-length mirror behind her bedroom door. A school night, so both her children were home. She could count on Jeremy's honest opinion. Elizabeth, in all of her Goth regalia and anti-mom sentiment wouldn't share her thoughts—if she took an ounce of interest in what her mother looked like.

She shook her head. Worry about Elizabeth would have to take place another time. Tonight was for the theatre.

Addie had intended to go with basic black, but Stanley James specialty store had this incredible blue concoction on sale. Okay, time for the unveiling. Addie opened the door and glided toward the den where the TV volume blared the latest blockbuster movie. She didn't get Jeremy's fascination with action flicks.

"Wow, Mom." Jeremy's pitch jacked up a couple decibels higher than his usual low register.

"Is it too much? I can change into the black I wore last year."

"I'd say it's perfect." He got up off the sofa, rising to his almost six feet, and circled her. "I'll be surprised if you don't pick yourself up a guy."

"Eeew. What's with you, Jeremy?" Elizabeth slouched farther back onto the leather sofa.

"Where are you with homework, guys?" Elizabeth hated when her mother asked, but Addie had learned that without pushing, her daughter didn't do her work, or she turned it in late.

"Mine's done." Jeremy made for the kitchen, his favorite room in the house.

No problems from him. It really wasn't Elizabeth's fault she had issues. It was her father, who only showed interest in his son. Addie should've left him sooner, before he psychologically damaged his daughter. Guilt burned a sour hole in Addie's stomach.

"What about you, Elizabeth?"

"I've got a couple of chapters to read in my English lit book. I'll get'em done."

"Probably not while watching this movie. Read in your room then you can come back to the television." Boy, it was hard being the disciplinarian.

Jeremy wandered back into the living room. "Are you driving, Mom?" He took a bite of a red juicy apple.

"No. Pete Talmadge said he'd pick me up."

"Good, then I don't have to worry about you drinking and driving." Jeremy laughed at how he'd turned around her usual lecture to her children.

The doorbell chimed.

"That's probably Pete now. Don't wait up for me." Addie ruffled Jeremy's hair and reached out to hug Elizabeth, who pulled back from the gesture. Addie glanced at Jeremy. His shoulders hiked in that what-are-you-gonna-do-shrug. She turned away, headed to the entry hall where she unlocked and pulled open the front door.

"Wow, Addie. Look at you." Pete eyed her up and down.

"That's two wows. The dress must work."

"Who was the other one from?"

"Jeremy."

Pete helped her into a cape. "You're stunning."

"Thanks. Let's go see how much money we can raise." She slid her hand into the crook of his arm, a smidge of remorse for using him raising its head, but she pushed it away. Just the way she shoved aside the memory of the uncomfortable conversation with board member James Duffy she'd held this afternoon. He'd refused to say anything to her about why he steadfastly supported Clay and wouldn't listen to her money concerns. She and the theatre needed this night to be a success.

◆ ◆ ◆

Mike Riley gripped the champagne glass. How the hell had he allowed Cindy to browbeat him again into putting on a tuxedo and coming to another fancy shindig? The women in their low-cut glittery dresses and the men in their expensive tuxedos mingled in the crowded theatre logia. His finger stole up to loosen the collar. He didn't usually fasten the top button. He'd refused to go the bow tie route and wore a western string tie, otherwise he'd have strangled for sure.

"Mike Riley, what am I going to do with you?" His sister-in-law, draped in something gold with a glass of champagne in her hand, waltzed up with his brother Pat close behind.

"You don't need to do anything, Cindy. I'm here like I promised."

"But you wore your western boots." Her pretty face wore a definite frown when she made eye contact with him.

He lifted a boot and glanced down. They were clean. He hadn't tracked in manure or mud. "They're my best ones." He took a quick swallow from his glass. What he'd give for a beer, rather than this piss poor, fizzy white wine.

Cindy shook her head at him and slid her free arm through one of his. "Come on. I want you to meet someone."

He dug in his heels. "Now wait just a damn minute. You didn't say anything about meeting anyone. Just that I had to come and spend money. I've done both, and now you should let me go home."

"She's little, bro, but it's easier to give in when she's made up her mind. It's what the kids and I do." Pat slung an arm around Mike's shoulder and nodded sagely, as if the two years Mike had on him at forty-seven didn't matter.

"Okay. Okay. I give. Who is it this time?" Please let it be a man friend. He was tired of Cindy's matchmaking efforts.

"She's beautiful." His sister-in-law said with something of a sing-song pitch.

Okay, not a guy.

Cindy handed her glass to her husband and then tugged at Mike's string tie. Pat rolled his eyes when Mike looked at him for help.

"She's smart, a friend, and Cowtown Theatre's executive director. I've really enjoyed getting to know her since joining the board a couple of months ago." Cindy retrieved her glass and led them around the concourse. "I don't remember you ever coming here before I started on the board, Pat. How about you, Mike?"

"Nah." Mike shook his head.

"How can you have grown up in Fort Worth and never come to Cowtown Theatre?"

"We spent our time on horseback, rodeoing," Mike said.

"Well, I know, but seeing plays and musicals is an important part of being well rounded."

"I didn't interfere with you bringing the kids, now did I, Cindy?"

She smiled. "No you did not. As if you could've stopped me." A short chuckle popped out of his sister-in-law's mouth. "Addie will be mobbed with people, but I'm sure she'll give us a moment."

Directly ahead, eight to ten people clustered in a group.

"Excuse me. Pardon me." Cindy politely elbowed her way through to the center of the crowd. Pat and Mike followed along like dutiful puppies, making their own apologies.

Mike stopped. He worked to close his mouth, which had dropped open. A raven-haired woman in a long, strapless dress stood before him talking with a short, white-haired man. Her voice had a low mellow tone with only a hint of a Texas accent, unlike his and Pat's which left no doubt as to their state of origin.

"Mr. Simmons, we can't thank you enough for your support. Your money is allowing us to provide ten scholarships for children to attend our summer program."

"Glad to hear that, Addison. Mother asked me right before she died to spend some of Daddy's money supporting the arts. I've tried to follow her wishes. I'm sorry I can't stay longer, but I have an early morning meeting." He took her hand and in a European fashion kissed it. Lingering way longer than necessary to Mike's way of thinking. Not that it mattered to him one whit. Still...

"Addie, I want you to meet some people." Cindy pushed up close to the woman with the sultry voice and blue eyes that matched the dress.

"Hey, Cindy. Your decorations are a hit. I've heard rave reviews." The executive director smiled at his sister-in-law.

"We had fun. Glad people like what we did. Addie, I want you to meet my husband, Pat."

"Thank you for sharing your wife with us." The woman extended her hand, and it was lost in Pat's large one. "She's a great addition to the board."

"My pleasure, Ms. Greer. She tells me she's enjoying herself."

"Oh, please, call me Addie. I feel like I know you from what Cindy's told me. You're a pediatric oncologist. Must be heart-wrenching work sometimes," she said with something of a tremble in her voice.

"Yes, but often just as uplifting when you see the will these little patients have to battle the disease. They and their families make you appreciate your blessings."

"And this is my brother-in-law, Mike." Cindy pulled him forward.

Now those blue eyes fastened on him as they had his brother. Mike's pulse skipped a beat. Hell. Why had he worn his stupid boots? He wished he had on a highly polished pair of shoes like the ones Pat wore. Even one of those strangling bow ties. Anything to make him seem acceptable to this woman.

"Cindy mentioned that you're a detective." She emphasized the job title.

"Yes, ma'am." Mike held the woman's hand longer than necessary, too. She was gorgeous, and the warmth sent from her sparkling eyes and smiling face spread through him. If he'd worn his western hat, he'd have yanked it off and fiddled nervously with the brim.

"You and Pat certainly chose very intense professions."

"You might say." He was like a teenager with his first crush. A waiter passed by, and he set his half-empty glass on the tray. Wouldn't do to drop it. He'd look like the ass he felt.

"You didn't finish your champagne, detective. Don't you like it?" A small crease formed between her eyebrows, apparently worried the champagne they'd chosen had failed to find favor with him. She tipped her head, waiting for him to answer, as if it were important to her.

"Well, ma'am, I just prefer beer."

A laugh burst from her mouth, and the corners turned upward, a small dimple winked at him. The laugh morphed into a giggle, which she tried to smother with her fingers. Fingers he'd love to taste, as well as her rose-colored lips.

"I'm so sorry, detective. I'm not laughing at you."

"No?" He couldn't help but smile at her, even if she were making fun of him.

"Addie, I'd love it if you could join us for supper one night soon." His sister-in-law's voice broke through.

Mike blinked a couple of times and raised his head. A smile played about his sister-in-law's mouth. Her eyes twinkled, as if she'd discovered a secret. Cindy broke the spell Addison Greer had wound around him. For a while there, no one else in the whole theatre lobby had existed except the lovely executive director. She was a potent personality. Little wonder so many people thronged the theatre this evening.

Vibration from his phone drew his attention from Cindy and Pat's conversation with the woman. "Excuse me." He nodded at Pat and turned away. Must be a busy night. He was a couple of detectives down on the list or he'd have never come to the fundraiser at all.

He spoke into his cell. "Riley." Hell. Someone had discovered a body out behind an east-side elementary school. He disconnected. "I'm sorry, folks, I've got to run."

"I'm sorry, too, Mike." Cindy leaned up and kissed him on the cheek. "How about I find a time the four of us can get together for supper? Okay?"

What could he say to that? He'd like to have supper with Addison Greer, just not with Cindy and Pat present, but he'd take what he could get. "Sure, Cindy, if Ms. Greer's willing."

♦ ♦ ♦

"It's Addie, and I'll look forward to the next time." She smiled what she hoped was one of her most encouraging smiles.

He touched his forehead as if to tip a hat she bet he wore most of the time. His boots knocked on the stone floor as his rapid steps carried him toward the door. An interesting man. Maybe Jeremy had been right about tonight. She turned back to Cindy and Pat. "Has he gotten called out on a murder?"

Pat nodded. "Probably so."

"Hopefully, that won't happen next time. I'll see if we can't work it out so neither of you is on call, Pat." Cindy shook her head. "That won't be easy, but my brother-in-law is a neat guy and worth the effort."

"Ms. Greer, pardon me for interrupting, but I'd love to talk with you if you have some time." A tall, distinguished-looking man with silver hair stepped into their circle.

Jonathan Harding was someone Addie wanted to talk with, too. She introduced the three. "Cindy is one of our board members."

"We don't want to monopolize you," Cindy said. "It was nice to meet you, Mr. Harding. Come on, Pat. There are still a couple of auction items crying out for my bid." She looped her arm through Pat's and headed toward the tables.

The Rileys walked away, and Addie turned toward Mr. Harding. "I'm pleased you could come tonight."

"So am I. Let's wander over to the bar. Neither of us has

a drink in hand. Doesn't seem right."

Addie laughed and walked along beside the older investor. She hoped she'd be able to convince him to put a considerable amount of money into the theatre. After getting her white wine and his Scotch, they settled onto one of the banquettes near the plate glass windows.

"Will it be too chilly for you here?" Harding's gaze trailed across her bare shoulders.

"No, I'm fine, thank you. What can I tell you about our theatre to convince you of the good work we do here and how much satisfaction you'd get from your involvement?"

And so the evening went.

Addie talked with almost everyone there at least once. She'd visited longer than she should have with an old friend, Katherine Thompson, and made a point to introduce her to Cindy, Pat, and to Jonathan Harding. Kate and Addie had been friends since meeting at a camp in East Texas the summer after they were in second grade. The Rileys and Mr. Harding could be important in her life, and she wanted them all to know each other.

◆ ◆ ◆

The last patrons left, and Charlie Haskins, the police officer Addie usually hired when an event was taking place at the theatre, flipped the lock on the front door.

"Thanks, Charlie." Addie patted his arm.

"No problems tonight, Ms. Greer."

"I'm sure that's in part because of your presence. This is a case of the old adage, *An ounce of prevention...*"

Charlie chuckled and laid a hand on his stomach. "It's more than an ounce in my case." He didn't exactly bulge over his belt, but he was a large man.

"Roger will have your check for you in the morning, Charlie, if you can stop by."

"No problem. I'll be here until the last of the staff drives off." He nodded and ambled toward the back areas of the theatre.

The staff and board celebrated with a champagne toast. Just a hasty count of bids added to what they'd made on ticket sales indicated they'd raised a couple of hundred thousand. They weren't out of the woods, but the situation wasn't as bleak as before the evening began. Addie hadn't gotten a commitment from Harding yet, but he'd agreed to meet with her next week. She had to reel him in. If she couldn't, this might be the last year for the theatre.

CHAPTER TWO

Friday, October 5

Everyone else had already arrived at Cowtown Theatre the morning after the fundraiser before Clay did. He'd wanted to blow the day off but thought better of it. No reason to rile Addie more than necessary. Well, well. Clay stopped to take in Missy Alexander's considerable charms. Bent over a table she was trying to shove out of the way, Missy, the youngest of the ensemble girls, wore a tank top and yoga pants that left little to the imagination. One cute ass. Clay squeezed his hands together in anticipation of the coming fun.

He stepped right up behind her before he spoke. "Need some help, Missy?"

She jumped, "Oh," and turned toward him, putting her delicious little orbs within easy reach. "Clay. I didn't hear you come in."

He dropped his eyes to her boobs then slid up to her lips and finally to her big blue eyes.

He resisted the urge to brush against her. "You know, Missy. I've been watching you."

"You have?"

Her whisper warmed places in Clay he liked to have

warmed. She tried to lean away, but she didn't have room. He placed both of his palms on the table behind her, bringing his growing erection within an inch of her body.

"I've been thinking you might be ready for more important work in our next production. How would you like that?" He let his eyes roam across her face and down to her breasts again.

"Oh, my gosh." Her voice rose an octave. "I'd love an opportunity to show you what I can do." Clay liked the breathy quality of her voice.

"I'd like to see that, Missy. I'll call you, and we'll set up a private audition. I wouldn't want to take a chance of embarrassing you if it didn't work out." He trailed his fingers down her arm.

"Thank you, Clay. I know I can do it. You won't be disappointed." She threw both arms around him in a grateful hug.

Her sweet little body pressed against him sent an electric charge through his system.

"Clay."

He jerked back from the girl and glanced over his shoulder. Who would be standing near but Shannon DeWitt? Crap.

"Run along, Missy." He squeezed her hand. "We'll visit later."

"Thanks." She literally skipped off into the theatre proper.

"That didn't look good, Clay." Shannon's tone was sharp.

"Addie almost didn't hire Missy for the ensemble because she's so young."

He crossed to the woman. "Stay out of what's not your business, Shannon."

"I believe this is my business. I'll add this little interlude to what I'll talk with Addie about." She stormed away.

He'd have been better staying at home today aside from the wonderful little brush up against Missy. Clay didn't need this hassle from the DeWitt woman. He spun on his heel and slammed out of the building, climbed into his car, and headed to the little store where he bought his stash. He wasn't out, but he'd need some more when Missy came over to visit. Anticipation brought a smile to his face.

After parking in the run-down strip shopping center, Clay stepped into the small establishment, pausing to give his eyes a moment to adjust to the dimness. Then he headed toward the back of the store but jerked to a stop. Well, hell. Elizabeth Greer all decked out in flowing black skirts and top with black hair with a red streak slithered around the end of an aisle. What was she doing here? This could be interesting. Her mother was always so high and mighty. *Yeah. Let's see what you're up to, Miss Goth.*

"Elizabeth." A young man with a backpack slung over one shoulder approached her.

Clay shifted, but only a little so that he didn't lose sight of her.

"What are you doing here?" Censure filled the boy's voice.

"Don't tell me you cut school, Jeremy? That's so un-goody-two-shoes of you." She swung away from him. Her skirt swirled, and her long black hair, so like her mother's, swished through the air. "Why can't you leave me alone? I have my own life."

"I saw you cutting across campus, and I followed you."

"Mr. Bainbridge will never notice I'm gone. I waited until he'd checked roll." The girl's tone of voice and disregard for the rules brought a smile to Clay's face. This could prove interesting.

"Come with me." Jeremy took the girl by the arm. "If we go now, we can get back to class without being caught."

She jerked out of his grasp. "I haven't finished my business here. I'm not going."

Clay stepped closer, pretending to look for coffee on the shelf. He didn't want to miss a word of the intriguing conversation. If the daughter's business was what he thought it was, Addison Greer had just lost her power over him.

"Come on, Elizabeth. Let's go. I've heard they sell drugs here." He lowered his voice, but Clay could still make out what the boy was saying.

"No. Really?" She planted one hand on her well-endowed chest and looked up at her brother with a false innocence.

"I haven't said anything to Mom."

"Well, don't. What she doesn't know won't hurt her. If she'd loved us at all, she'd have stayed with Dad."

"Don't be a jerk. Dad left her for a chick barely older than you are now." He shook his head. "You are so messed up."

"Yeah, I'm so messed up Dad never wants to see me, but you, the golden boy, he parades out before his friends. At least he does until he finds out about you." She brushed past him. "Leave me alone. I have stuff to do."

Her brother stared after her for a moment before he trudged from the store. Clay trailed after Elizabeth. Sure enough, she slid between the curtains separating the front of the store from the back. So little Miss Elizabeth had a yen for marijuana, huh? Wait until she tried some of his special blend. He was about to become her best friend and she, his. He wasn't certain how he'd use her, but he would. First thing to do was get his hands on a little more cash.

◆ ◆ ◆

Later in the day, Clay returned to the theatre. He stuck his head in the fag accountant's office. "Hey, Roger, my man. Got a few minutes?" Roger paled when he saw Clay. Such a wuss. Why did Roger Garland care if people found out he was gay? So many in the business were. It should've been no big deal.

But he was terrified, and that fear played right into Clay's hands. Roger was always good for extra cash.

"I hear we did all right last night, Rog." Clay plopped on the corner of Garland's desk. Roger leaned back farther into his chair.

"I… uh…yes. I believe we did." He removed his glasses and rubbed his eyes before sliding the frames back in place.

"Did your *friend* enjoy the party last night?" Damn, the guy got even paler, if that was possible. This was too easy.

Roger ran both hands ran through his hair. "What do you want, Clay?"

"Two thousand."

"God, man, you're bleeding me dry." He dropped his head into his hands. "When?"

"As soon as possible." Clay shoved off the desk.

"I've already deposited the cash we took in last night. I won't be able to get my hands on anything until tomorrow."

"I'll stop by in the afternoon. That work for you?"

"Yeah. But lay off after that."

"Sure, man. This will hold me for at least a couple of weeks."

Roger nodded, not making eye contact. Clay pulled the door behind him. A laugh he couldn't contain blasted out. Roger was a weak sister.

Clay headed home to get ready for his date with Linda Alexander, the board member he had in his pocket. He had a few things to do for her to ensure she stayed there. He picked up supper from the market including her favorite wine.

An attractive fifty-year-old, she loved playing the aggressor. Fancied herself as some sort of cougar. It didn't matter to Clay what she looked like or whether she was a good lay, he needed her vote to maintain his position of power over Addie. That he intended to do at any cost. Tomorrow he'd contact Elizabeth and get something going with her. He poured a large glass of wine, heated the food, and lowered the lights to wait for Linda's arrival.

♦ ♦ ♦

Sunday, October 7

"Mom, you got a minute?"

The depth of her son's voice never failed to surprise Addie. "Sure, hon." She set her Sunday paper aside and patted the seat on the couch next to her. "What's on your mind?"

"I haven't seen Elizabeth this morning." Jeremy dropped on the sofa, his elbows resting on his knees. The blue plaid shirt brought out the color in his eyes, which matched Addie's.

His tone piqued her curiosity. "She spent the night with Sonya. Why?"

"Oh, yeah, I'd forgotten."

Addie leaned forward and brushed his blond hair out of his eyes, where it promptly returned. "You worried about going to your dad's today? Elizabeth won't be back until you return."

"Yeah, but it's so shitty, Mom." Jeremy straightened and cut his eyes at her. "Sorry."

"I can hardly argue with you there. But it is what it is, what it's always been. Your father...well, he's a horse's ass, but he's your father."

Addie gulped a sip of coffee from her mug then set it back on the end table next to her. This was a tough topic, particularly on what she'd looked forward to being a quiet Sunday morning. "The last time we went to court over custody issues, this was what we set up. First Sunday you go over there. It's not as if you have to go for the whole weekend. If you don't want to do this anymore, you don't have to. You're old enough a judge would side with us."

"Then we've got the expense of the lawyer and the headlines." He slumped down on his spine, resting his head against the back of the sofa. His blue jeans emphasized the length of his legs. Her son had his father's height, for sure.

Leave it to Jeremy to think of the cost and publicity side of the situation. If her ex fought, it could get nasty. At least it was last time.

"Mom, I hate this. I hate what it's doing to Elizabeth," he said in a fierce tone, one fist pounding his thigh.

"Elizabeth doesn't blame you, Jeremy." Addie patted his knee. "It means a lot to me that you worry about her."

"Well, don't you?" He bounced off the sofa, crossed the room and then spun around toward her. "If you don't, you need to take a good look at her."

"She doesn't dress the way you or I would choose." Addie couldn't stop the scolding tone from coming through. "But she's still the same person inside."

"Lots of people who dress that way do drugs, Mom." He glared at her from across the room.

"Oh, Jeremy," Addie sat forward. "You're being stereotypical, and you shouldn't suggest your sister is involved just because of the way she dresses."

He shook his head for a moment then glanced back at her. "Okay." He slammed his fists into his pockets. "You sure you don't mind me taking your car to Dallas? I could hop on the train."

"No, I'm staying at the house today, catching up on our personal finances and probably reading a few scripts."

"Always looking for the next show, huh? I'll call you when I leave Dad's."

Addie got off the sofa and hugged Jeremy. "I'm proud of you. You're a good son and a good brother." She stepped back. "Not to mention talented. I can't wait to see you in *The Music Man*. Your rehearsal schedule is about to pick up, isn't it?"

"Between all our schedules, we probably need to get another car."

Her mouth curved up into her I'm-one-ahead-of-you smile that she didn't get to use often but tickled her no end when she'd bested her kids in something. "Funny you mentioned it. That's why I'm doing a little accounting work with our finances today. See what we might be able to come up with."

"That'd be great." He hugged her, lifting her off her feet.

Addie laughed. "Put me down, you crazy boy, before you hurt one or both of us."

"Dad should really pony up for our wheels."

"Yeah, but don't mention anything about it to him. He'll just say I'm squandering the money he does send." She patted him on the back then handed him the keys. "Head on over there, sweetie, and be careful."

"Thanks."

Addie waved to her son from the front porch, pulling her sweater-jacket around her against the chilly fall breezes. It had warmed up from earlier in September when the freak cold front hit, and now was seasonally cool. The teeter-totter temperatures continued. She went back inside, determined to find the money for the kids to have a car.

Her cell sang out. Cindy Riley's name flashed on the screen.

"Hey, Cindy, what's up?"

"I'm so glad I caught you, Addie. I know this is short notice, but something of a miracle has happened. Neither Mike nor Pat is on call for the rest of the day. I was afraid it might take months to find a time when we could all get together. Are you free today?"

Addie's blood crashed in her ears her palms grew sweaty at the thought of seeing the detective again. "Well, I..." Addie stuttered. Cindy ran on as if Addie hadn't spoken.

"It's Sunday, and I almost didn't call because of your kids, but I was so excited to find a time with both the guys available, I decided to jump on the opportunity." She stopped and laughed. "Guess, I should shut up, so you can get a word in."

Addie's heart thudded a little quicker. Try as much as she had, she'd not been able to get the detective out of her mind. Absurdly crazy reaction on her part. "Well, I..."

"Please say you can, Addie. We can do any time that works for you."

"I don't know." Her phone beeped. "Cindy, let me get this. It's Elizabeth. I'll call you back. Thanks for thinking of me." She clicked over her hand tight on the cell. "Elizabeth, are you okay?"

"Sure, Mom. The project Sonya and I are working on for one of our classes is taking longer than we anticipated. She'd like me to stay over."

"But tomorrow is a school day." Why was it as mom she always had to play the spoiler with her daughter?

"I know. But the assignment is due tomorrow," she said with a slight sing-song pitch, "and if we can keep on it, we'll have it completed on time."

Elizabeth's use of "on time" was a key to get to her mother, and it worked. Moreover, as much as Addie hated to admit it, some of her motivation to acquiesce had a lot to do with accepting the opportunity to see Detective Mike Riley. "Her parents are going to be there? And you know I'll check."

"Yeah, I know, Mom, and yes, they'll both be home." Her inflection said she was the most put-upon teen in the history of the world.

"What about clothes for school tomorrow?"

"We'll swing by and pick up something. Take maybe fifteen minutes."

"Okay, Elizabeth, but don't go out tonight. Call me when you're about to go to bed and call me when you're on the way to school in the morning." Addie's stomach tightened at the possibility she was making a mistake to trust her daughter.

"Sure, Mom. Thanks."

"I love—" The phone went dead. Addie stared at her cell, a sense of confusion washing through her about whether she should be mad at Elizabeth for hanging up on her or glad she was free to tell Cindy yes. Was she wrong to do this? Her heartbeat fluttered. Heat rose in her cheeks. She hadn't been out with anyone not related to business in a long time. She couldn't even remember the last time she'd experienced this stomach-dropping anticipation.

Jeremy would be all right. She'd leave him a note after she knew the details, so he wouldn't worry if he got home and found her gone. What was she going to wear? A laugh bubbled out. She didn't even know what the plans were yet. She punched in the keys for Cindy's number.

"Hey, Cindy. Thank—"

"Please don't say no, Addie."

"Then I'll say yes." A little thrill of excitement shoved her voice into a slightly higher range than usual.

♦ ♦ ♦

At four that afternoon Addie, dressed in jeans and boots, and Mike rode in the back seat of Pat and Cindy's SUV. Plenty of space between her and the cowboy detective, but Addie couldn't keep from shooting glances his way. The four of them headed out to the Stockyards where they parked in one of the public lots and got out. The chilly wind rustled the trees as they strolled the brick streets of North Fort Worth, making Addie grateful for her leather jacket.

Sometimes when you lived in a city a long time, you forgot to take advantage of its unique heritage. In Fort Worth, that was the Northside with its Stockyards and cattle drive.

"You don't go to the Fort Worth Stock Show and Rodeo every January?" Cindy stared at Addie as if she had grown two heads.

"We went some when the kids were little but not anytime recently. Why? Do you?" Addie paused and looked in one of the shop windows. The fringed leather skirt in a warm pumpkin color made her think of pie.

"Yeah, the family's had box seats for years. When Mike and Pat were younger, they both
rodeoed."

Addie glanced back at the men who'd stopped at another window displaying saddles and stuff she couldn't name. She and Mike lived not just in different worlds but different universes.

"Pat," Cindy threw over her shoulder, "remind me we need to invite Addie to the rodeo in January. She's not been in a long time."

"You're not a rodeo fan, Addison?" Mike asked when he and Pat joined up with the women.

Addie laughed. "I hesitate to tell y'all this, but when I go, I usually root for the animals."

"You've got to be kidding. And you a Fort Worth gal?" Pat asked in his strong Texas twang.

"You know Fort Worth is where the west begins, don't you," Mike teased. "The phrase is emblazoned on our newspaper."

"Yes, but I'm more from the culture side of our 'Cowboys and Culture' slogan."

"Well, we'll have to see what we can do about that then,

won't we." Mike moved up to walk with her, and Cindy dropped back. In his blue jeans, white shirt, brown leather jacket, boots, and white western hat, Mike looked more a cowboy himself than a big city police detective.

"Perhaps so." *Silly woman. He's just talking about the rodeo.* Still her face heated, and her stomach did that stupid spiraling thing. Definitely been a long time since she'd experienced the sensation. Not entirely unpleasant and she admitted, exciting.

They continued along Exchange Avenue, not talking about anything in particular, just walking. Occasionally, their hands brushed together. Once Addie tripped on the uneven sidewalk, and Mike was quick to take her elbow. His strong grip made her feel secure.

They were almost past a restaurant when Pat hollered, "Hey, anybody ready for barbecue?"

"Anytime anywhere," Mike stopped and looked back.

"And, Addie, he really does mean what he said," Cindy said.

The four entered, and the smells of hickory smoke and beer greeted them. A bit of cigarette smoke from back in the day clung to the walls.

"Mike's been known to eat barbecue a couple of times a week." Cindy slid into a booth. Country-western music blared from a jukebox in the rustic restaurant with logs for walls.

"I guess I'm more apt to do that with Mexican food." Addie took the other side and scooted over. "I don't eat a lot of beef, and I find a lot more options there."

"Well, we don't have to eat here." Mike leaned back in the booth. "Fort Worth's not short on good Mexican food restaurants, particularly up here on the Northside." He made to slide toward the edge.

Addie stopped him with a hand on his arm. "We don't have to change on my account. I'm a born and bred Texan, and I have to eat smoky grilled ribs slathered in sauce a couple of times a year."

Mike's hand covered hers. "Good. We'll do Mexican next time."

◆ ◆ ◆

"Hey, Mom. Your note said Stockyards. Not exactly your thing. Did you have fun?" Jeremy sprawled on the sofa the TV tuned to a football game.

Addie dropped down in the rocker, started the gentle motion, and smiled. "Yes, Son, I did. I had a surprisingly good time."

"Was it business? Your note said something about one of your board members."

"Not business, strictly pleasure. I was with Cindy Riley, her husband, and brother-in-law—we took in the Stockyards and ate barbecued ribs. Messy, but so yummy."

Jeremy sat up on the couch and leaned forward. "You had a date?"

Addie glanced at him and away. Her son seemed startled. "Well, not exactly. It was more like four friends hanging out."

"Mom, you went on a double date." Jeremy laughed. "You have to realize that's what that was. Who was the guy? Did you like him? Are you going again?"

"Gosh, Jeremy. Twenty questions." How should she answer him? Mike had talked about a next time, and she'd love a next time with him. She was quite—to use an old-fashioned term—smitten with Cindy's western-hat-wearing brother-in-law.

"Mom. Talk to me. Who is this dude?"

Addie laughed. "This *dude* is a homicide detective."

"Wow." Jeremy fell back against the sofa cushions, as if the idea she'd been out with a cop tipped the picture he had of his mother on its end.

"Yes, quite wow." She stood. "Now, I'm going to work on those finances like I promised, to see if we can get you and Elizabeth some sort of vehicle." The possibility of a car would get her off the hook with her inquisitive son.

"Okay, but I'm still going to want to know more, especially if you're going to see him again."

Addie rose and leaned down to ruffle Jeremy's hair. "I'll keep you posted if anything develops." She started out.

"Hey, why isn't Elizabeth home yet?"

"She and Sonya had a project due tomorrow. They're pulling a late night."

"You're letting her spend the night when we have school tomorrow?"

"I know I don't usually do that, but I was excited she was talking about getting a project done on time and wanted to reward that behavior. I hope it works. Don't stay up too late."

◆ ◆ ◆

Tuesday, October 9

Clay paced his office at the theatre. Garland had gotten hold of the extra money as he'd promised, and Clay had turned it into more marijuana cigarettes. The odd little Goth girl would come crawling for them. He didn't find her look appealing but having her as an ally just might come in handy in his war with her mom. It wouldn't take much to get her hooked if she weren't already.

James Duffy's backing was certain, because Clay kept his drug habit a secret and on occasion even supplied the jerk.

Linda Alexander was still his for the taking. Well preserved for fifty. Even naked she looked damn good. Her husband must be a real asshole. She was so grateful for Clay's attention she'd do anything he asked. And had. Memories of their sexcapades made him smile.

The hang-up in all this was still Shannon DeWitt. She was the swing vote. If he couldn't get her to change her mind and continue to support him, well, he'd have to do something. He couldn't afford to lose this job.

He'd had a bad string of luck at the tables and been forced to borrow money from people who didn't understand about late payments. The thugs who visited him made it plain what would happen. When Addie asked about his split lip and black eye, he'd told her he'd tripped and fallen. Next time he wouldn't get off so easy.

No, he had to bring DeWitt around. First, he'd talk to her again. There had to be some way he could convince her. Time was moving on. The next board meeting was Monday of next week. He had to know where he stood with the bitch before then. His stomach clenched when he pulled out his cell and looked up her number. She picked up after second ring.

"Hey, Shannon."

"Hello, Clay."

She didn't sound very encouraging, but he pushed through. "I wondered if we couldn't talk again."

"What for?"

Hell, she was going to be a hard-ass. "I'd like an opportunity to try to change your mind about how to vote on my job at the board meeting."

"I don't think there's any reason for us to talk more."

"Aw come on. You've always struck me as being a fair-minded person. Give me another shot at this." Clay struggled to keep the whine from his voice.

"All right," she said with tone of resignation. "I'll listen to you again, Clay, but I'm not going to change my mind. I'm just doing this so you can't later complain you didn't get a fair hearing."

Clay tightened his fingers on the cell. Bitch. "Can you stop by the theatre around eight-thirty?" Everyone would be gone by then, and that gave him time for some preparations if the talk didn't go well. Keeping his job was essential if he wanted to avoid another run-in with those thugs who worked for the men he owed money. "I have an early supper appointment, so that will be fine. See you then."

Her cell went dead. It seemed apropos. If she didn't support him, she'd find she'd made a hell of a big mistake. In the meantime, he had preparations to make.

◆ ◆ ◆

Clay's phone rang at exactly eight-thirty.

"I'm out front, Clay, but the door is locked."

"I'll be right there to let you in." He'd locked the front door, not because that was the policy when most of the staff had left the building, but he didn't want her sneaking in on him. He wanted to be ready, and he was.

"Come on in, Shannon. Sorry it took me a while to get up here. I was in the costume room checking on a couple of pieces."

"Let's get our talk over and you can get back to work." She slapped her gloves against the palm of one hand.

"Come on back with me. I want to show you where some of our money has gone."

She cocked her head as if considering his request then nodded. Clay ushered her toward the workroom in the rear of the building. Their steps echoed on the concrete floor. He hoped their talk didn't go badly, but if it did, he was ready.

The costume room was large, with an extensive collection from various shows throughout the years. Clay's favorites were from musicals he'd performed in off-Broadway productions.

"Here's one of Dolly's hats. You want to try it on?" He maneuvered Shannon in front of one of the many mirrors.

She dodged away. "No thanks, but it is a great looking hat. I remember the production. Isn't it one you went over-budget on?"

Heat spread up Clay's neck. He clenched his fists, crushing the brim, before he gained control. Who'd she think she was to question him about what he needed for a great production? He laid the beautiful, feathered creation on a shelf.

"Yes, Shannon, it was. From a creative standpoint it was worth every cent."

"But you didn't stay on budget, Clay. It can't matter how creative you are if you can't stick to the budget."

Crap. She didn't sound much like she'd support him against Greer. DeWitt wasn't leaving him any options. He walked behind a large shelf unit filled with bolts of material. "Come look at this, Shannon. It might help change your mind."

"Okay, but I don't have much more time. So make this quick."

Clay struggled not to laugh at her choice of words. "Come over here. He stepped behind her, so she was close to one of the support columns. Her head turned right and left.

"What do you want me to see?"

He slid a gun from its hiding place under the bolts of materials, and when she faced him, he leveled it directly at her chest. No way to miss this close.

"Clay. What are you doing?" She stepped back but ran

into the column. Her face drained of color. "Let's talk." Her hands extended in front of her. She took two steps closer.

"We have talked, Shannon. You said the wrong words."

Blam.

The shot propelled her back. She hit the column and in slow motion slid down to the floor. A large blossom of red bloomed on her chest.

Clay's hand trembled. His heartbeat fast enough to jump from his chest. He'd hide the gun and he'd shower when he got home and burn all his clothes. No one would ever know. He'd get to keep his job and have money for those weasels threatening him.

CHAPTER THREE

Wednesday, October 10

Mike Riley pulled up in front of Cowtown Theatre. The flashing red and blue lights from the patrol cars gave the late afternoon an eerie appearance. Why couldn't someone else have picked up this call? He'd only seen Addison Greer once since meeting her at the fundraiser with Cindy and Pat. He'd hoped to see her after the Stockyards, but he'd gotten busy. Flu took out several detectives. Maybe a good thing now he hadn't seen more of her.

Still his mind flooded with memories from the two times he'd been with her. His stomach did an unusual roll. She'd been gorgeous in that long, blue gown, the color exactly matching her eyes, her shoulders bare. No jewelry. She hadn't needed any. He swallowed convulsively. She'd been hot in jeans and western boots, as well, though clearly she was a city slicker. He settled his white hat more firmly on his head and pushed aside thoughts of what might have been.

"Detective Mike Riley." He flashed his identification for the young patrol officer standing guard on the front door.

"The body's in one of the back rooms."

"Thanks. You're keeping a record of everyone who comes

in?"

"Yes." The officer nodded.

The stark glass lobby contrasted with its dressed up frou-frou appearance on the night of the fundraiser. He shoved away his memories of Addison. No place for that now. Somebody had killed a board member, and his job was to find out who. This could be awkward with Cindy on the board. He'd look at everyone remotely involved, including Cindy. Pat would be mad as hell, but that was the job.

Mike's gaze scanned the people gathered at one end of the atrium, looking for the dark-haired woman who'd so caught his interest. There she was. Her eyes opened wide, and color drained from her already pale face when she saw him. She hugged a young girl and spoke to a man who looked toward Mike. Then the lady in question moved in his direction. Shoulders back, head high, beautiful. Addison Greer walked into his homicide investigation.

"Detective Riley." She didn't extend her hand and neither did he. Her eyes were red as if she'd been crying.

If she were going to be formal, so would he. "Ms. Greer, sorry to see you again under these circumstances." He shoved his hands in his pockets. What he wanted to do was drag her into his arms. Same reaction he'd had when he first met her. But he sure as hell didn't date anyone involved in a case. Too bad she rattled his balls.

"Me too. I can hardly believe what's happened."

Her chin trembled, and she blinked against the moisture filling her eyes. She must've been close to the victim.

"My people and I will do anything to help you find who did this." Her hands twisted together. Then perhaps she became aware of what she was doing because she shoved them behind her.

"I'm sorry for your loss." A noise behind him pulled his attention to the doorway. Rick had arrived. Wonder how she'd react to him. Most women practically swooned at his Latin good looks. Mike gestured toward his younger partner whose rapid strides brought Rick to Mike and Addie—Ms. Greer. Hell. She was right to keep things formal.

"Rick, this is Addison Greer, the executive director of the theatre. Detective Martinez is my partner."

She didn't offer to shake hands with Rick either. The pallor never left her face.

"Detective." She nodded. "I was telling...Detective Riley, my staff and I will do anything to help."

"Thanks, Ms. Greer. We appreciate that. The sooner we find who did this, the sooner you can get back to normal."

"I'm not sure we'll ever get back to normal—whatever that is—after this but thank you." Pain seeped through her low voice.

"Can you get us a personnel list with addresses and phone numbers?" Mike asked. Giving her something specific to do would probably help her get through this initial shock. "And how about some space we can use to interview everyone?"

"Yes to both your questions. I'll give some directions to the crew to set up...what? Two separate areas?"

"Uh, that will be fine." *Come on, Riley. Get your big head in this game. The vic deserves your best.*

"Detective Martinez and I will check on the body." A shudder shook Addie, but he plunged on. "Then we'll start those interviews. Officers will make sure no one leaves. We appreciate your cooperation." Mike stalked away, Martinez following in his wake.

Mike mentally slammed a fist up against his head. What an idiot he was where women were concerned. After the murder of her husband, Mike had followed Jill Barlow to Vermont one winter, nearly freezing his tail off. He was glad he'd gone; they finally got the men responsible. But he should've learned his lesson about women involved in his cases. Now he was in the same situation with Addison Greer. Hankering after a woman he couldn't pursue. Just not gonna happen a second time.

They stepped into what must be one of the costume rooms, judging from the clothes hanging from portable racks against all the walls. Bright colors, sequins, feathers, leather breast plates. At lot to take in, and at first glance Mike didn't detect anything to suggest this was a murder scene.

"Back here, Detectives." An officer gestured them around a shelving unit. They moved in his direction and walked around the end of the unit. Stacks of material, now blood spattered met his gaze.

"Good afternoon, gentlemen." The ME, wearing slacks and a jacket, crouched near the body, her hands encased in gloves. "Looks like we've got ourselves a murder."

"How'd we get you?" Rick asked.

Sandra Dyson didn't come out as often as her assistant MEs.

"Just lucky, I guess." She laughed in a voice roughened from too many years of smoking. "Well, actually not so lucky for Drew, who was scheduled for this shift. His kids gave him chicken pox."

"Hell of a deal." Mike looked at Rick then asked, "Do we know who discovered the body?"

"The woman in charge of costumes was in here working for most of the morning," the officer said. "She left for lunch, returned, and worked some more. Said she'd begun to notice a smell but figured they had the skunk back that sometimes got under the building. Then she needed a piece of purple material and came around behind this shelf." The officer shook his head. "She fell apart, screaming, when she realized the victim had been back here the whole time she worked."

"What can you tell us so far, Sandra?"

"Nothing official until after the autopsy, of course."

"Of course." Mike pushed, "But?"

"Gunshot wound to the heart at pretty close range. I'm guessing she might've known her assailant. No defensive wounds. Killed sometime between yesterday evening and three this afternoon when she was discovered."

"Okay, good. That's helpful. Keep us posted on when you do the autopsy. Rick or I will be there."

"Sure. Possibly tomorrow, but I'll let you know."

"Rick, let's go interview the staff, find out how many knew our vic and how well."

"So what do you think?" Mike settled into his desk chair and opened a folder. They'd let everyone go home with the warning they'd have follow-up questions. He'd interviewed half the staff and board members they'd been able to get hold of. Rick had taken the other half, including Addie and Cindy. She seemed concerned about the executive director, leaving her side only when they each talked with Rick.

"I didn't find anyone who spoke ill of our victim, did you?" Rick asked.

"Nope." Mike looked at the notes he'd made. "She'd served on the board for quite a few years and seemed to be universally liked."

"There appear to be two camps in the theatre." Rick picked up a headshot of Addison and one of Bennett. "At this point, I can't tell which has more validity, but it seems like there's money and power and secrets involved."

"Yeah, that's what I'm getting. All good motives for murder. You liking anyone for it yet?" Mike asked.

"Well, unless your sister-in-law hired someone—just joking—" He raised both hands as if to ward off an attack when Mike felt his eyebrows crawl to the top of his head. "She's got an ironclad alibi for the approximate time of the murder. She and your brother were on a plane returning from visiting NYU with their kids. She didn't get the message until after they landed, which is why it took her so long to get here."

"Apparently most of the board members were on

Addison's—Ms. Greer's—side in an issue concerning the artistic director."

"Addison?"

Count on Rick not to miss anything. Here goes. "Cindy dragged me and Pat to the theatre's recent big deal fundraiser, and I met Addison Greer then."

"Big deal—like black tie?" Rick didn't even try to hide the smirk across his face.

"Yeah." Mike nodded.

"Did you have to rent a tux?" Rick rocked his chair back on two legs, studying his partner.

"Actually, I own one. I've worn it to a couple of cancer fundraisers with my brother. Pat said if you wore it twice it was cheaper to buy than rent."

"You wear those fancy, shiny shoes I've seen in movies?"

Mike laughed. "Nope. Drew the line at those. Wore my good boots."

"Thank God." The two front legs hit the floor. "I was afraid you'd gone all society on me. Have you seen the executive director since?"

Mike nodded once. "Had supper with her, Mike, and Cindy about three weeks back."

Rick's eyebrows drew together while he stared at Mike. "Anything else you need to tell me?"

"Might have, given the right opportunity and the time. You know how short-handed we've been because of the flu taking out so many detectives. But, of course, not now."

"Okay, then." His partner nodded then slapped the table.

"Back to business. You pick up on what the beef was between Greer and Bennett?"

Mike nodded. "Yep. Several overheard them arguing. Bennett said..." Mike glanced at his notes. "Bennett told her, *Don't fuck with me, Addison. You'll lose.* Ms. Greer was heard to say..." Mike flipped the page over. "*You mess with this theatre, and I'll make you sorry.*"

"Well, if Bennett was our vic, I'd definitely say we have to look real close at the executive director." Rick scanned his notes. "However, from what I picked up, DeWitt had recently been a supporter of the artistic director, so maybe Greer's still a probability. She could have needed to get rid of DeWitt."

"I just don't see her as a killer. Besides—" Mike started.

"Yeah, yeah, I know, women generally don't use a gun. They poison." Rick tapped his pencil against the pages of his notes. "I was going to say, before you rushed in, if DeWitt changed her mind, then that makes Bennett look suspicious."

"Let's keep digging, Partner."

♦ ♦ ♦

Mike twisted open the cap from a longneck beer bottle, then sank into his old leather chair that wrapped itself around him saying welcome home. He and Rick chucked it in for the day around nine p.m. Mike had picked up fried chicken and eaten in his truck on the twenty-minute drive out to the ranch.

He turned on the radio and closed his eyes, bleary from reading all the statements. Ultimately, they'd figure it out.

Because of where Shannon DeWitt had been killed, it made sense to pursue all her connections at the theatre, which meant the staff and board members.

The loud bleat of his cell made him jerk, and he blinked his eyes open. God, he hoped he didn't have to go back out.

"What kind of jackass are you to interview my wife?"

"Well, hello to you too, Patrick."

"She'd never kill anyone. You've known her almost as long as I have. Did you have to put her through that?"

"Give it a rest, Pat." Cindy's voice came in the background. "He was just doing his job."

"You didn't even have the decency to talk with her yourself."

"Of course, not. That would've been questionable." Again Cindy's voice. "Here, give me that phone." Sounds of a scuffle then Cindy in a normal volume. "I'm sorry, Mike. Pat's being a jerk."

"I'm glad you understand why I didn't—"

"Of course." Long pause. Cindy continued in a softer voice. "It's just all these years you've dealt with homicides, we've never been touched by any of the less glamorous details."

"I get it, Cindy. I'm sorry you're caught up this time."

"Rick interviewed Addie and not you. Same reason?"

"Sure. Just cleaner because I'd met her."

"Guess we won't be going for another dinner anytime soon. Damn. I was sure I saw some sparks fly between you two."

Mike didn't see what he could say to that. His best plan

was to ignore the tightening in his groin every time he thought of Ms. Addison Greer.

"Mike, you don't really think she had anything to do with this, do you?"

"I'm not at liberty to say."

"What possible motive could Addie have, for God's sake?" Cindy's voice rose in pitch with each word she spoke.

"From what we've heard, DeWitt was a supporter of Bennett and a crucial board vote was coming up regarding him." Mike took several swallows of his beer.

"Yes, but before Pat and I flew out to New York, Addie told me Shannon had come around. Addie would be able to fire him. She'd needed just the one extra vote, and that was Shannon's. The other two board members hanging with Clay couldn't save his job."

Mike sat forward and set the bottle on the table in front of him. "Who all knew that story, Cindy?"

"Gee, I'm not sure, Mike. I'm sorry. I left town right after Addie told me, so I don't know who else knows. And I'm sorry Pat gave you such a hard time."

"No sweat." Mike laughed. "Nothing new there. He's done it all my life. Besides, he loves you and was making sure no big bad cop took advantage."

"Well, I'll tell him he owes you a drink."

"Make it a steak and we're even." Mike chuckled at how Cindy got his brother to do whatever she wanted. Pat always thought it was his idea.

"Maybe Addie will be able to come along." Wistfulness

touched her words and tone. She had to know better.

"We'll see how the investigation goes, Cindy."

"Dammit, Mike. You know she couldn't have done this."

"Good night, Cindy." He disconnected. The hell of it all was Mike didn't know whether Addie might or might not have killed DeWitt. Just because generally a female didn't use a gun to kill, didn't mean Rick and he wouldn't consider the possibility of every woman connected to the theatre as a possible suspect. Hell, he wanted to clear Addie. With every fiber of his being, he wanted her to be innocent.

But good cop that he was, he'd follow the evidence, even if it pointed him to the beautiful Addison Greer. He slugged back the rest of his beer. That'd put a real dent in the matchmaking Cindy seemed so all fired set on. If he could corroborate what Cindy told him, maybe then....

♦ ♦ ♦

Thursday, October 11

"Cowtown Theatre." Generally, Addie didn't answer calls at work, a secretary did, but she'd already sent her home. Addie pushed the button before it registered she didn't recognize the number.

"Hello, Addison. This is Jonathan Harding."

"Mr. Harding. Hello.

"Please, Jonathan."

"Of course. What can I do for you?"

"I'm hoping you'll have lunch with me tomorrow."

"Well, Jonathan, you've probably heard we've had some trouble here at the theatre."

"Yes, and I'd like to talk with you about that. You have to eat, and it will do you good to get out of the mess for a while. I was thinking of the Chisholm Trail Club."

Addie sighed. One of her favorite places, and maybe it would be good to get the prospective of an outsider. "Thank you, Jonathan. I'd like that very much, but I'd like to put it off until next Friday. Would that be okay?"

"Yes, if that's the best we can do."

"What time?"

"I thought a little later—they won't be so busy, and we'll be able to visit. How would two work for you?"

"Fine. I'll see you Friday, November second, at two then."

"Let me swing by and pick you up, Addie."

"No, but thanks. I have meetings beforehand."

"All right. I look forward to next week then."

"Goodbye, Jonathan." Addie disconnected. Was she making a mistake? She couldn't hope to get money from the man when they were in the middle of an investigation of a murdered board member. They'd be lucky not to lose any of their regular donors.

Several board members had mentioned they wanted to talk about some sort of memorial for Shannon. She'd been on the board for ten years. What effect would her death have on the vote regarding Clay? If she'd been alive, Clay would be gone. Addie would have had enough votes to send him packing.

She opened the bylaws document to see exactly what it said concerning board vacancies. Using her turquoise pen, she read, highlighted, and circled. "Damn. That's how I remembered it." She ran both hands through her hair then stretched her arms over her head, trying to loosen the tension. "We've got to act like we have the same number of board members as we did before Shannon was killed. So I'm still short of the required one more than a majority."

She slammed the booklet closed and shoved it across her desk. What idiot wrote the bylaws this way? Updating them now took on more urgency. However, always it was about time and board members who were volunteers.

Addie rested her elbows on the desk, her fingertips rubbing her temples where pain pounded like a hammer on a nail. Not surprising, what with all the stress resulting in a severe lack of sleep.

The only good thing about that was she caught Elizabeth sneaking in late last night. Well it wasn't good that Elizabeth was sneaking in, only that Addie had caught and grounded her. Her main talent at the Fine Arts School was art, but she was one of the townspeople in the school's production of *The Music Man*, in which Jeremy played the lead. Many days they stayed after school together. That was all Addie allowed.

She tried to be a good mother, and she seemed to be succeeding with one child but not the other.

Addie looked up at a knock at the door. "Come in." She opened the lower desk drawer, pulled out a box of generic headache pills, and popped a couple in her mouth. Mike Riley stuck his head around the door as she swallowed. She choked on the water. He hurried around her desk and patted her on the back.

"You, okay? People aren't generally thrilled to see me, but they don't usually choke."

Still gasping, all she could do was nod her head while tears trickled from her eyes.

"Seriously, you okay? I can do the Heimlich."

Finally, Addie gulped and whispered, "I'm okay." While she thought she might like to see how the good detective's arms felt around her, the Heimlich wasn't exactly what she had in mind.

She took another swallow of water and breathed in deeply. "Okay. I'm fine, now." She wiped tears from her eyes, certain from the heat she felt that red covered her face. "I'm sorry for the unorthodox greeting. I was taking a couple of pills for a headache. Have a seat, please." She waved to one of the chairs in front of her desk. She should've worn something nicer than warm-ups, but she'd had no appointments out of the office and wanted to be comfortable. "Do you have any more information about the murder?"

"We're still investigating." He lowered himself into the chair she'd indicated. "I wanted to follow up on something I've heard—"

"I'm sure it's about the fight Clay and I had," Addie jumped in. "I think everyone heard us. The door was open."

"Yes, we heard about it from almost everyone. Seems like you said—"

"That if he messed with the theatre, I'd make him sorry. I guess if he were the one dead, I'd be your prime suspect."

"Yep." He nodded.

"Why do I get the feeling there's something more here." Addie fiddled with a pencil, rolling it back and forth across her desk. It made a clicking sound as it passed underneath a silver ring on her right hand.

"It's this whole issue about your intent to fire Clay Bennett. Is that your intent?"

Addie hiked up her shoulders and released them before leaning back in the chair. "Detective, the theatre is having money problems. It's important to be able to put on shows that come in on or under budget. Clay Bennett has trouble ensuring that happens. I've talked with him several times and documented those chats in his personnel file."

"As I understand, you can't fire Bennett without a supermajority of the Board."

"That's right. I had no reason to want Shannon DeWitt dead. She told me she agreed with the firing."

"Is there any way you can substantiate that?"

"Probably not. I told a couple of people. Pete Talmadge, Cindy Riley. But that's just my word." She dropped her head into her hands. "This is such a nightmare."

"With her gone, can't you do what you want?"

She sat up and looked directly at the detective. If only she'd met him at another time. "No. The bylaws are written in a screwy way. So even though we have a vacancy, we have to operate as if we have all of the members. I'd have to get James

Duffy or Linda Alexander to support the firing, and I don't believe there's any likelihood of that happening."

Mike nodded. "Okay, I think that explains things for me. We will find who did this, Addie. Have faith."

"Thank you."

Mike stood. "I've got work to do, and I'm sure you do to. Take it easy." He opened the door and left her office.

"Oh, my goodness." Addie groaned and collapsed against the back of her chair. Did he realize he'd called her by her nickname? She straightened her shoulders. Eventually, they'd move past all of this. She hated to think someone associated with the theatre had killed Shannon, but she'd been attacked here, and that made it likely. If that were true, Addie knew a murderer.

CHAPTER FOUR

Friday, October 12

"Let me pay for that."

The teen swung around at Clay's words. "Why? Do I know you?" Her eyebrows canted together over her nose.

"No, but I know who you are. Addison Greer's daughter, Elizabeth. Am I right?"

"How do you know my mom?"

Elizabeth stood as if she were ready to sprint away, balancing on the balls of her feet. The long skirt swirled around her ankles. He'd use his practiced smooth moves to make her trust him.

"I work with her at the theatre. How is she as a mom? She's sometimes a hard-ass at work." He rubbed a hand through his hair. "Shit. I probably shouldn't have said that to you."

The girl's shoulders visibly relaxed. He'd hit the right note with her.

"Nah. You nailed her. She grounds me for no good reason. Sometimes, you just have to bust out, you know." Her feet rocked side to side like to some internal music, while her fingers rifled through the cellophane-clad multicolored candy sticks.

"Sure do." Clay nodded. "You make up your mind?" He nodded toward the bin.

She yanked her hand away. "No money."

"Like I said, I can get it for you." Her eyes squinted at him as if she were trying to figure out his angle. Ultimately, her desire for the sweet overcame any hesitation she had, and she nodded. "Thanks."

He paid for her candy and gum for himself and then walked out of the little store with her. "How old are you, Elizabeth?"

She stuck the candy stick in her mouth. After a short pause, "I'm eighteen. Why?"

"The way you're holding the candy it looks like you'd like a smoke."

She leaned against the side of the building. "Oh, yes. What'd I give for a real cigarette right now. I'm out and don't have enough money for a pack. Hell, I couldn't pay for this stupid candy."

Clay pulled out a pack and lit a cigarette. "Take a drag." He held it out to her.

Elizabeth didn't hesitate but took the cigarette and pulled the smoke into her lungs, blowing it out on a long sigh. "Thanks. Boy, gum and candy just don't touch that."

"Come on back to my apartment, I've got a pack I can let you have."

He read her face as if she were speaking words, her concern about going off with a relative stranger—she wasn't a stupid girl—warring with her desire for the smokes. He read it in her eyes, the way she glanced around, and the way she rubbed her hands through her long skirts. Ultimately, the nicotine won out.

"Okay, seeing as you know my mother. You won't tell her though, will you?"

"Not a chance, sweetheart." He pulled her arm through his and headed for his car.

By the time they arrived at his apartment, he could tell Elizabeth had warmed up to him. She'd chatted about school, an art project she had in the works, her brother, and the musical they were in. Upstairs in the apartment, she plopped on his sofa and lit up another cigarette. All he had to do now was make sure she got the one with the marijuana laced with coke.

"You want something to drink, Elizabeth? Soft drink, beer, something harder?"

"Beer would be good." She lit another cigarette from the smoldering end of her first.

At the rate she was going, he'd have her agreeing to do anything he asked. She puffed away like she was starving. When she was close to finishing it, Clay crossed over to her. "Here's the beer and another smoke. He held his lighter to the tip of his special brand.

She drew in deeply.

"How do you like that?"

"Thanks, Clay." She drew in again and leaned back against the leather sofa. "Oh, this is really good. I appreciate you doing this and listening. No one listens to me."

"What about your dad?" He crossed one black slacks-covered leg over the other, resting his ankle on his knee—oh so relaxed—and puffed on his laced stick.

"He's a big deal lawyer in Dallas."

Clay didn't like hearing that, and his foot jiggled on his knee. "What kind of law does he practice?"

"I don't remember, but he's made a lot of money and has a big house. Not like I get to see it or the money. Only my almighty brother does that." She drew more of the drug into her lungs.

"Sorry your parents are split. What happened?"

"My stupid father brought his young bitch into our home and did it with her in Mom's bed. She caught them. As I said, he was stupid. Mom kicked his ass out right then."

"Sounds like you have issues with both parents."

"Mom's so controlling, and Dad doesn't want anything to do with me. Maybe because his girl was only a little older than I am now." She studied the cigarette between her fingers. "Good smoke." Her eyes narrowed when she cut her gaze back at him.

"Let me get you another one." He rose and crossed to the desk After pulling one out of the drawer, he crossed back to the sofa. "You mean your father doesn't want to see you?" Clay didn't consider himself paternal in the least, but what was the matter with this girl's father? A screw-up as far as he could tell.

"Because I'm a girl. He only wanted a boy. I could tell before the divorce. After... it was hard to miss when he just had Jeremy come visit and not me."

Clay lit the cigarette and handed it to her then slouched

down on the sofa, next to the girl. He dropped his arm around her shoulder. "That's crappy. No one should treat you like that."

She looked up, and he'd caught her just like that. A little hint of coke in with the marijuana, a listening ear, and he had her. He trailed his fingers lightly up and down her arm. Elizabeth relaxed into him. He moved his hand up to her neck and massaged his way there and around her shoulders. She relaxed even more.

"Oh, that feels good, Clay."

"There's more where that came from but not now. I have work to do, and you need to get home. If you try not to get on your Mom's bad side, she'll give you more freedom, and we'll be able to spend more time together. Smoke and hang out. If you'd like that."

"Well, yeah. Are you sure you want to spend time with me?" Her eyebrows flew up in disbelief.

"Very sure." He leaned down and kissed her on the forehead. He moved slowly, not wanting to spook her. "Come on. I'll drop you off close to your house. No reason for you being any later than necessary. Okay?"

"Thanks."

He held his hand out and helped her off the sofa. She stumbled into him. But he didn't slide his hands down to her rear and pull her close. Maybe someday, but this was too early.

◆ ◆ ◆

Addie messaged her friends to confirm she'd be at their

get-away. They always booked two rooms, and over the last ten years had hung out in some unique bed and breakfasts. Addie hadn't been sure she'd be able to go, what with everything that had happened, but she needed the time to recharge her batteries. And she counted on some good advice about Elizabeth from her friends. Kate and her daughter had spent years in counselors' offices after her husband's death on 9/11. To this day, Kate still picked her cuticles.

"You two are certain you'll be okay here for the weekend?" Addie checked over the items she was taking to the B&B in Irving.

"Sure, Mom. We've got rehearsals. We've got money." He grinned. "We won't starve, and we won't get into trouble."

"Speak for yourself, Jeremy."

Addie spun around to her daughter.

Elizabeth laughed. "Kidding. You go and have fun. Tell your buddies we said hi."

"Don't worry, Mom. I'll watch out for her." Jeremy picked up her small suitcase and pretended to stagger. "What do you have in here?"

"Oh, you." She flipped her scarf at him. "It is not heavy, though with the cold front that's swung in, I packed a couple of sweaters. I've got my laptop and cell, so if you need anything, I'm within quick reach."

"What's in this shopping bag?" Elizabeth hauled it out to the garage.

"Snacks and wine." Addie laughed.

"Is Kate bringing her apple cake?" Jeremy literally licked

his lips. "You should ask her and her daughter to Thanksgiving this year. She could bring it with them. Pumpkin pie and apple cake. Sounds like some good eating."

"I like your idea, Jer. I'll ask. Maybe they'll come if they don't have other plans."

"Well, either way, if there's any cake left from this weekend; bring it home, will you?"

Addie laughed. After hugging both kids, she climbed in the car. "I'll see what I can do. Now be—"

"Careful, don't do drugs, or drive with anyone who's been drinking, and no sex." Jeremy and Elizabeth repeated the litany in unison.

"Guess I've said that a few times, huh?"

"Yup." Elizabeth rolled her eyes.

"Now get out of here, Mom." Jeremy patted her shoulder through the rolled down window.

"I love you both."

"Back atcha. Go." Jeremy shook his head.

Addie laughed again, backed down the driveway, and pulled into the street.

♦ ♦ ♦

"Boy, I thought she'd never leave." Jeremy pushed the button to lower the garage door and walked into the kitchen.

"I can't get over how long Mom and her three friends have known each other." Elizabeth held a glass under the ice dispenser, filling the room with the clink of cubes exploding, then poured herself a soft drink. "You want one?"

"Yeah, thanks." Jeremy got the chips from a cupboard. "Grab the salsa."

"Sure thing." Elizabeth joined him at the kitchen table.

"We have friends we've known since elementary school, but still... They met at camp, went to different schools, and still managed to keep in touch."

"Oh, yeah, that camp she sent us to that time." Elizabeth stuck a chip into the dip.

"I don't think we ever disappointed her like we did when neither of us wanted to go back the next year."

"Yeah, but it was suffocatingly hot, and we didn't have air conditioning. What was she thinking?"

"And they had snakes and alligators." Jeremy shuddered. "Not my favorite companions." Now was as good a time as he was apt to get to talk privately with his sister. He wasn't looking forward to it, but she worried him. He swallowed a big gulp of soda and burped loudly.

"Jeez, why do you guys think that's so cool?"

He laughed. "So how are things going with you, Elizabeth?"

"Fine."

"What about school. Are you cutting any more classes?"

"Not since the last time you caught me. So what is this? You're not my boss."

"No, but I worry about you."

"Well, don't. I'm fine. Now unless you want to be late for rehearsal, we need to shove off. That must be Tommy honking now." Elizabeth grabbed a jacket and sauntered toward the garage.

Jeremy sighed, picked up the empty dish of salsa, ran some water, and left it in the sink. "Be right there." That didn't go as well as he'd hoped, but maybe her knowing he was concerned would keep her from stepping too far across the line. He'd keep an eye on her this weekend.

♦ ♦ ♦

She'd been looking forward to this weekend with her childhood friends, one of several trips they scheduled a year. The drive to Irving took about an hour, and the traffic was beastly, but worth it for Addie to get a visit with her best friends at one of their favorite bed and breakfasts. When they didn't have time for a longer trip, this was where they generally stayed.

"So tell us about this detective." Devon Moore had her own cosmetics company in Dallas. It was a perfect job for her because she was always done up—even when they'd gone to camp.

"There's nothing to tell." Addie almost wished there were.

"Cowboy type." Kate cut the apple cake.

"Oh?" Kim Denison filled mugs with coffee and set them on the table in Kate and Addie's room. Kim had the longest drive of any of them, coming from Wichita Falls farther up in North Texas. "How do you know that? Have you met him?"

"I didn't get to meet him, but I saw him at the theatre fundraiser a while ago. He wore a string tie and boots with his tuxedo. All he needed was a western hat to be all hero type. Based on conversations with our girl here, I put two and two together." Kate handed a plate and fork to each woman. "Eat up."

"Coffee and wonderful cake. Great way to end an evening." Devon licked icing off her fork.

Aside from a few contented moans as they consumed the cake, Addie's friends were silent. Maybe they'd drop the subject of Detective Riley. She hoped so. It wasn't as if she had anything to say. They'd had little contact. Maybe things would have been different if someone hadn't murdered Shannon. Guilt surged, curdling the cream-cheese icing. How could she think that?

"They still haven't found who murdered your board member?" Kim asked. "The story hit the Wichita Falls newspaper. Of course, maybe it was a slow day because I've seen nothing more."

"No." Addie pushed the cake around on her plate. Hard to enjoy now.

"The homicide detective interviewed our friend here." Kate took the last bite of her cake. "Why did he do that?"

Devon sat forward on her chair.

"Well, they interviewed everyone connected to the theatre, even his sister-in-law." Addie sipped her coffee.

"His sister-in-law?" asked Kim.

"Can you imagine?" Devon finished her cake.

"He was just doing his job." Addie didn't want them to think badly of Mike.

Kate rose and carried her cup to the kitchenette. "Anyone want some more?"

"Yes, I do." Addie got up and followed. She needed to re-direct the conversation. "Where should be go shopping tomorrow?"

The others all spoke at once.

Thank God. The subject caught everyone's attention and she, and her friends argued over the merits of their favorite places.

"Tomorrow night we're playing Bunko, so don't shoot your wad at the malls." Kim said. Devon dragged Kim from the sofa. "Okay. I need my beauty sleep, so I look great when we hit the shops tomorrow."

"See you for breakfast in the morning," Kim hugged Addie and Kate before heading to the door, "and you should be prepared to shop till you drop."

Addie locked the door after the two women left for their room, which was just down the hall. "We're very lucky, you know?" She glanced at Kate whose eyebrow skimmed her hairline. "Sure, we've all gone through rough times." Addie hugged her friend. "And you, maybe the worst." Addie couldn't imagine how her friend and her daughter had managed to go on with their lives after Kate's husband had been killed in Tower One on 9/11.

"I get what you mean, Addie. We're still friends after all

these years. Remember all the letters we sent when we were kids?" Kate climbed up on one of the two double beds in the large room.

"It wasn't as easy to keep in touch then as it is now."

Addie smiled. "Boy, I did not want to go to camp that year, but Mom and Dad insisted. They needed a place to stash me for the summer while they traveled. Best thing they ever did for me because I met you, Devon, and Kim."

"Don't go maudlin on me, or I'll cry." Kate sniffed.

"Oh, you." Addie threw a pillow at her friend who broke into laughter. Each time one of them calmed down, the other burst out. Finally, Addie crawled off the bed and made her way to the kitchenette. "I'm getting a glass of wine. Otherwise, after all this, I'm never going to fall asleep. Want one?" She held the bottle toward Katherine.

"Yes, thanks. Did Devon say anything to you about her business?"

"She mentioned if things didn't improve, maybe not being able to go later this year when we talked about going to Hot Springs for a week. I figured she was generally grousing about business." Addie drifted around the room, sipping her wine. "She always talks like the bottom is about to drop out, but nobody is a better money manager than Devon." Addie set down the glass. "I'm gonna clean my face." She stepped into the bathroom.

Kate followed and leaned against the doorframe. "Yeah, but this time she may be serious. She told me before you arrived, she's having trouble making the books balance. Can't figure whether her bookkeeper is skimming or something else is going on."

"I hate to hear that. It's such a pain when people don't do what they're supposed to." Clay Bennett's face swam before Addie's closed eyes. When she got home, she'd need to put together the job application form, so they could start looking for his replacement. As soon as Detective Riley solved Shannon's murder, her theatre family could get back to normal.

"Okay, your turn." Addie stepped past Kate, crossed to her bag and pulled out her pajamas. "I'm going to read a bit before going to sleep. Will the light bother you?"

"Of course not. I know that's the only way you can go to sleep. Besides, we now have all these cool little lights or e-readers that don't bother anyone else. I hope things work out for you at the theatre, sweetie."

"Thanks. Me too. Who do you think will make the first purchase tomorrow?"

"My money's on Kim. Her husband's family is rolling in old ranching money. They seem to have been totally unaffected by the recent economic downturn."

"We'll see. I just might get an early start on Christmas gifts." Addie clicked on her e-reader.

"When was the last time you bought anything for Christmas before Thanksgiving?"

"Well, I could start." She rolled her eyes. After having seen Elizabeth do it so much, she had no trouble mimicking the look.

"Right."

Addie ignored her friend's comeback and directed her gaze to the lighted page of her e-reader, but her mind's eye only saw gorgeous Mike Riley dressed in his tux, boots, and string tie.

◆ ◆ ◆

Wednesday, October 17

After a couple of visits and an unlimited supply of the drugs, Clay had hooked Elizabeth. Now to start backing off so she'd do anything he asked. It was time to put into effect his plan for the gun. Knocking from the porch made him smile. Elizabeth was right on time.

He opened the door. "Hi."

"Hey." She threw both arms around him. "I've missed you."

Clay's glaze darted over the apartment complex. Only that old man taking his trash to the dumpster. He slid his arms around the girl and ushered her into his apartment. "It's only been a few days, Elizabeth." He yanked a strand of her long black hair, so like her mother's.

"But you have stuff I can only get here with you." She dropped her book bag on the sofa and headed for the refrigerator.

Clay smiled at how much at home she appeared to be here. Elizabeth lifted out two bottles of beer from the refrigerator. She handed him one before carrying hers toward the chest in the entry hall. She pulled open the top drawer, set down her bottle, and turned back toward him, resting her hands on her slim hips. "Where's your special blend of cigs?" Small frown lines sprang up between her eyebrows.

"Listen, Elizabeth. I'm sorry. I don't have any of those smokes today. You know they're expensive." He took two swallows of the icy beer.

Her frown deepened, and she stomped to the windows where she took several large gulps of the golden brew. After a while, she turned around. "How much are we talking? I might be able to help. It's almost time for my allowance."

Yes, she'd be able to help. "Bring me what you can, and we'll see what we can do."

◆ ◆ ◆

Friday, October 19

Addie rode the escalator up to the second floor in the building that held the Chisholm Trail Club. Despite being in a modern, shiny glass building, the appointments of the dining room were distinctly old world. Dark mahogany wood pillars and paneling.

"Welcome, ma'am." The tuxedoed maître'd stood erect at the entrance.

"I'm meeting Jonathan Harding."

"Oh, yes, Ms. Greer. Right this way."

Before she reached the table, Jonathan stood, and to her surprise greeted her with a kiss on the cheek.

"I'm so glad you could make it, my dear." He waited until

she sat in one of the large comfortable leather chairs before he took his place at the table covered in beige linen over black. "Would you like to start with a glass of wine?"

"I don't think so, thank you." Addie, glad she dressed in her best black suit with the royal blue silk blouse, spread her napkin in her lap. The scent of the pink carnations in the crystal vase in the center of the table wafted toward her. "These are lovely."

"Let's pretend this is an early dinner rather than a late lunch. I've taken the liberty of ordering for you. Besides, I really want you to try my favorite Sauvignon Blanc."

Ordered for her, huh? An unusual liberty when they didn't know each other well. "All right. Just one glass." Nevertheless, Jonathan ordered a bottle. The clear color sparkled in the fine crystal. She raised it to her lips, sniffed, and then sipped. The cool liquid caressed her tongue. She set the glass on the table. "I have to admit this is quite excellent. How did you learn about it?"

"I have friends who own a small vineyard in California. I first bought it just to be supportive. You know how it is."

Addie nodded, impressed that Jonathan would take that action.

"The wine turned out to be one of my favorites. I've invested in their vineyards and don't miss an opportunity to introduce others to what I think of as an outstanding wine."

"How lucky for you the Club stocks it."

"They don't regularly yet. I've found that sometimes we have to make our own luck." He took another sip, seemed to roll it on his tongue and then swallowed. "I have it flown in for the Club and my home. I'm hoping enough others will begin to ask for it that Henri will order it directly from the vineyard."

Addie leaned back in the chair and studied her dinner partner. Jonathan must be considerably wealthier than she'd understood. Their salads came and the conversation continued on general topics. The main course arrived—sea bass, which was Addie's favorite. She wondered if he knew or was just lucky. Hmm. Jonathan turned the conversation to the theatre.

"Have things begun to take a more normal turn for you at work?"

"We had the costume room professionally cleaned so it's usable again, though I confess to always getting a slight chill whenever I enter. If we had enough money, I'd reconfigure the area. Change the walls, put something else in there, so it wasn't such a constant reminder of what happened." She couldn't repress the shiver that ran through her at the thought of poor Shannon lying there by herself for part of a day.

"Let's talk about money." Jonathan smiled at the server who stopped to refill their wine glasses. "The fundraiser last month seemed a huge success. Was it financially?"

"I'm glad you had a good time, Jonathan." Addie smiled with pride at their accomplishment. "Yes, we did very well, but of course, we were already in the hole. So now we're out of the red, but we don't have enough capitol for the rest of the year's shows."

"And you're missing a board member. How is that position filled?" He sipped his wine and studied her across the top of the crystal.

"Word of mouth. A current board member or the staff will run across someone who expresses an interest in serving and a willingness to help support the theatre financially and/or with their time. I'll ask that person if they're willing to serve when a term expires, or we have a vacancy."

Jonathan didn't say anything, just nodded his head.

Addie took a quick sip of the luscious wine, set the glass down. No more of that. She needed a clear head to negotiate with this extremely smart man. She leaned across the table and cocked her head. "So, tell me, Jonathan, are you perhaps interested in a position on the board?"

She refrained from physically crossing her fingers, but mentally did so. His support would probably make the difference between a successful year or not. She held her breath.

"The short answer is yes."

Addie let out a long sigh, and a smile spread across her face. She relaxed against the comfortable chair with the high back.

"But there are some conditions."

"What are they?" Addie couldn't imagine him asking for something she couldn't provide. His own parking spot perhaps?

"I'll be an active member of your board, and I'll contribute five hundred thousand—"

She straightened, both hands flying in front of her mouth, and gasped. "Wow." Was he serious? This would be fantastic and fix their problems for some time.

"Yes, but remember I have conditions."

"I'm sure we can work this out, Jonathan. Tell me." Addie leaned forward again, daring to hope they could resolve this.

After taking a sip of his wine, Jonathan twirled the glass on the cloth, almost as if he were nervous. Addie had never met a more self-assured man in her life. What was bothering him?

"Well, I'm very attracted to you, Addie."

Oh my. Addie leaned into her chair.

"Hear me out." He raised his hand, as if to keep her from fleeing. "You're beautiful, articulate, cultured. I have many engagements where it would be beneficial to me to have someone like you on my arm. If you will agree to accompany me the majority of the times I ask—I'm not unreasonable and realize there may be some conflicts with schedules—then I'll accept a seat on the board and take care of your theatre's financial worries." He leaned back in his chair.

For a moment, Addie sat in stunned silence. Why would this attractive and powerful man feel he had to bribe someone to go out with him?

"Well, Jonathan, I'm flattered, but there must be lots of women dying to have you as an escort."

"But I want to go out with you. I'm sixty, Addie, and what, you're maybe forty?"

"Thanks for the compliment, but for the record I'm forty-five."

"Still a significant age difference. Men must be falling all over themselves to get your attention."

Addie chuckled. "I have to tell you, Jonathan, no one has

done so much for my self-esteem in a long time. To be truthful, I've only dated a few times since my divorce. Between my children and work, play times have been in short supply. And no one caught my interest." Her gaze fastened on the glass windows.

Why would Mike Riley's face flit across her mind? Nothing could come of whatever slight attraction she might've sensed. So far as she knew, she was still a suspect or at least a person of interest, as they say on TV.

"Addie." His voice called her attention back to her dinner companion. "I won't expect anything of a sexual nature from you, merely your presence."

Her cheeks grew warm. Did he mean he wasn't interested that way?

He reached across and took her hand. "Not that I'd be averse to that happening if we grew to care about each other that way, but that's not part of the deal I'm offering. When do you think you might be able to give me an answer? Twenty-four hours perhaps?"

Addie squeezed his hand and then removed hers. Her fingers drummed lightly on the beige tablecloth. Damn, she was actually considering this. The money and his good sense on the board would be invaluable. He was only asking for a little of her time. She could make this work. The next board meeting was in a few weeks. It would be helpful if they could replace Shannon at the first opportunity.

"Addie?"

"Jonathan I can give you an answer today."

"That would be wonderful if the answer is yes."

"First, I want to tell you about a situation and see where you might stand." She explained the deal with Clay Bennett, how she wanted to fire him because of his squandering of the budget and his questionable behavior with the ensemble girls.

"To fire Bennett, I need one more board member's vote. With Shannon's death I lost that."

"You're asking if I'll be that vote?"

"Yes, I am."

"And if I say yes, do we have a deal?"

Addie nodded. She hoped she wasn't making a mistake. But it seemed like such a win-win, for her, for Jonathan, and the theatre.

He raised his glass. "Then, my dear, we have a deal."

Addie raised her glass and clinked with his. "A deal."

◆ ◆ ◆

Saturday, October 20

"How are rehearsals going, Jeremy? You and Elizabeth have been really late the last couple of nights." Addie chopped half a clove of garlic for the spaghetti sauce. It was one of their family traditions, Saturday night pasta supper, but harder and harder to make happen as the kids got older. Now it was more like monthly.

Jeremy plopped onto one of the kitchen bar stools. "We've had to do some switching around. A couple of kids had injuries and dropped out. So we're re-blocking, and you know how that goes." His mouth screwed around, and his eyebrows flew skyward, giving him an almost comic look.

Addie reached across and ruffled his hair. "Get the cheese from the refrigerator and grate it, please. How are you doing with the River City number?"

"Pretty good. He rose from the stool, ambled over to the refrigerator, and removed the package of fresh mozzarella. "My theatre teacher gave me some tongue twisters to practice. It makes the words in the song seem not so fast. We've got the cutest kids from a neighboring elementary school filling in with the townspeople."

He snatched a scoop of cheese from the bowl and plopped it into his mouth. Addie whacked his knuckles with a wooden spoon. "No snacks."

Jeremy laughed. "There's this one little girl. She has blonde pigtails. Maybe third grade. She's a good little dancer, and she's always telling the other children when they aren't getting it right." He set the bowl of cheese on the table and then reached across and snagged a couple of olives. "How much longer until supper is ready? It's hungry in here." He rubbed his stomach in an imitation of what he used to do as a small boy.

Addie blinked her eyes. He wouldn't be happy to see tears. "Good news then. I'm popping the garlic bread in the oven. Go tell you sister we're ready, please."

As soon as her kids turned seventeen, Addie allowed them to have wine at home. Not often, but she thought it was a safer initiation into the drinking world than they'd get on their own with friends. Oh, she wasn't naïve enough to believe neither of her children, as high school seniors, had taken a drink away from home, but she had an agreement with them never to get in a vehicle with a person who'd been drinking, or to ever to drive themselves if they'd taken a drink. They just had to call, and she'd come get them.

Anytime. Anywhere. No questions.

Jeremy returned to the kitchen. "She'll be here in a minute." He picked up the wine, opened it, and filled the first of the three glasses.

By the time Addie had served the pasta and gotten the salad from the refrigerator, Elizabeth came in and pulled out her chair. "Smells good, Mom."

"I'm glad we could pull this off tonight. We've missed several Saturdays. How do you think rehearsals are coming for *The Music Man*, Elizabeth?"

Elizabeth shot a glance at her brother. "Didn't you ask Jeremy?"

"Yes, but now I'm asking you."

"No one makes sauce like you, Mom. Can you get me a little more?" Jeremy held up his plate.

"Sure, dear." Addie took the plate and left the table.

"So, Mom, what's the news on the murder?" Jeremy asked.

"The police are still investigating. They haven't made any arrests. It's just all so sad." She set his plate in front of him. Addie wished he hadn't brought up the subject. She picked up her fork, but the loss of Shannon in that way and at the theatre made her slightly ill. She shoved the spaghetti around on her plate.

When they were almost finished eating, Jeremy said, "We'll clean up, Mom, since you cooked."

"Well thanks, guys. Did you tell your father about the show, Jeremy? I think he might like to come. At least, let him make the decision."

"I'll call him. Okay, you're out of here. Take a glass of wine, go read a book, or watch one of your TV shows." Jeremy put his palms on his mother's shoulders and guided her toward the kitchen door.

"Thanks, guys. I love you, too. Holler if you need me for anything."

◆ ◆ ◆

"I'll rinse, Elizabeth. You fill the washer."

"Thanks, Jeremy." She heaved a big sigh. "You redirected Mom when she asked about rehearsal. I didn't know what to say because I didn't know what you'd told her." She took the plates as Jeremy handed them to her and slid them into the washer.

"I didn't give you up, Elizabeth." Maybe he should have. "But don't you think you ought to tell her before she goes to a performance and learns then that you're not in the show? Cause that's what will happen if you miss one more practice." He scrubbed the saucepot.

"Yeah, I'll get there. I will." She put the left over sauce in a container and set it in the refrigerator.

"What happens to you? We arrive at rehearsal together, and then I never see you again. I covered for you a couple of times even said you'd gotten sick. But I can't keep that up. You said you were going to stick with this."

Jeremy closed the dishwasher and turned it on. He took hold of his sister's arms. "Look at me. What happened?"

She didn't make eye contact with him. He shook her arm. "Elizabeth?"

"I met someone." Her voice was soft, not the loud volume she'd had ever since she'd been a little girl.

"Like a boyfriend?"

"We're not both gay, Jeremy, so yes, kind of like a boyfriend, though not really. But a friend. Speaking of telling people, when are you telling Dad?" She grabbed a sponge and washed off the kitchen table.

"That's another issue, Elizabeth, but right now we're talking about you. Who's the guy? Where'd you meet him?"

"He makes me feel special. He treats me good, Jeremy. I think I might be falling for him." She dropped the sponge in the dish on the counter next to the sink and faced him.

"Well, good. I'm happy for you, but you can't let him make you cut school or the rehearsals."

"It'll be fine, Jeremy. I'll do better. I promise. Thanks." She gave him a quick hug and took off toward her room.

Jeremy ran a hand through his hair. Hell. Was he making a mistake?

CHAPTER FIVE

Monday, October 22

Monday morning first thing, Addie walked straight into the office of Roger Garland, their accountant. "We are about to be hit with an infusion of cash."

"What're you talking about?" He looked up from his computer. "You rob a bank?"

"Of course not. What would you say to an extra five hundred thousand dollars, Roger? What will that do to all of our red ink?" She was too excited to sit and paced back and forth in front of his desk. She'd dressed up today, navy slacks and matching long-sleeved top, a navy and green long sweater, and short boots for the announcement.

"Addie, are you nuts? Where are we going to get that kind of money? The fundraiser didn't even bring in that kind of dough."

She made herself stop, sinking into one of the chairs in front of his desk. She probably did look a little...well, crazy. The smile on her face made her jaws ache.

"Do you remember meeting Jonathan Harding at the party? Tall, distinguished-looking gentleman?"

"Yes. Kind of an older guy with a really great looking

head of silver hair."

Addie smiled. Roger was already going bald in his mid-thirties, so he had an appreciation for anyone with lots of hair. "Yes. That's the one. Well, Mr. Harding is going to join our board, and he'll bring five hundred thousand dollars with him." Addie sprang from the chair and spun with her arms flung wide. "Oh, doesn't that just sound fantastic!"

Roger laughed. "That solves our problems for this year and provides a cushion even into next year."

"Yep. Do I look a little smug?"

"Well, you look very contented with the turn of events."

"I need to send out an announcement to the board members adding his appointment to the agenda." She started for the door.

"Does this mean with Harding joining the board, you'll go ahead with a vote on Clay?"

Addie turned back to Roger. Did he look hopeful? Was he also one of the people Clay held under his thumb? She nodded.

"Good luck."

Guess that answered that question. "Thanks. Show me any bills you're going to pay first and then bring me a draft of a new budget with the infusion of cash. We'll want to share that with the board. That should be way more fun to put together, huh?"

"You got that right. Good job snagging Harding."

Roger had already turned back to his computer, a big smile on his face, before Addie got through the door. She went to her office to work on drafting a message to the board about

Jonathan. Besides his money, he'd be a good addition, what with his head for business.

◆ ◆ ◆

Thursday, October 25

Fall in Fort Worth provided no shortage of events and fundraising galas for all kinds of worthy causes. Big Brothers and Sisters, the Bridge Association for kids who had nowhere else to go, and research for practically every disease known, to name a few. Jonathan Harding had told her he supported many of them. The first Addie was attending with him was An Artists' Christmas for Camp Fire. The second was for Alzheimer's research. The list included several other events.

Addie had been once before and remembered it as a fun evening with great paintings and photos and pieces of artwork to bid on, a lavish sit-down dinner, dancing to a great band, and an auction of large ticket items like a trip to Paris for two or season tickets to the Cowboys. Nothing she'd be bidding on, but she might look for a new piece of art for the lobby of the theatre.

"Hey, Mom, a limo just pulled up in front of the house." Jeremy bounced into her room without knocking.

"Must be Mr. Harding."

"You look great, Mom."

"Thanks." She kissed her son on the cheek "Don't wait up. I may be late." Jeremy was hot on her heels when she headed to the front of the house. The chimes rang, and she opened the door. "Hello, Jonathan. Come in. This is my son Jeremy. Mr. Harding."

"Very nice to meet you, sir." He extended his hand.

"Nice to meet you, too. Don't worry about your mother. I'll look after her. May I help you with your coat, Addie?"

"Thank you." There were only a few things from her marriage with Judson Greer she appreciated. Two of them were her children, the third her house, and the fourth, this coat. A ranch mink stroller, many years old, but quite perfect for a benefit held on this unseasonably cold October night.

Addie stopped before going outside. She turned back to Jeremy. "Have you seen your sister in a while?"

"She's in her room with the music blasting."

"Can you give me another moment, Jonathan?"

"Certainly. Jeremy and I'll visit."

Addie went down the hall to the other side of the house where the kids' rooms were. As she approached, the bass bonged in her chest. How did Elizabeth stand that? Addie knocked once and entered.

"Elizabeth, I'm leaving."

Her daughter glanced at her and waved then turned back to the sketchbook in her hands. Addie let out a long breath and went out of the room, pulling the door behind her.

"Okay, I'm ready, Jonathan. Good night, Jeremy."

Jonathan held open the door but turned back to Jeremy. "Nice to visit with you. Good luck with your show. I'll get your mother to tell me when it is. I'd like to see it."

"Thanks, sir. Y'all have fun."

The door closed and Addie hurried to the limo with Jonathan's arm protectively around her back. It was nice. She'd been independent for a long time.

"I loved the blue dress you wore for the theatre fundraiser last month, but you're amazing in this green."

Addie smiled as she climbed into the limo. He remembered what she'd worn. When Jonathan joined her on the back seat, she said, "Thanks for being kind to my son. His father is not too thrilled Jeremy wants to go into performing professionally."

"Frequently sons don't want to follow in their father's footsteps."

"Do you have sons, Jonathan? You sound like you're speaking from experience."

"Let's start with a glass of champagne to celebrate our arrangement, and then I'll tell you about my sons."

Addie nodded. There was apparently more to this man than just a large bank account. Of course, she knew he was successful. She'd done a little research. He was a native Texan, grew up in Houston. His father had drilled oil wells and made a bundle.

She took a cautious sip of her drink, regretting not taking time to eat a piece of bread before leaving home. Lunch was a long time ago and supper would be late. She'd have to go easy on the liquor. Wouldn't do to get rip-roaring drunk on the first outing with the theatre's benefactor.

"I married my high school sweetheart. She gave me two sons. The oldest was a police officer and killed in the line of duty." His lips thinned.

Addie instinctively clasped his hand in hers. "Jonathan, I'm so sorry for your loss."

He patted hers and left his on top. Maybe she shouldn't have initiated that contact, but her heart ached for him. "What about your wife and other son?" *Please don't' let him still be married.* She'd never even thought to check that. If he were, she'd have to renege on their deal, and the theatre would lose his gift.

"It was devastating. My wife never got over it, slowly wasting away until she died five years ago."

"I'm so sorry." Addie blinked to keep tears from falling.

"You have a gentle heart, Addie. The final blow was when our younger son also decided to go into law enforcement. The idea she might lose him the same way was too much."

"I guess you didn't want him to do that either."

"No, but you can't stand between a man and what's in his heart. We all must choose." He lifted his glass from the side holder and finished off the clear liquid. "I apologize for starting our evening out on such a dark note."

"Don't apologize on my account. I asked. You answered. Where's your son live?"

"He's in Houston, married to a wonderful woman, and they have a son."

"Good." She smiled.

The limo pulled into the covered area in front of the Fort Worth Hotel. "Looks like we've arrived," Jonathan said.

A valet opened the door, and by the time Addie was

stepping out, Jonathan had reached her side. With a hand on her back again, he ushered her through the crowds and into the lobby. The marble floors gleamed. Massive columns strung with tiny lights reached to the two-story ceiling.

They rode up the escalator to the second floor, checked their coats, and got another glass of champagne. Large vases of carnations and hydrangeas filled odd corners in the outer room. Addie didn't have to lean close. "How delightful. Nothing beats the scent of carnations."

Jonathan steered her past a roadblock of people. The soft notes of the orchestra filtered to them from inside the main room. They wandered through the various art exhibits. Jonathan introduced her to people he knew, and she did the same. No one seemed surprised to see them together.

Interesting.

A large painting of bluebonnets caught Addie's eye, and she studied it from both close up and at a distance.

"Do you like this one especially?" Jonathan stopped next to her.

"I'm thinking it might work in the theatre lobby. I'll have to keep an eye on how the bids go. Many people may think it's too ordinary. I mean Texas Bluebonnets, but still..."

"Addie."

She turned to find Cindy Riley and her husband Pat crossing toward them. Addie reminded them they'd met Jonathan at the theatre fundraiser.

"Since then, Jonathan and I have run into each other at several other community events," Pat said, shaking the man's hand.

"I was pleased to hear you'd be joining the theatre board," Cindy said.

"Thanks. I'm looking forward to serving. I think Addie runs an excellent organization which provides an important service to our town."

Cindy laughed. "You've got him indoctrinated all ready, Addie. Good for you."

The two couples chatted for a while longer but were sitting at different tables. Jonathan had purchased an entire table and invited people who worked with him. Before they went to sit down, Addie wrote a bid on the bluebonnet painting. She'd been right, not many people had bid on it so far. She crossed her fingers and let Jonathan lead her into the dining room.

The meal was scrumptious. Filet mignon not overcooked. Grilled asparagus. Wild rice. And for dessert, cream brulé. Before the dancing began, Addie excused herself and went to the ladies' room. "Hey, Cindy. Wasn't that meal wonderful?"

Her friend, who was reapplying lipstick, made eye contact with Addie in the mirror. "Absolutely. This is one of my favorite events."

"You and Pat go to a lot of these?" Addie thought they must have considerably more money than Pat's brother Mike. A police detective probably wasn't too high on the pay scale.

"We go to about five or six a year. We try to vary what we attend but always come to this and, of course, cancer prevention. Now I'm on the board, I won't miss our Cowtown

Theatre Night of Stars events. Have you known Jonathan long?"

"Actually, no. I knew of him but only met him at our event."

"How fortunate you got him to come on the board."

"His money and his expertise will be invaluable."

"Are you bidding on anything?" Cindy slipped her lipstick into her small silver clutch.

"Actually, I am. There's a lovely bluebonnet picture I have my eye on for the theatre lobby."

"Well, let's go see how you're doing?" Cindy opened the door and sailed through. Addie laughed as she followed her.

◆ ◆ ◆

Saturday, November 3

Mike climbed off his horse, surprised to see the dust from a car heading toward his house. He took time to unsaddle Blackie. "I'll be back and bring you an apple." He rubbed his horse's nose and then walked around to the front of the house. "Cindy, is everything al; right? You were driving like a bat out of hell." He gave his sister-in-law a quick hug. "Did I know you were coming?"

"No, you didn't, but I know you and Saturday mornings. Not much interferes with your ride except a dead body. It was so cold last night that I took a chance all the murderers stayed inside." She laughed.

"As it turns out you're right. I need to finish brushing down Blackie. I'll go in with you to grab an apple for him. You fix yourself a cup of coffee, and I'll be along."

"Well, I'm certainly not standing around out here in the cold. I'll occupy myself. Take your time."

What the hell was this all about? Cindy didn't come out here very often. She really wasn't a ranch kind of person. Guess he'd find out.

He finished putting away Blackie, who was appropriately appreciative of the apple, and Mike went toward the house to see what bee had gotten in Cindy's hair.

"I saw you coming and poured you a fresh cup." Cindy was perched on a bar stool in the kitchen, a cup, and the newspaper in front of her.

"Thanks." He took a quick swallow. "You make good coffee, Cindy. Not that I'm not glad to see you, but why'd you come out?

"I saw Addison Greer last night."

"Okay. I'd expect since you're on the theatre board, you'd see her pretty frequently."

"Pat and I attended a black tie fundraiser for the Alzheimer's Association."

"I think y'all hauled my ass there one time."

"Yes, and you threatened to disown us if we took you again."

"Now, Cindy, I still go to the cancer things with you and, hell, I even went to the Cowtown Theatre Night of something last month." He took another swallow of coffee, closed his eyes, and envisioned the brunette in the royal blue strapless dress. She'd dazzled him with her beauty and charm. Hell of a note since she was now a person of interest in a murder investigation.

"Mike, where'd you go?"

He set his cup down and glanced at his sister-in-law. "Just savoring the flavor." Cindy didn't need to know it wasn't her coffee. "So you drove all the way out here to give me an update on Pat's and your social calendar?"

She set her cup down and folded her hands in front of her. "No, dear brother-in-law of mine. I came to tell you we ran into Addie at the fundraiser, wearing a gorgeous gold number I'd almost kill to have—"

Mike stiffened.

"Joking, joking."

"Okay, you came to tell me what Ms. Greer was wearing." Mike laughed. "I gotta tell you Cindy, I'm lost. What are you getting at?"

"Addie was there with wealthy oil tycoon Jonathan Harding. We also ran into them a few days earlier at the Camp Fire Artists' Christmas. She was wearing green then."

"Okay. Well, I don't quite get the point of your information. You think I've taken a sudden interest in Ms. Greer's wardrobe?"

"The point, Mr. Detective, is if you're going to sit on your hands while this investigation continues, you're running the risk of losing any chance you might've had of forming a relationship with Addie."

Mike rose from the stool, walked to the coffee maker, and poured himself another cup. He downed half of it before turning back to Cindy. "I can't have a relationship with Ms. Greer as long as she's a person of interest in the investigation. Even if I wanted a relationship," he added for good measure.

"Right. Solve the damn murder, Mike or you're going to miss out one very good woman."

◆ ◆ ◆

Monday, November 5

Mike re-read the coroner's report. A .38 did the damage. They had the bullet, and if they could find a gun they'd be able to match it up. "Not a lot else from the autopsy either, Rick."

"Yeah, disappointing."

"We've got to find the weapon." Mike flipped through the pages of the report again before straightening the sheets and put them in the folder.

"One of the ensemble girls hinted that Bennett had come on to her, and when she protested, said he'd get her fired. She needed the job, so she never reported him."

"Why did she now?" Mike asked.

"Maybe I made her feel safe. I don't know."

"What say we go have another talk with Bennett?" Mike stood and pulled his jacket off the back of his chair.

"Right behind you."

They made good time getting from downtown to the west side of Fort Worth where the theatre stood. They walked in, nodding to a couple of the staff and made their way to Bennett's office. Mike knocked once and pushed open the door.

"Mr. Bennett, we have a few more questions for you if you have time." Mike stopped in front of the desk. Rick stood by the door, as if he thought the man might make a run for it.

Bennett stood. "Sure. I'd ask you in, but you already are. Have a seat." He waved to the chairs in front of his desk.

Mike settled into one, but Rick stayed where he was.

"What can I do for you gentlemen? Have you reached any conclusions about the sad loss of our Ms. DeWitt?" Clay settled behind his desk, cluttered with papers, files, and catalogues. He'd apparently been in the middle of a project.

"We're still gathering facts." Mike crossed one leg over the other and pulled his small notebook from his inside jacket pocket. "Do you own a weapon, Mr. Bennett?"

"No. We have a few in props for theatrical purposes, but I don't personally own a weapon. Never have seen the need. In most instances, I'm capable of defending myself. I have black belts in several martial arts."

"I see. I've heard you and Ms. Greer have a few areas of conflict. Do you want to comment?"

"As in any organization, we have our share of gossipers. You can't believe everything you hear, Detective."

"So there's no truth to the stories you and Ms. Greer have had words?" Rick stepped in closer. "Over funding issues?"

"We've had professional disagreements. I'd hardly call them conflicts." He gestured to the piles on his desk. "As you can see, I have work to do. Is there another way I can help you?"

"A couple more questions, Mr. Bennett. Is there any truth

to the rumors you've been coming on to some of the female ensemble members?"

Bennett laughed. "Let me be frank with you, Detective, I'm rather sought after by some of the young girls. But being entirely professional, I tell them no. Some of them get their feelings hurt and say things that aren't true. I'd never do anything inappropriate."

"Are you aware of any other staff members who own a weapon?" Mike held his pencil above the pad, ready to note any response.

"I'm afraid I can only offer you rumors on that subject."

"You tell us the rumors and leave us to decide about the truth of them," Mike said.

"I've heard Addie—Ms. Greer—has a weapon. Again, just rumor."

Mike noted the remark in his book. *Well, hell.* He glanced at his partner. "Anything else, Detective Martinez?"

"No. This will do for now." He, too, closed his book.

Mike stood. "Thank you, Mr. Bennett, we may be back."

◆ ◆ ◆

"Anytime, Detectives. Would you mind closing the door as you leave?" The door shut with something just short of a slam, and Clay reached for his cell. It was time to move the action along. "Elizabeth, can you meet me in the next fifteen minutes or so?"

"I've got one more class, Clay."

"Be there for the attendance then slip out. You've done that before. I've got something you're going to love."

"Oh?" Her voice shook with excitement. "You've got more of those special smokes?"

"Yeah."

"But, Clay, I can't pay for them right now."

"We'll think of something. I'll meet you at the apartment."

"Yeah, okay. I'll be there."

Clay disconnected and headed through his office door. "I'll be back in a while, have an errand to run," Clay said to the receptionist in the box office. Always better to be up front in case anyone wanted him for something. He drove quickly to the small apartment complex in a mixed area of Arlington Heights, known for older homes and brand new McMansions. Owners tore down existing buildings and put up new. The apartments fell into the older category. His was just a one bedroom but suited his needs.

Clay entered and poured himself a drink. This next piece was crucial to his ultimate success. He opened the drawer with the cigarettes with the drug already added—the drug which would lower Elizabeth's inhibitions. With the way the girl felt about her mother, Clay might not have needed to use it, but better safe than sorry.

Where was she? Clay paced to the window and looked out. He had a tight opening to get things done if the detectives went directly to Greer's house. He stopped in front of the window. There she was, hurrying up the street. Good.

"Clay, Clay. It's me. Open up." The knocking on the door blended with Elizabeth's words.

He opened the door, and she burst through, her long skirt and silky over-blouse flying. "I was almost caught getting off campus." Her chest heaved as she worked to catch her breath.

"But you made it. That's all that's important. Do you want a drink before we sample these smokes?"

"Yeah." Her gaze locked on the cigarettes lying on the coffee table.

"Have a seat, Elizabeth, while I get that for you." He came back with two glasses of whiskey and handed her one. "To you, Elizabeth, a beautiful woman." He toasted her then threw back the alcohol. It didn't burn as much as the first had.

Elizabeth only sipped at the liquor, but still her cheeks turned pink from the drink and his flattering words. If she dropped the Goth get-up, she would be beautiful. She looked a lot like her mother.

"Ready for the smoke, Elizabeth?" Clay picked up the off-white stick and waved it under her nose. She leaned toward it as he moved it away.

"How am I going to pay for these?" She laced her fingers together as if to keep from grabbing for what he offered.

"Let's enjoy our smoke first, and then I'll tell you." Clay flicked his lighter. The tip glowed red as she drew the drug in. Her eyes closed, and she smoked the entire thing.

"Oh, God, that's good." Elizabeth sat up and flung her arms wide.

"Want another?"

"Well, sure." The girl leaned her head against the back of the couch.

He didn't want her too far gone to understand his instructions or be able to follow them. "Let's talk about paying for these, Elizabeth, before we have another."

"Okay. I'll do whatever you want me to but give me the second smoke."

"Patience, dear. I want your help to play a practical joke on your mother. You up for that?"

"What kind of a joke?" Frown lines formed between her eyes.

"You do what I ask, and you get a supply of this candy."

"Oh." She stared at the sticks lying on the table. "Okay, tell me what you want me to do." She leaned forward as if just being closer to the cigarettes made her feel better.

Clay got off the sofa and went to the sideboard. He lifted out the gun, using a pencil to keep his prints off,

Elizabeth's eyebrows rose, her lids opened wide, and she straightened up.

"Don't worry. It's not real, but we're going to pretend it is for now. You hide it in your mother's house. When someone comes asking about it, you pull it out for all to see."

"That's it?"

"Yep. And I'll keep you supplied with this stuff for the next month." Clay picked up a cigarette, lit it, and pulled deeply into his lungs. "Want another?"

She nodded. He handed her the cigarette, which she

put in her mouth. Clay's lighter flared, and he held it toward her. "Are you going to help me out?"

Elizabeth leaned forward, but Clay moved the lighter away. "What's your answer? Will you help me play this joke on your mother?"

Elizabeth nodded, and he put the flame against the tip of the cigarette. She took a deep draw, held the smoke in her mouth before pulling it into her lungs. Her eyes closed and when she opened them, they appeared glazed. "When do you want me to do this, Clay?"

"I want you to take the gun home right now. I'll drop you off close to the house."

Elizabeth finished the drag then wobbled her way to a standing position. "I'm ready."

"Here's what we're going to do." Clay dropped the weapon into a paper bag. "When you get home, hold the end of the sack and empty the gun into a drawer. Then if you hear anyone asking about a weapon, you can point them to where it is." Clay forced a laugh. "Your mom's going to be so surprised. It'll be a great joke." Elizabeth's high-pitched giggle joined his deeper laugh. Oh, yeah, this should take care of his problems at the theatre with Addison Greer.

♦ ♦ ♦

Tuesday, November 6
The doorbell rang. Addie stopped reviewing the newest

budget Roger had put together, allocating the influx of cash from Jonathan. She left the laptop open on the living room coffee table. It wasn't late afternoon yet, but it was already getting dark. Darn Standard time. Switching back and forth was so disrupting. Always a tough transition.

Addie stifled a yawn. It usually took her two weeks to adjust. She flung open the door without looking to see who it was. Mistake. She could've used the slight warning before seeing Mike Riley standing on her porch.

"Detective. How can I help you?" She stood with one hand on the door-frame, hoping her voice didn't sound as wispy to him as it had to her.

"May, I come in, Ms. Greer?"

"I'm sorry. Yes, of course." She stepped back. "Can I get you iced tea or coffee?"

"No thanks." He took off his white western hat and held it in his hands.

"Well, come into the living room. I was just doing a little budget work." She gestured to one of the wingback chairs and returned to her place on the sofa in front of the laptop.

"Family or theatre?" He sat on the edge of the chair.

"Oh, theatre definitely. Sometimes I think I'll never get caught up with it all."

"I'm sorry."

"Oh, no, this is really a good thing. Our new board member brings not only great expertise but also a wonderful financial contribution. Now, we're figuring out the greatest need."

"So you've already replaced Ms. DeWitt?"

"We will officially at the next board meeting. It may seem inappropriately fast, but I think everyone will be quite happy when they see who it is and look at the revised budget."

"May I ask who the new member will be?"

"You understand it won't be official until the board votes, but Jonathan Harding has agreed to join us."

His eyebrows rose. "The oil man?"

"That's right. Do you know him?"

"I've heard of him. Your organization is fortunate if you're getting an infusion of his kind of wealth."

"Absolutely.

The front door banged open. "Thanks, Tommy. Mom, I'm home." Jeremy breezed through the living room, making a beeline for the kitchen. His usual behavior.

"Jeremy, we have a visitor." Her son slid to a stop and whipped back around.

"Huh?"

"Detective Riley, this is my son, on his way, if I'm not mistaken, to raid the refrigerator."

Jeremy displayed all the manners she'd instilled in him. He walked into the living room and held out his hand. "Jeremy Greer. Nice to meet you, sir." If he remembered that this was the man she'd gone on a date with, he gave no indication.

"Mike Riley. Don't let us keep you from something I did when I got in from school every day. Mom always had fresh cookies. My brother and I put a real hole in our parents' food bill."

Addie imagined they did. Both he and Pat were over six feet and solidly built.

"Wow, you were lucky. I get mostly cheese and crackers or fruit and chips."

Addie shrugged her shoulders. "Not a good mother, I'm afraid. I've always worked, so there've been few of those nice homemade touches. Have you seen your sister?"

"She's not here?"

"Well, I've not seen her come in, but she's been known to slip by me." Addie looked at Detective Riley. "Elizabeth is always watching her weight, so she steers clear of the kitchen when she gets home."

"Mom, Elizabeth and I have to go back for rehearsal. We're into technical, so we're doing the regular times, rather than right after school. Can you drive us?"

"Sure. What time do you need to be there?"

"Seven-thirty."

"We'll get an early supper, and then I'll drop y'all off."

"What play are you doing, Jeremy?" Detective Riley asked.

"*The Music Man.*"

"He's playing the lead." Addie couldn't help but brag.

"Good for you. Don't let us keep you. I was mighty hungry when I got home."

"Jeremy laughed. "Yeah. Nice to meet you, Detective Riley."

"You, too."

Jeremy went on toward the kitchen, his book bag slung

over his shoulder. Addie returned to the couch while Detective Riley remained standing. "He's such a good kid. Always does his homework first opportunity he gets, either before or right after rehearsals."

"He does lots of that kind of thing?"

"Do you know much about theatre or what it takes to get a musical performance ready, Detective?"

"Actually, no. I take it Jeremy's doing a musical?"

She laughed. "Yes. You know, 'Seventy-Six Trombones,' 'You've Got Trouble' 'Till There Was You'."

He looked down, twirled the hat in his hands then glanced back across at her. "I'm more into country music."

"I see. Well, perhaps if you're not busy, you can make one of their performances. Jeremy and Elizabeth are in a fine arts school, and the shows are quite professional."

"I'll think about that." He set his hat on the coffee table and pulled out his notebook. "I don't want to take up more of your time than necessary, but I have a few more questions about Ms. DeWitt's murder."

"All right." She closed the laptop and pulled a leg up underneath her on the sofa, leaning back. He always seemed to find her in warm-ups. Could be because she wore them so often when she wasn't going to be about town working on fundraising for the theatre. "Have a seat and ask away." Riley settled into a chair Addie had always considered large, but he dwarfed it and didn't look too comfortable perched, as he was on the edge.

"I want to know more about the conflict between you and your artistic director, Clay Bennett."

Addie nodded. "Sure. It was unfortunate we played it out in such a public manner."

"What was Ms. DeWitt's role in all of that?"

"I felt Clay was being a spendthrift, seldom coming in on or under budget. More times, he went over. Well, that action, if ignored, will lead the theatre into bankruptcy. I wasn't about to ignore his behavior. My job is to protect the theatre, our financial supporters, and fans."

"And Mrs. DeWitt?"

"I've explained this, Detective."

"I'd like to hear it once more."

Addie couldn't keep the sigh inside before she repeated her earlier story. "I wanted to fire Clay. Unfortunately, the bylaws state I have to have the concurrence of a supermajority of the board. A number of board members supported my intention, but I still needed one more vote."

"Which side was Ms. DeWitt on?"

"Originally, she was on Clay's side, but she'd recently changed her position and supported the firing."

"Did many people know that?"

"I told Pete Talmadge, our stage manager, and your sister-in-law. I believe Shannon planned to tell Clay, but I don't know that for certain."

"With Ms. DeWitt out of the picture, where does that leave you?"

"Again our bylaws, which must be amended, state we will

operate as if all positions are filled. Without Shannon, I wouldn't have a supermajority. So where are you going with this line of questioning?"

"We're trying to determine motive?"

"Oh, my God." Addie jumped off the sofa. Rapid steps carried her across the room from the detective. She spun around. "You think I might've killed her?"

"We're looking at everyone connected to the theatre, Ms. Greer."

"Well, I didn't kill her. She was a wonderful woman, had served us well for many years."

"One last question, Ms. Greer, and I'll be out of your hair."

"What?" She planted her feet a little apart and crossed her arms over her chest.

"Do you own a weapon—a gun?"

"No, I don't. I don't even know how to shoot one."

"Mom."

"Elizabeth, hello, dear. When did you get home?

"A while ago. I came in the back." Elizabeth stood in the archway as if she couldn't decide to enter or not.

"We're going out for an early supper, and then I'll drop you and your brother for rehearsal."

"Okay."

"I'm sorry. Detective, this is my daughter Elizabeth. Detective Riley." What would he make of her dress and make-up?

She nodded and came into the room. "Hi."

"Nice to meet you, Elizabeth." He took her hand when she extended it.

"Get started on your homework until we leave for supper." Elizabeth turned to go.

"Are we finished here, Detective?"

"Mom." Her daughter had stopped and then turned around.

"Yes, dear?

"I heard him asking about a gun."

"Yes, that's right, and I told him I don't have one. We've never had one."

"Well, yesterday, I was looking for scissors and—" She walked over to the small table placed next to the chair in which the detective had been sitting. Slowly she slid open the drawer. "What's this?"

Mike leaned over then straightened. He looked at Addie and Elizabeth then the drawer.

The hair on the back of Addie's neck rose. "What?"

Mike used his pencil and lifted out a gun.

Addie stepped back. Her hands flew in front of her mouth. "Oh, my God. Why didn't you tell me as soon as you saw the gun, Elizabeth?"

"I figured it was a prop, but when the detective asked, I thought I should speak up."

"You did the right thing, Elizabeth." He turned to Addie. "I'll take this downtown, and we'll get it checked. In the meantime, you should come with me."

Addie was stunned into silence. What was happening to

her life? He couldn't really think she'd killed Shannon, could he?

"Hey, Mom." Jeremy yelled from the den. "Remember we have to eat early because we've got to get back to school for rehearsal."

CHAPTER SIX

Tuesday, November 6

Addie rested her elbows on the gray metal table and propped her chin on her clasped hands. The room was so cliché it seemed like a joke. Two chairs on her side of the table, two chairs on the other. A large plate glass window faced her. TV crime shows being a favorite of hers, she assumed someone might be watching.

Detective Riley had escorted her in and then left. His white hat didn't seem to fit him as well as when she'd first met him. Remaining calm through the waiting challenged her need to be up and doing. She resisted twiddling her thumbs while she waited for Riley to come back and question her about the gun.

Why hadn't Elizabeth said something when she first discovered the weapon? What had she been thinking? At the sound of the handle twisting, Addie glanced toward the door. Riley and his partner entered.

"Ms. Greer, you remember my partner, Detective Martinez?" Riley pulled out the chair directly across from her.

"Ms. Greer." Martinez took the other seat.

"Detective." Addie tilted her head in his direction.

"My partner tells me you claim to know nothing about

the .38 caliber loaded Smith & Wesson he found in your house."

"I don't know what your partner told you, Detective Martinez," Addie straightened in the chair, "but let me assure you I don't know anything about that gun."

"Your daughter knew exactly where the weapon was." Mike Riley looked at his notes rather than at her.

Addie rubbed one hand down her face. "I can't explain, Detective. What makes you so sure it was the one used to kill Shannon?"

"We'll ask the questions, Ms. Greer." Martinez stated.

"It's all right, Rick," Detective Riley shot his partner a glare then focused on her. "We'll know for certain when we get the ballistics report." He leaned forward. "If you don't know anything about the gun, do you have any ideas about how it ended up in your living room?"

"I wish I could tell you, but I was stunned when Elizabeth pointed it out this afternoon."

"Were you stunned it was there or that your daughter fingered you, Ms. Greer."

Mike shoved back from the table. "Rick." His tone held censure.

"You know, Detective Martinez, if I were guilty, I don't believe I'd be very inclined to cooperate with you. That was a dreadful thing to say. Neither my daughter nor I have anything to do with the gun." Addie squeezed her hands together. It wouldn't help her case to slug Martinez, but that would make her feel a great deal better.

"So how do you think it go there?" Martinez continued

the questions.

"I. Have. No. Idea." She leaned forward emphasizing each word.

"Can you give us a list of everyone who's been in your house since the murder?" Detective Riley lightly beat his note pad with a pen.

"I suppose I can come up with that. But, Lord, I can't think any of those people would have brought in a gun."

"If it's not you, then someone else did. You can't have it both ways." Martinez insisted.

The door flew open, and Addie's head snapped in that direction, and the detectives turned also. She didn't recognize the average height, mustachioed man who entered first, but she did the second.

"Jonathan?"

"Addie, this is Douglas Peterson." Jonathan made the introductions. "He's a criminal defense attorney." Both men wore what appeared to be high-priced suits, similar to what her ex always wore.

"Ms. Greer, have you been charged with anything?"

"I don't believe so." She glanced at Mike. "Have I, Detective Riley?"

"No, ma'am." He rose and faced the lawyer. "I'm Detective Mike Riley, and this is Detective Martinez. Are you representing Ms. Greer?"

"Yes, if she agrees." He looked directly at Addie.

"Well, I..." My God. How much would a lawyer cost? Did she really need one?

"If you're concerned about my fee, don't be. Hand me a dollar, and we have deal."

"If I'm arrested..." A shudder ripped through her system. "If I'm arrested, it would surely cost more than a dollar."

"Give him a dollar, Addie. Better to be prepared. I'll pay for anything else." Jonathan crossed his arms over his chest.

"I can't let you do that."

"Ms. Greer." Peterson held his hand out.

Addie huffed, "Okay," and reached for her purse on the floor. She pulled out a dollar and extended it to the lawyer. "But we haven't finished this discussion, Jonathan."

"That's quite all right, my dear." A smile of satisfaction crossed his face.

"Now, Detectives, do you have any more questions for my client?" Peterson asked.

Mike looked at Rick who shook his head. "We'd like that list of people who entered your house between the murder and this afternoon when we found the gun."

"I'll put that together for you."

"Then we're leaving." The lawyer helped Addie up. "Gentlemen."

He turned and, along with Harding, ushered her through the door and out of the building.

Addie settled next to Jonathan in the back of the limo, her hands twisting in her lap. He'd insisted they follow the lawyer back to his office.

"Let's get this settled, Addie, and then I'll take you back to your house."

"I appreciate that. I rode to police headquarters with Detective Riley, so I don't have my own transportation. But, Jonathan, I can't let you pay for Mr. Peterson."

"There's nothing to discuss about this issue. Just because you're innocent is no reason to assume you don't need quality legal representation."

"Thank you for the vote of confidence, but think about how this will look, Jonathan, when it gets out. And you know these things always do."

"Hopefully, that you have a fairly good-looking sugar daddy." He laughed. "Your expression is priceless, Addie." He reached for her hand and folded it between his two. "Not to worry. No one will think that."

"Of course, they will. That's not flattering to either of us. You clearly could have anyone you want on your own merits, discounting your gazillions, and to imply the only way you can have my companionship is by paying for it is ludicrous."

"I think that may be the nicest complement I've had in many a day." He released her hand with a final pat. "In point of fact, isn't that what I've done with the money for the theatre? You accompany me to all these social events, and in exchange I've given the theatre five hundred thousand."

"Don't you believe in what we're doing at the theatre?" Addie withdrew a bit.

"Yes, I most certainly do."

"Well then, the way I see it is, you've secured yourself a position on the non-profit board of an organization you believe in—much like many others on the board, I might add—"

"And you attend the fundraisers and galas with me, because...?"

She smiled at him. "Because it gives me an opportunity to get dressed up, the events are fun, and they're for a good cause. And I like you. We're friends, Jonathan, and friends help each other out."

"That's all I'm trying to do with Peterson, Addie."

"But letting you pay for my lawyer implies other ties than we have. I'll see him because he's expecting us and pay him for his time today, but I'll find a lawyer I can afford. If I decide I need one." She rallied a smile for him. "That's not to say I'm ungrateful to you for springing me today. I am appreciative. The time in that little room was grim." She couldn't suppress a shudder.

The limo drew up in front of the gleaming, tall, glass building. Addie had been in it before for lunches with donors. She and Jonathan rode the elevator up to the thirty-ninth floor. The elevator doors opened to reveal glass on either side. One seemed to enclose a conference room. On the other, a receptionist sat at a large counter with lush leather chairs grouped around mahogany tables behind her.

Jonathan identified himself and Addie, and within moments, a woman escorted them down one of the halls to the left. She knocked once and opened the door for them. They entered a large corner office with two walls of floor to ceiling windows.

"Ah, you made good time. Jonathan. You and Ms. Greer have a seat on the sofa there. Do you need anything to drink? I can have coffee, iced tea, or something stronger brought in."

"No thank you, Mr. Peterson." Addie remained standing. "And thank you for getting me out of that dreadful interview room, but I can't afford your services."

Peterson's gaze went directly to Jonathan, who shook his head and shrugged his shoulders. "She's too damned independent for her own good."

"If you'll bill me for your time today, I'll pay you right away." Addie searched in her purse. "Send it to that address, please." She extended a card and after he took it, she shook hands with him. "Thank you again, Mr. Peterson."

"You're welcome, and good luck to you, Ms. Greer."

◆ ◆ ◆

"Well, that's a hell-of-note." Mike dropped back in his chair.

"Interesting for sure."

"My sister-in-law indicated something was going on between Ms. Greer and Mr. Harding. Looks like she nailed it."

"An innocent person doesn't need an attorney, especially such a high powered one as Peterson."

"Come on, Rick. This can be a scary process for someone not versed in the legal system."

"Yeah, I know. I'm just pissed at them swooping in here and clearing out with our only person of interest."

"Well, we won't know that until we get the ballistics report. In the meantime, as soon as we get the list of everyone else who's been in the house, we'll have another group to check out."

Rick stretched. "I'm for calling it a day. Want to grab a beer?"

"Thanks, I'll pass this time. Going to stop by my brother's house."

"Work or pleasure?"

"A little of both."

Mike headed for his truck and drove to his brother's large gray, clapboard house with white shutters in the Rivercrest area of town. Pat had worked hard as a pediatric oncologist, and he'd done well for himself and his family. Mike rapped with the metal knocker. He hadn't called ahead.

For all he knew they might be heading out for some cultural event or to an activity at the kids' prestigious private school.

"Mike. What are you doing here? Well, shoot. That sounded really hospitable." Cindy grabbed his arm and pulled him inside. "Come in. Come in. We haven't eaten yet so I can easily set another place. Join us."

And that was Cindy, all whirlwind, social butterfly with a great heart. Thus all the charity work she did.

"Sorry to show up unannounced. Kids around?"

"No, they're with friends working on school projects. They'll eat when they get home. Pat's not on call, and I expect him home soon, so we decided to eat without them."

"Well, I won't crash your private evening then. I'll check with you tomorrow." Mike turned to leave. This wasn't a good idea anyway.

Cindy looped her arm through his and spun him around. "Come on back to the kitchen. I'm having a glass of wine while I finish the supper. Surely, I can twist your arm for a beer." She opened the stainless steel French door refrigerator.

Mike was sure it was top of the line. Everything Cindy had gotten in her redo of the house fell into that category. "Okay, yeah. Thanks."

"Grab a seat at the bar and tell me what's on your mind."

Cindy opened the oven door and pulled out the rack holding a covered Dutch oven. When she lifted the lid, the aroma made Mike's mouth water. He dropped his hat on one bar stool and sat on another.

She glanced over her shoulder at him. "Sure you're not tempted? Roast beef with potatoes and carrots."

Mike couldn't keep the smile off his face. "Cindy, it smells as good as what Mom cooked."

"High praise indeed. Well, if you won't stay, how about I fix you a to-go box?"

"Won't say no to that. Thanks."

"To ask again, brother-in-law of mine, what's on your mind?"

Mike took a gulp of the beer. Might as well get to the subject. It's why he'd come. "I wanted to talk with you a bit more about Addison Greer."

Cindy turned from the counter to face him. "Oh? Business or pleasure?"

Odd how she used the same words Rick had. He gave

the same answer. "A little of both."

"Okay, but I don't promise to answer everything you ask. Unless you're planning to haul me downtown." She turned back to the counter where she worked on his take-home. "And somehow I think your brother might take exception to that move, given we were out of town when the murder happened."

Mike fiddled with his bottle of beer. How to start? "How many times have you seen Addie with Jonathan Harding?"

Cindy slanted him a glance over her shoulder, and she couldn't hide the grin spreading across her face.

"Well, I think three times. You know non-profits hit the fall and winter season hard. So, yeah, they've been together at the last three events Pat and I attended. "May I ask why you're interested?"

"I had her down at police headquarters, questioning her about a weapon I found at her house earlier today."

"A weapon? My God. You took her downtown. To one of your little gray rooms?"

He nodded and took a swallow of the beer.

"How'd you get a search warrant?"

"Didn't have one."

"Well, I don't know much about what you do, Mike, but I watch TV. You can't go through someone's house without a search warrant. And you can't get that without probable clause."

"Her daughter pointed it out when I stopped by to ask some more questions."

"What?" Cindy spun around and crossed to the bar. She

pulled out a stool and sat. "How in the world did that come about?"

After Mike explained, Cindy reached for his hand, and squeezed. "The poor woman. I can barely stand to contemplate what that must have been like for her."

"All in all, she was pretty cool through the whole thing. She arranged for her kids to get to rehearsals, and then I took her in for questioning."

"You said, kids, plural. I thought her son was in a play and her daughter is the artist?"

"Both are in *The Music Man*. Her son has the lead."

"They go to that fine arts school."

"That's right."

"We should go see a performance."

"I don't know about that, Cindy."

"Don't you think, if you have any interest in the woman at all, you'll need to do a fair amount of ass kissing to make up for dragging her downtown? Going to see her son perform is small potatoes, my friend."

"Well, we'll see. Cindy, you know almost anyone is capable of murder, given the right motivation."

She hopped off the stool. "Now listen, Mike Riley, there is no way you can convince me that Addison Greer did this, and if you aren't careful you just might lose your doggy bag." She stalked back to the counter and finished putting a healthy serving of the meat, potatoes, and carrots into a container made especially for the job. She finished, flipped back around to him, and took a sip of her wine.

"So what does any of this have to do with Jonathan Harding? That's how you started this inquisition."

"Hell, Cindy, it's not an inquisition. I just wanted to know what her relationship with Harding was. He showed up at headquarters with Doug Peterson, a criminal defense attorney for her."

"Well, good for him."

"A high powered, high charging, criminal defense attorney."

"Well, if you need one of those, that's the kind you'd want. What's your deal?"

"She acted like she might not take him because of his fee."

"I'll help her if she can't afford him. I've read his name in the paper. He's good."

"You don't have to worry about that. Jonathan Harding seems to be paying the fee."

"Oh." Cindy took a rather large swallow of wine and coughed a few times.

"Yeah, that's what I thought. You don't pay for someone's attorney, unless you expect to get something in return, or perhaps are already getting something in return."

"Mike Riley, how dare you suggest that about Addie."

"Just the logical assumption, Cindy. You even made it."

"What made you ask about a gun in the first place?"

"Clay Bennett gave us the lead." Mike rose, crossed to the pantry, and threw his bottle into the recycle bin.

"Bennett? I can't believe you bought anything he said.

The board is firing his ass tomorrow."

"Really, I thought Addie didn't have enough votes to do that."

"My understanding is Jonathan is voting with us on the issue. And he's really pulled our irons out of the fire financially."

"Oh?"

"Yep, to the tune of five hundred thousand dollars according to the new budget that was emailed this afternoon."

Mike nodded. Addison Greer had a lot to be thankful to Harding about. Just how was she expressing her appreciation? And now an attorney to defend her? That pretty much cut the legs out of any other competition. Not that he was competing for her. She was still a person of interest. But if she weren't? That would make a hell of a lot of difference.

"Mike." Cindy sidled up to him. "Addie can't be bought with money. You're not out of this yet."

"I don't see how I can be in it, until we get this murder solved or at least determine she's in no way involved."

"Well, then what are you standing around here for? Get busy." She handed him the bag with his supper.

◆ ◆ ◆

Wednesday, November 7

Addie didn't look forward to talking with Elizabeth about the gun, but she had to. With Jeremy out of the way, working on a project at Tommy's house, this was an excellent time. She knocked on her daughter's door and pushed it open. "Elizabeth, can you come into the living room?" Without waiting for an answer, Addie turned and walked away. Would she follow?

"Be right there."

The cheery flames of the fireplace belied Addie's dread of the meeting. She backed up to the warmth, hoping to quell the chill running through her body.

"What's up?" Elizabeth entered and plopped on the sofa.

Addie drew in a deep breath and let it out, straightening to her tallest. "We need to talk about the gun."

"Oh... What about it?"

Had her daughter's face turned a slight pinkish tone? Hard to tell with all the Goth make-up on. "Why didn't you tell me about the gun as soon as you found it?"

"Like I said, I thought it was a prop." She fiddled with her full skirt. "Between you and Jeremy, we have props lying all around the house. Never occurred to me it was real."

"You didn't touch it?" Addie shuddered at what might've happened to her daughter if she'd handled a loaded gun. The news reported far too many people killed by guns they thought weren't loaded.

Elizabeth paused for a moment before answering. "No, I didn't touch the gun." She failed to meet her mother's gaze.

"Well, that's a relief." Addie crossed and sat next to her daughter on the sofa. "Do you realize what a difficult position this has put me in?"

"What do you mean?"

"If that gun turns out to be the one used to kill poor Shannon, the detectives will narrow their focus on me as the murderer."

"I'm sure it won't be the murder weapon, Mom." Elizabeth rose, paced the room, twitching her skirt. "You've been watching too many of your cop shows. Can I go now? I've got homework."

Addie sighed. "Okay. Run on." She dropped her head into her hands as Elizabeth scooted from the room. How did the gun get into that drawer? God, what a mess.

◆ ◆ ◆

Thursday, November 8

Addie's stomach growled. The board meeting had come and gone. The jacket of the red power suit she'd worn hung on the back of her desk chair, doffed as soon as she entered the office after the meeting. She'd worked through lunch and now, at almost six, her body reminded her breakfast was a long time ago. Still, she'd intended to knock out the last article for the newsletter, which went out monthly to all their supporters. She wanted to put the most positive spin on the recent staff change and welcome their new board member.

They didn't have a show either performing or rehearsing right now, and everyone else had gone. No interruptions would make this go fast. The kids wouldn't be home until late. Good thing she'd been able to get them a car. Maybe after how stressful everything had been of late, a quiet evening at home would do her good. As soon as she finished this article she'd pack it in.

Her office door opened, banging against the wall. Addie jumped up. Her heart leapt to her throat. Clay Bennett stood in the entry.

"Are you happy with yourself, Addison? You got what you wanted." He strode from the doorway to stand in front of her desk.

"I'm sincerely sorry things worked out this way, Clay. We were happy when we hired you and had high expectations of the relationship lasting." She clasped her hands in front of her to hide a slight tremble. Why hadn't she left when everyone else had? She slid her feet into the heels she'd kicked off under the desk. Every inch would help in this confrontation.

"Sure."

Clay moved to the side of her desk. Addie moved to the other end. What was his intent? Yell at her, bully her a little? Her heart thumped against the wall of her chest so hard the sound of it pumping inside her ears made her light-headed. She should've known he took the firing too calmly during the meeting.

He stalked her around the desk.

"You bitch." He advanced on her faster than she could back away. He grabbed her by the front of her blouse and hauled her up close to him. "You're going to be sorry you ever crossed me."

"Clay!" The word came out strangled-sounding. She scratched with both of her hands at his, trying to pull them away. He pulled the blouse so tight he cut off her breath. She couldn't pass out. No telling what he'd do then. He tightened his grip. Her eyes threatened to pop out. Then he slammed her against the wall. She slid down, her head ringing.

"Oh, what happened, Ms. Greer? Did you slip and fall?" he mocked. "Here, let me help you up." He grabbed her arms, squeezed until she couldn't stop a whimper from escaping. He yanked her roughly to a standing position.

Addie leaned against the wall, her legs struggling to support her. She gasped for air.

He yanked her hair and the pain brought tears to her eyes. Then he moved his hands down her front, as if he could smooth the wrinkles from where he'd manhandled her.

Addie bit her lip to keep from screaming. If he was calming down, which it looked like he might be—God, she prayed he was—she didn't want to set him off again.

"I just wanted to tell you goodbye, Ms. Addison Jones Greer. It's been a pleasure working with you." His hand clamped around her breast, and she sucked in a gasp. He smiled once and slammed her against the wall again before he spun on his heel and left.

Addie slid down the wall. One hand soothed her tender breast. One arm wrapped around both legs, and she sobbed. She'd never been so scared in her life. The office phone rang. Late for calls, and for the life of her, she couldn't get to it. The continued ringing brought on a fresh onslaught of tears. Finally, the sound stopped, and the utter silence in the building sent icy fear cutting through her system.

She crawled toward the desk, yanked her cell from the top, and scooted into the cubbyhole underneath. Her hand shook. Who should she call? Someone who could get in the building. Depending on how Clay left the front door, it might be locked. Pete Talmadge, their stage manager. Would he pick up? Could he come? She punched in the single digit for him, amazed she remembered it with the way her head spun. Someone picked up.

"Thank God."

"Addie? What's wrong?" His deep rumble turned on the water works again."

"Can... can you come?"

"Where?"

"Theatre."

"Sure. Where are you?"

"Office."

"Be there in less than ten minutes."

"Thanks."

Pete lived close to the theatre, but the ten minutes dragged on like sixty. Visions of Clay's face distorted in anger kept floating before her eyes, little hiccups continuing long after her sobs had stopped. She couldn't stop her body from shaking.

"Addie? Addie, where are you?"

She peaked around the side of her desk to find Pete's bear-like presence filling the doorway.

"Here."

He rushed to her side and knelt down beside her. "My God. Are you hurt? Your blouse is torn. What happened?"

"Scared." Terrified was more like it.

He put a comforting arm around her. The warmth of his body started to melt some of her fear. She told him what had happened. Pete's hand clutched her arm where Clay had grabbed her when she told how he threw her against the wall. She winced.

"I'm sorry. He didn't do anything else, did he?"

She shook her head, not mentioning her tender breast.

Pete sighed his relief. "Can you stand?"

"With your help." Her legs only supported her as far as her desk chair. She let her head fall back against the high back.

"I'm calling the police." His hand reached for the desk phone.

"No." She covered his with hers. "We've had enough of police lately. Clay just needed to let off some steam, and that's what he did. We shouldn't hear or see anything more from him."

Pete dropped the handle back on the receiver. "Well, I'm going to alert the staff he's not allowed into the building, and first thing in the morning we'll take steps to change the locks."

She nodded. "I've never had a gun, but I wished for one tonight." She forced a smile.

"Probably a good thing I don't have one, I'd have shot him. That would have for certain brought on more police." Addie forced thoughts of Detective Mike Riley away. She'd actually considered calling him tonight, but she couldn't manage all the numbers. Pete being on speed-dial was definitely a plus.

"Come on. I'll drive you home."

"No. My car is here. Would you follow me though?" She was such a wimp.

"Of course, if you're sure you can handle the drive, and I'll see you safely inside."

She shut off the computer. Maybe she'd work on that article at home. Or maybe she needed a night with a good bottle of wine. She'd never been so physically scared for her safety in her life. When Jud broke up the family by sleeping with that secretary in their bed, she'd been afraid she'd be unable to provide for the kids by herself. But this...she gritted her teeth against the tremble threatening to take over her body. *Okay, Greer, get a grip. It's over and you're safe.*

CHAPTER SEVEN

Friday, November 9

"What do you mean you don't have any more smokes, Clay? I cut class for them."

"Well, you can hang out with me babe, but no smokes."

"You said if I hid the gun for you, I wouldn't have to worry about having money for the smokes anymore."

"How did that go by the way?"

"You dropped me off close to the house, and I got there before super brother or Mom. A cop showed up asking about a gun. I bounced in and did just what you asked."

Clay paced back and forth. God, he'd liked to have witnessed that. "How'd your sweet mama handle that?"

"She was surprised. Asked me why I didn't tell her about it when I first saw it."

"And..." Crap, this was like pulling weeds to get the girl to tell the story.

"I told her I assumed it was a prop from the theatre, which you'd told me it was. It's a good fake, because it fooled the cop, and he hauled her downtown for more questioning right then."

"How long was she gone?"

"I don't know, maybe a few hours. We left for rehearsal, and she was home when we returned.

"Too bad she didn't have to spend the night. That would've made the joke really fun."

"On the way to school, Jeremy called that rich dude she's been going out with, and he got a lawyer to spring her." She spun from the windows and stalked up to Clay. "Yesterday when Mom asked me again, I told her the same story. So, I did my part. You have to do yours. Where are my smokes?"

Clay patted her on the shoulder. "You did good, kid. Not your fault they didn't keep her longer. I intended to keep you supplied for a month, but I need money now. My supplier has gone up on me. Not my fault."

"I don't have any extra cash. Mom's tightened down, and I have to account for every dollar she gives me." She dropped onto the couch, holding her heard between her hands.

"Ever try your hand at a little shoplifting? You pick up a couple of items at some of those high-end boutiques, sell 'em online, and then you've got the dough for me. No sweat and pretty fast turn-around."

Elizabeth stared at him. Was she going to take the bait? It didn't matter to him whether she got the money. If she got pinched for shoplifting, that'd hurt her mother, and that's all he was interested in doing. Damn bitch. Firing him. He'd make her sorry.

"All right." Elizabeth stood. "I'll try, but it may take me a couple of days. Can't you at least give me one to get me through?"

The hands she held out to him shook. Clay took pity on the loser. "Sure, babe. We'll share my last one. How's that?"

"Better than nothing."

Clay pulled open the drawer, blocking her view so Elizabeth couldn't tell how much stash he had, and lifted out one. "I'll even let you take the first drag." He held out the cigarette. Her hands trembled as she placed it between her lips. He flicked the lighter. Her eyelids fluttered closed, and she drew the drug deeply into her lungs."

"Ahhh." She exhaled. "So good."

"Yeah. There's more where that came from. You just need to get a little dough." He pulled on the cigarette. Yes, this little deal with Elizabeth was going to turn out good for him, whatever happened. Stupid bitch Greer would get what was coming to her and then some. He needed her to suffer. If she weren't careful, he'd hit her more than through her daughter. The anticipation of torturing Addie made his heart race. Last evening was nothing compared to what he could do to her.

◆ ◆ ◆

Saturday, November 17

Without Elizabeth realizing he was near, Jeremy followed her down the street. He'd dropped her off at the mall to shop with Sonya with the understanding he'd return to drive them to rehearsal in an hour. If he hadn't gotten stuck in traffic, he'd have missed his sister coming out of the mall and walking west. Where the hell was she going? Jeremy parked, locked the car, and set out on foot.

She passed by the movie theatre and left the mall parking area. Up ahead was a set of apartments with a gated entry. Elizabeth punched the button and said something into the intercom he couldn't hear. The gate swung open. He'd have to time it right to slip through before it closed without her seeing him. Whew! Close, but he managed it and then crouched behind a parked car. Hell, he hated spying on Elizabeth, but he didn't feel he had any choice.

He poked his head around a pillar. His sister was heading for the stairs. At the top stood a man, smiling as if he were waiting for her. He was familiar, but Jeremy couldn't quite place him. His stomach clenched when the guy took her hand and drew her toward one of the apartments. *Shit.*

Jeremy glanced around. It wasn't a bad apartment complex, nor was it the best, but behind closed doors, anything could happen. Should he run up there and drag her out? Maybe he'd call on her cell and tell her he had to pick her up at the mall earlier than planned.

She might not get the message.

She might ignore his call.

She might kill him for following her.

Screw it. She was his sister. Even if she slugged him, he'd look after her.

Jeremy tore up the stairs and pounded on the door before he lost his nerve. Silence from inside. He pounded again. Finally, it swung open partway. The man stuck his head in the crack.

"What do you want?"

"My sister."

"You must have the wrong apartment."

The man spoke with such authority, Jeremy glanced around, but this was the apartment. More to the point, this was the man Elizabeth had met at the top of the stairs. Jeremy shoved his foot in the door just before it closed.

"No. I don't have the wrong place. My sister is Elizabeth Greer, and she's inside. Now let her go, or I'll call the police." God, he didn't want to do that, but Elizabeth was leaving with him now, or else. Jeremy shoved the door. His looks deceived most people. While slender, but he was strong. He had to be to lift girls in dance class. He forced his way in, glanced around spying his sister sitting on the couch. "Are you okay?"

"I was better before you burst in here like some avenging angel." She took a long pull from the cigarette held between her fingers. "What the hell are you thinking?"

He waved a hand in front of his face. Didn't like smelling that with his sister here. "You have two choices. You come with me now, or I'll call the cops."

"Miss Greer, go with your brother. We can schedule this lesson some other time."

"What kind of lessons?" Jeremy glanced at the man.

"Acting lessons."

Just like that, it hit Jeremy who this was. Clay Bennett, his mother's artistic director, or former AD. She'd fired him.

"Why'd you say she wasn't here when I asked?"

"I didn't want to interrupt our lesson."

Jeremy snorted, grabbed his sister's hand, and hustled her across the floor. She stopped and dropped the cigarette into the ashtray. "Sorry." She seemed to be addressing Bennett, not Jeremy.

"I'm sure Mom can help her with acting lessons. Come on, Elizabeth." He pulled her through the door, not letting go until they reached the car. "Get in." She flounced past him and yanked the door from his grasp, slamming it shut. At least she hadn't tried to run off. He'd been afraid she might. No time to figure out how to handle this. He jumped in and turned the key.

"Jeremy."

"No, we're not talking until we get home, but then, Elizabeth, we're having this out." He curled his fingers around the steering wheel, focused on getting them home safely. That was the first hurdle. Next, talk with his sister to see what was going on. After that, decide whether to tell his mother or not. Because it involved Bennett, Jeremy was more inclined to tell her than if Elizabeth had been with a high school kid.

Explosions of pain hit behind his eyes from the stress of too many decisions. He was afraid of what his sister might say. What was she into? Somehow, Jeremy doubted this was about acting lessons. On top of that, they had to be at rehearsal soon, which didn't give him enough time to complete such an important discussion with her.

Fifteen long minutes passed, and Elizabeth refused to say anything.   She was so damned stubborn. Not one word of explanation passed her lips.

Jeremy pulled his cell from his jean pocket. "I'll call Mom

and get her to come home right now." He was bluffing, because, in truth, he'd really prefer not disturbing his mother. With Bennett out, she was swamped. If Elizabeth were in danger, there'd be no question. In the meantime, he had to get her to talk.

"Jeremy you don't want to call Mom to come home and find it's all over nothing."

"Yeah, but I won't know it's nothing if you don't tell me what's going on."

A long sigh escaped then her lips pressed into a straight line. "Okay, okay. It's what Clay told you. Acting lessons."

"What? Why wouldn't you tell Mom or me? And why are you taking them?"

She hung her head. "I didn't want to embarrass the family. My art is good, but on stage, well...You shine. I didn't want to be a dud."

Her words were spoken so softly Jeremy almost missed what she said. Hell. He slid his cell into the pocket of his jeans. "Is this because of Dad?" While he'd never been too thrilled with Jeremy's interest in the theatre, he'd never wanted anything to do with his daughter.

"I just thought...please don't tell Mom."

"I'm pretty sure I smelled marijuana in there."

"I just had a regular cigarette."

"Which Mom doesn't know about."

"And she doesn't need to. I was using it as a prop."

"Really?"

"Yeah. I know I've been kind of a flake of late. I'm just

never as good as you are on stage, and painting's not so grab-the-headlines as acting. You act, sing and dance. Hard to compete. Anyway, Sonya suggested lessons would help. I decided what the hell, it can't hurt and might do some good."

For the whole speech, Elizabeth sat still with her hands clasped in her lap, her head slightly down. Jeremy hated to be suspicious. He really wanted to believe his sister, but he wasn't naïve either. "How are you paying him?" No teenage girl should've been in the apartment of a grown man. He didn't know how old Bennett was, but the whole deal made a snake-like feeling curve up his back and across his shoulders.

"He's not charging me the regular amount because of Mom. I sold a few of my things online."

"That was clever of you." Maybe he could work a compromise.

"Jeremy, please don't say anything to Mom. I think the lessons are helping, and they're fun."

Jeremy ran both hands through his hair. What was the right thing to do? Could she be this good of an actress? She seemed sincere. "Okay, if you'll only take the classes at the theatre—"

Before he finished, Elizabeth jumped off the sofa and flung both arms around him. "Thank you, thank you. You won't be sorry. You're the best brother."

He held her away. "I'll be watching, Elizabeth. No more sneaking off. You don't get any other chances." He gripped her shoulders to emphasize his point. "Got it?"

"Got it. Let's head to rehearsal."

Jeremy raised his wrist. "Hell. We better not hit any lights, or we'll be late.

◆ ◆ ◆

Tuesday, November 20

Addie walked in the house, kicked off her shoes, went directly to the small wine bar, lifted a bottle of Sauvignon Blanc, and filled a glass. She had a sip before moving to the sofa and lifting out the script from her satchel. With Clay out of the picture, directing the next show fell to her, and maybe the next one, until the board hired a new artistic director. It had been quite a few years since she'd done this part of the business, but some things you didn't forget.

Truth be told, she was looking forward to dabbling in the directing end for a change. Fortunately, for her, the show, *Thoroughly Modern Millie*, was one of her favorites from college and from a tour.

She settled into the chair and set the glass on the table. The table with the drawer that held the gun. Damn. How could the weapon have gotten there? Elizabeth, when they'd talked, hadn't been very enlightening. Addie hated to think one of the people who'd come into her home had brought it. Even if they brought it in, why didn't they take it when they left? Pain spiked in her head the way it did every time the issue crossed her mind.

After another sip of wine, she opened the script. The front doorbell chimed its soft, warm tone. What now? She came home early so as not to be disturbed. The bell rang twice more before Addie got there and flung it open.

"Elizabeth?" Her daughter stood on the front porch next to a uniformed policeman. "Charlie?"

"Hey, Ms. Greer." The officer pulled off his cap.

"What are y'all doing here? Is something wrong?"

"I picked her up after she shoplifted a silk scarf at the new boutique in the Center."

"What? There must be some mistake." Addie was afraid to remove her hand from the doorframe, fearing she'd collapse.

"Afraid not. May we come in?"

"Oh, yes. Of course." Addie stepped back, and the officer and her daughter entered. Elizabeth flounced to a chair in the living room and flopped in it. She had the grace to, at least, hang her head. "Have a seat, Charlie, and tell me what happened." Addie sat on the sofa and indicated the officer should sit next to her. He remained standing.

"I'd just finished lunch at a little sandwich shop next to the boutique and stepped out on the sidewalk when Elizabeth burst through the door with a staff member hot on her heels. I stopped her and then asked the clerk what the problem was. She said Elizabeth had taken a scarf without paying for it." Charlie's tone of voice suggested he'd rather be anywhere but in her living room telling her this.

"I told her I'd meant to. I stuffed it in my pocket while I was trying to get my wallet out." Elizabeth's voice held that whiny sound that tightened Annie's gut and made her nuts.

"How much was the scarf? Where is it now?" Addie

asked, still trying to make sense of what Charlie had told her.

"Twenty-five dollars. The store got the scarf back, and because Elizabeth is still seventeen and I know her, the manager agreed to let me bring her home and not to press charges."

"Thank God. And thank you, Charlie."

"She's not allowed back in the store either. I'm thinking the young lady needs some sort of community service to impress on her the gravity of her actions."

"I can assure you that will happen." Addie walked with him to the door and held it open. "Elizabeth, is there anything you'd like to say to Officer Haskins?"

Her daughter stood. "Thanks, Officer."

"We all make bad decisions, Elizabeth. The trick is not to repeat them. See you, Ms. Greer."

"Elizabeth, come with me." Addie walked her daughter into the kitchen where she fixed them both a drink. "Everything's bearable with iced tea, right?" Her daughter cracked a small smile and dropped into a chair.

"Whatever possessed you to shoplift? You didn't have enough money on you? What were you thinking?

"Mom, slow down on the questions, will ya?"

"Help me understand. Then we'll talk about consequences because there certainly will be those. I don't think you understand how lucky you are that Charlie Haskins was the policeman to get involved with this."

"Yeah, I do get that, Mom." Elizabeth sipped her tea.

"Okay, I'm listening. Answer my questions. Say

something."

"The scarf was the same color as your eyes. I saw it and thought how great it'd be for your birthday."

"My birthday?" Addie hadn't given much thought to her impending forty-sixth. Falling so close to Christmas, it frequently got overlooked.

"Yeah. Like I said, I stuffed it in my pocket while I got out my wallet. Then the stupid girl yelled and ran at me. I don't know, I guess I panicked and ran out."

"Okay." Addie stood. She pressed the palms of her hands against her eyes and prayed she made the right decision. "To begin with Elizabeth, I'm grounding you from anything but school and play rehearsals for six weeks. No shopping. No movies. No visits with friends. No cell. After I do a little research, we'll find a community service project. I'll give you some options, but there will be no option about whether you do the work or not. Got it?"

"Yeah."

"You might want to consider a 'yes, ma'am' in this instance, Elizabeth."

"Yes, ma'am."

CHAPTER EIGHT

Tuesday, November 20

The crisp air cooled Mike's skin. The wind billowed out his jacket as he rode back up to the barn. He and Blackie had been out all morning. The peace of the countryside healed his spirit. Rick and he had completed a particularly grueling case that sucked the life right out of him. The jury had come back with a guilty verdict late yesterday afternoon.

It was one of those shit-awful ones where a crazy woman claiming to do what God instructed, killed her children. Three kids all drowned, one after the other. The husband had just flown back to the Middle East for a third tour when it happened. He'd been gone so much he didn't realize how messed up his wife had become. How would he ever recover from this?

A white SUV was parked near his house, dust still trailing out along the dirt road. "Looks like we've got company, Blackie." Mike unsaddled his horse before heading up to see if his sister-in-law came by herself or whether Pat had come along for the ride.

"Mike. Glad you're here," Cindy hollered from his porch, as if she were afraid he'd run off.

He laughed. "Why'd you come out if you didn't think I'd be here?" He shook his head.

"I called on your cell but never reached you. Figured I'd take a chance." Her voice had a hint of excitement, something she was bursting to say.

"Is everyone all right?"

She stepped through the front door, dropped her coat on a chair and made straight for the kitchen.

"You want some coffee?" he asked. A 'duh' question if there ever was one, because Cindy was a bigger coffee fiend than he was. Must not be bad, or she'd have told him right off what had put the burr under her blanket.

"Need you ask?" She reached for the coffee canister but handed it to him. "I'll let you do the honors." She slid up on one of the seats at the bar. "Why'd you take a leave from your phone? Are you feeling okay? Pat was worried."

"Ah, so Pat sent you out here?"

She laughed. "Well, let's just say he was glad to hear I was coming. We read the paper this morning."

"Yeah." Mike didn't talk about on-going cases. Cindy and Pat only knew what they read in the paper. He sat on a stool next to his sister-in-law.

"How are you doing?" She glanced at him and away.

"I'm glad it's over. It may be the worst case I've ever worked." He gritted his teeth so hard they hurt.

"I hope the woman never sees the light of day again."

"She won't. I hope her husband gets counseling, but how the hell do you get past something that horrendous?"

"Poor man," Cindy whispered. She stared out the window, a tremble taking over her chin. "I really need that cup of coffee now."

"Based on the aroma drifting this way, I'd say it's ready." Mike crossed to the counter,

and filled two mugs. She added the cream he always kept on hand for people who visited. He drank it black.

"Wonderful." Cindy set the mug on the counter. "That helps."

"Did you just come out to check on me?" He settled back on a bar stool next to her.

"Well..."

"I'm really okay, Cindy. You learn in my business life goes on. Otherwise, you'd walk around all the time with your chin on the ground and your heart bleeding."

"You're a good man, Mike Riley. I'm glad you're my brother-in-law."

"Thanks. Now why don't you spill what else is on your mind." He rose and refilled their mugs then returned the pot to its holder.

Cindy added cream, took a good size swallow then straightened up. "Okay. Have you seen or talked with Addie...other than for business reasons?"

"Because I'm talking with her about *business reasons,* as you so quaintly call a murder investigation, is the very reason I'm not talking with Addie—Ms. Greer—about anything else."

"Well if the business reasons didn't exist, would you be interested in talking with or seeing her?"

How was he going to answer that? He'd love to see the beautiful Addison Jones Greer as often as she'd agree. He wanted to see if the spark he'd felt at the gala and then in the Stockyards couldn't be fanned into something more. But he couldn't pursue her.

"Ms. Greer is a person of interest in a murder investigation. I can't see her, even if I wanted to."

"Are you telling me you're not interested?"

"Cindy, for God's sake. Don't you listen? Addie is a person—

"Of interest. I heard you." Her voice raised. "But. If. She. Weren't?"

Mike flung himself from the stool and plodded to the sink where he sloshed the leftover coffee down the drain. He heaved in several long breaths. Cindy meant well, and God knew if things were different, he'd make a play for Addie, despite Jonathan Harding's presence in the mix.

But the situation was what it was. When he and Rick solved this case...if the spark was still there, then maybe he'd chance pursuing her.

"Mike Riley. Mike? Where'd you go?"

He turned around to find Cindy standing only a few steps behind him. Huh. He did check out there for a moment.

"Are you okay?"

He nodded. "Yeah, Cindy. I'm fine. This discussion is concluded."

She jammed her fists on her waist. "You'll be sorry if you lose out on her because of an overblown case of ethics. You know Addie didn't kill Shannon."

"I don't know that in the sense of being able to prove it. I have to be able to prove it, Cindy. Or rather, prove she did."

Cindy spun on her heels, stomped out of the kitchen, and grabbed her coat. The slam of the front door was her last word on the subject.

◆ ◆ ◆

"You got a minute?" Jeremy asked his sister after school.

She grabbed an apple from the kitchen counter. "I'm busy, Jer. Catch you later."

He took hold of her arm when she sidestepped around him on the way to her room.

"I don't think so." He swung her around, directing her to the barstool.

She huffed out a big sigh. "Okay. What do you want?" She planted herself tentatively on the stool.

"Shoplifting? What the hell were you thinking? Money's tight, but I've never known Mom not to be able to find a way to get us something we really needed."

"I liked the scarf. Thought it'd be pretty with Mom's eyes. It was for her birthday." She bit into the fruit then wiped the juice from her chin.

"Right. Mom's birthday. Which isn't until next month."

"Yeah."

"I'm so not buying that. Were you going to sell it?" Hell, her face flushed. That must have been what she'd planned.

"And use the money for what?"

"I told you. Acting lessons from Clay."

"I hate to think of what kind of lessons you were getting from Clay, but I'd bet money it wasn't acting."

Elizabeth lashed out at him, striking him on the cheek. "Hey!" He rubbed his face.

"It's not like that. Anyway, he's an old guy. Give me more credit than that." She flicked her wrist up and down and rubbed her hand. "And I'm sorry I hit you."

The last came out so softly it was almost as if an afterthought.

"Well, you must be getting something from your time together." Jeremy walked away from his sister, ran a hand through his hair. "I haven't said anything to Mom about you hanging out with him, but I will if you don't straighten up. If I catch you meeting with Clay at his apartment, I'm going to Mom. I hope you're not into drugs, but if you are, that has to stop. Now." He paced away from her then marched back into her space.

"And another thing, if I see anything else to make me suspect you're using, I'm talking with Mom. Got it?" He stood in front of her, fists on hips, and held her gaze.

Elizabeth nodded.

"We've got rehearsal tonight. I expect you to go and to stay the whole time." His sister nodded again. "Be ready by the garage door in ten minutes." Jeremy ran to his room to grab his script. Was he doing the right thing? Guess he'd see.

♦ ♦ ♦

Wednesday, November 21

The next day, Addie pulled into her garage. For a moment, while the door rolled down, she rested her head on the steering wheel. It had been a killer day with auditions for the next show. While she knew what she was doing, she'd forgotten how gut wrenching it was to pick between people who were equally talented, and you liked. She had some tough decisions to make tonight if she wanted to post the cast and start rehearsals on Friday.

She was determined to schedule them, so she'd still be able to see her kids. Kids. Yeah right. Her *kids* would leave for college next fall.

Addie dragged herself out of the car and shoved at the door, barely getting it closed. Damn Clay Bennett for making her fire him. Why couldn't he watch the stupid budget like everyone else had to do? Up the couple of steps into the kitchen and straight to the wine bar where she lifted out the opened bottle from last night. The glass stopper was a souvenir from the girls' weekend. She poured a full glass and took a healthy gulp, savoring the warmth as it trickled down to her belly. One more sip and she let out a long sigh. Whatever was required to keep the theatre afloat, that's what she'd do.

Jeremy would understand. He and Elizabeth were already at their own rehearsal. Would Elizabeth be all right? Addie didn't know what was going on with her daughter and couldn't seem to break through the wall of ice between them.

Addie unbuttoned her blouse as she made her way to her bedroom and kicked her heels into the closet. Stripping out her slacks, she slid on a pair of yoga pants, one of the most comfortable things she owned. A tank top with them was all she needed. The changeable Texas weather had given them a warmer than usual fall day. She refilled her wine glass and, with a legal pad in front of her, set about the exacting task of casting *Thoroughly Modern Millie*.

The doorbell rang, making her jump. The kids had their own keys. Besides, they'd come in through the garage. The bell rang again. Could she ignore it and pretend not to be home? *Don't be stupid, Addie. Go see who it is.* Setting the pad on the ottoman, she approached the entryway.

Addie peeked through the side window. Her heart literally jumped into her throat making her pulse beat wildly. Detective Mike Riley stood on the porch, his hat throwing a shadow over his face. What did he want? Well, best way to find out was to open the door, which she did. "You here to arrest me, Detective?"

He stared at her for a full thirty seconds. What was the matter with him? Did she look so bad? Addie glanced down, and heat flooded her face. Not an outfit she'd choose to wear when greeting the good detective.

"Sorry to disturb you, Ms. Greer." He removed his hat, twirling it around and around. "Had you already gone to bed?" His voice sounded hoarse.

He must think she was wearing her pajamas. "No, Detective. Doing a little theatre work, casting the next show.

Can I do something for you?" She crossed her arms over her chest then took them down. That had done nothing but emphasized she was braless. Last time she ever opened the door dressed like this again.

"May I come in?"

"Yes, of course. I'm sorry." Jeez. They'd both been staring at each other. "Wasn't thinking clearly, I guess." She led him into the living room. "Can I offer you anything? I'm having wine."

"Thanks, but I'm on duty."

"Of course." Why else would he come here? "How about coffee or iced tea then?"

"Coffee would be nice."

"Come on back to the kitchen." Padding ahead of him in her bare feet, Addie wished she'd put on shoes. Wished the yoga pants and tank top fit looser. Wished he hadn't come on business. "It'll just take a couple of minutes." She went through the steps automatically, adding the grounds to a filter she didn't remember setting in place. Why had he come?

"I hate to put you to this much trouble. I forgot everyone doesn't have a pot ready at all times."

With his white western hat in one hand as he leaned on the counter, he couldn't have looked sexier if he'd tried. Addie turned her back on him, got the mug from the cabinet and a spoon from the drawer. She set them in front of him, never making eye contact, afraid he'd see her reaction to him in her eyes.

"Nothing smells as good a fresh coffee." *Way to go,*

Addie, with the scintillating conversation.

"You got that right."

The steam curled up from the cup after she'd poured. "Do you need anything else, cream, sugar? You don't strike me as a man who'd use any of the little pink packets." Crum. That made it sound like she'd been thinking about him. Just because she had was no reason to let him know.

"Black's just fine." He lifted the cup and took a healthy sip. She couldn't drag her eyes from his throat as he swallowed.

"You make a good cup of coffee, Ms. Greer. I needed that."

"It must be a tough job, Detective." She shot a glance at him from under her eyelashes. That seemed a safe way to look at him, but no... that weird tingling still hit in her stomach. That foolish, schoolgirl butterfly thing, which she hadn't experienced since the year she'd met her ex-husband.

"Unfortunately, we don't always get to interact with nice people."

"I didn't kill Shannon, Detective."

"We're looking into proof, Ms. Greer. You never have gotten us that list of everyone who came into your home between the murder and when we found the gun."

She paced the space between the bar and the sink. "I'm sorry. I meant to do that earlier. Not sure how I've forgotten. When my children come in this evening after rehearsal, I'll ask them. Do you have to have the list tomorrow? It's Thanksgiving."

"Friday will have to do then."

"I'll drop off the list."

"Is the theatre closed Friday, or will you be working?"

"We're just off tomorrow."

"I can pick it up from you there. You won't have to deal with parking issues downtown. Your theatre doesn't have that problem. What time would work best for you?"

"We'll have a lunch break between twelve and one and then another break around two-thirty for about fifteen minutes. Either of those will be fine."

"You don't go out for lunch?"

She smiled. "Generally it's a working lunch when I do, trying to raise money from someone or a foundation."

"That must get old, always searching for the next donor."

She took a swallow of wine then set the glass on the counter. "Only if you don't believe in the cause."

"And you see the cause as what? Providing entertainment?"

She finished her wine, drinking faster than she normally did. "That's probably a longer answer than you want to listen to tonight."

"Maybe another time then. Thanks for the coffee." He walked from the kitchen toward the front of the house. At the door, he turned. "Good luck with your casting. I'll see you either at noon Friday or at your afternoon break."

She stood with one hand on the door the other on the jam. The porch light made dark circles under the man's eyes. Yes, it must be a difficult job. "I'll have the list for you. Though for the life of me, I can't imagine anyone I know bringing a gun into the house."

"Sometimes, even people we know well can surprise us." He set his white hat on his head, turned, jogged down the front steps, and climbed into his dark color, late model truck. She stood there until she could barely see the taillights in the distance. *Okay, enough mooning, woman. You have work to do before the kids come home.*

♦ ♦ ♦

Addie set aside her legal pad with an audible sigh, raised her hands over her head, and stretched for the ceiling. She'd done it—cast *Millie*.

The sound of the garage was followed by the door-opening buzz. Must be the kids home from rehearsal. "I'm in the living room, guys." She rose and ambled toward the kitchen, the point of stopping off for Jeremy whenever he entered the house. One of his legs had to be hollow. "Can I get y'all anything?"

"How about popcorn, Mom?" Elizabeth asked.

Surprised but pleased by the direct request from her daughter, Addie agreed and got out the pot and corn. She and the kids had long ago decided the pot made it best. Memories of eating popcorn a couple of times a week, which had been a regular part of their life, made her smile. When had that ended?

"Don't you love that?" Jeremy hung over the island. The distinct sound the corn made as its hard shell cracked open shooting out the puffy, white kernels filled the kitchen.

"Grab the large white bowl, please, Elizabeth. This is just about ready." White puffs peeked their heads above the lid. Her daughter set the bowl close and Addie emptied the pot. Jeremy added salt. Addie's mouth watered while she drizzled melted butter over the steaming snack. Parceling out separate servings for everyone, she left some in the large bowl for seconds. This couldn't have worked out better. She and her kids carried their popcorn, napkins, and drinks into the living room. Iced tea for her and sodas for the kids.

They all munched in silence for a bit. Addie dreaded bringing up the subject of the gun, but she'd promised Detective Riley—she'd get information for him. "I hate to interrupt this nice time together to talk about difficult stuff, but I've got to put together a list of everyone who came into the house between the time when Shannon DeWitt was murdered and when the gun was found here. Can y'all help?"

"Sure." Jeremy shoveled a large handful of corn into his mouth. "Tommy Henson came one afternoon to help me work lines."

"Sonya Lowry came over twice. We worked on a school project together."

Addie had celebrated Sonya's arrival. It meant Elizabeth was doing schoolwork.

"I put our housekeeper, Sue Patterson, on the list. She came every Friday between those dates. Anybody else you can think of?"

"Your stage manager stopped by when we were headed to rehearsal one night." Elizabeth suggested.

Addie wrote the names down, but of course, Pete didn't have anything to do with the murder. Nobody else she knew could have either. Could they?

"And don't forget Mr. Harding," her son added.

"But he wouldn't—"

"Doesn't Detective Riley want the names of everyone?" Elizabeth threw a white puff into the air and caught it cleanly in her mouth.

Addie nodded her head and added Jonathan's name to the list. This was so absurd.

"You've got Tommy's cell number, don't you?" Jeremy stood.

"Yes. Where are you going?"

"Refilling my bowl and then off to bed. I don't know of anyone else. See you in the morning. Looking forward to turkey tomorrow."

She blew a kiss in Jeremy's direction. "Elizabeth, has Sonya changed her number since you last gave it to me?"

"Nope." She rose. "Mom…

"What is it Elizabeth?"

She shook her head. "Nothing. I'm off to bed too."

Addie quickly went to her daughter and gave her a brief hug. She'd found she could sometimes get away with a hug if she kept it short. "Thanks for your help, honey."

"Yeah, sure." Elizabeth slouched down the hall toward her room.

Addie bit her tongue to keep from reminding her daughter to stand up straight. That kind of advice never went over well. If they had something of a truce, Addie didn't want to be the one to throw a stick in the spokes.

CHAPTER NINE

Thursday, November 22

Thanksgiving morning dawned warmer than usual with a forecast high of seventy-five degrees. It had just been she and the kids for many years. If they didn't have company like Kate and her daughter, who had gone skiing this year with some of Blair's friends, Addie didn't cook at home. They went out for the meal. This year was no exception with a one o'clock reservation at Kennedy's, a nice restaurant on the west side of town they all liked. The time of the meal changed, depending on when the big football game was on TV. Some years the kids had a week off for the holiday, and when that happened, they took a trip.

Good thing that wasn't the case this year. She'd have had to disappoint them. Because of picking up rehearsals, Addie wouldn't have been able to leave town. Oh sure, she'd escaped to Irving for the weekend with her friends, but that was before she fired Bennett. And no way to compare that to a Colorado or Vermont trip, both places the family had spent Thanksgiving in the past.

"This is a really great buffet, Mom." Jeremy sat down with his second helping of everything.

"I never can decide whether this is a good deal for us or

the restaurant." Addie smiled at her son. "The owner must have a near heat attack when you walk in."

"Yeah, Mom, but you and I don't eat nearly as much as Jer does. If they charged by how much we ate, the way that old salad bar place down on Camp Bowie used to do by weighing the plate, that might be different." Elizabeth wore her traditional Goth look, with long trailing top and skirt over short boots. No coat or jacket since it was so warm.

"I'm surprised you even remember that place, Elizabeth." Addie sipped her iced tea.

"It was near the theatre and had the best ice cream of any I've ever had. I thought it was cool you let Jer and me walk over there when you had rehearsals."

Addie smiled at the memory of her kids when they were ten years old and everything seemed easier and safer. She'd never do that today.

"Pardon me, ma'am, do any of you want coffee with the desserts?" A server stopped by their table, with a pot.

"Yes, please." Addie turned over her cup.

Both kids declined.

"Jeremy, did you leave room for the pumpkin pie?" Elizabeth's gaze pinned her brother.

"You need to ask?" His eyebrows shot up in shock. "When have I ever turned down pie?"

Elizabeth joined Addie in a laugh, filling Addie's heart with content. She was proud of her kids and grateful for them. Maybe being caught shoplifting would act as a wake-up-call for Elizabeth, and she'd straighten up from now on. Hard to believe both would be away at college next fall.

"Okay, ladies, onward to the dessert table." Jeremy made a to-do about holding his sister and mother's chairs for them and leading them toward their quarry.

Addie had chosen coconut cake, a favorite that she seldom ate because she was so picky about how it tasted. Kennedy's was only place she indulged. Elizabeth had pecan pie and Jeremy had pecan and pumpkin.

"This is great eating." Jeremy licked his fork. But I love December, with all our birthdays and Christmas. The month of the big haul." He rubbed his hands together in anticipation. "How are we going to do to celebrate this year?" Jeremy alternated eating the two pieces of pie but making fast work of them.

"I don't know, Son. Finding a time that works with our busy schedules might be tough over the next couple of weeks. We don't need to do anything for my birthday, but maybe we can squeeze in a supper someplace to celebrate both of yours."

"Well, you may want to ignore your birthday, but we're turning eighteen! Celebrate!" Jeremy stood. "Can I get anyone another dessert?"

"You've got to be kidding." Addie shoved aside her plate with one bite of cake she reluctantly left, fearing she'd roll out of the restaurant if she ate it. "I'm stuffed."

"When I get back we'll figure out where and when to have the joint dinner." His long legs took him quickly toward the dessert table.

Addie glanced at Elizabeth and forced a smile. "After the

holiday, I'll find several options for community service for you."

Her daughter nodded. "I didn't figure you'd forgotten."

Jeremy returned, set a piece of chocolate cake at his place, swung a leg over the chair, and attacked the cake as if he hadn't eaten anything in a week. "So do you have suggestions of where to go?"

"How about Luke's downtown. They have steak and seafood." Addie sipped her coffee.

"Great. Something for all of us." The way Jeremy talked you'd never guess he'd just polished off a huge holiday meal. After a bit of wrangling, they put a date on their calendars.

"I hate to ruin the festive meal, but have you heard anything about who the police think killed Ms. DeWitt?" Jeremy scooped the last of the icing off his plate.

"You mean other than your mother?" Addie's joke didn't sound as funny as she'd meant it to.

"Jeez, don't say that," he said.

"Well, we should probably be straight with each other about this." Addie met her daughter and son's gaze. "So far as I can tell, I'm still a person of interest to them. Now I didn't kill her, but if they haven't found another likely candidate...well... Okay, enough said." She straightened in her chair. "Not going down that rabbit hole."

They filled the rest of their time together by sharing memories of earlier Thanksgiving dinners and trips. Addie pushed aside her real concerns about what would happen to her children if the cops arrested her for Shannon's murder. The idea of that and what would follow nearly made her gag. She excused herself to the restroom where she splashed water on her face. She had to keep it together. Holidays had always been special times to the family, and she didn't want to ruin this one.

◆ ◆ ◆

Friday, November 23

The day after Thanksgiving, Clay went to see who was pounding so loudly on his front door. "Elizabeth. I wasn't expecting you." The girl, young woman actually, pushed past him and turned with a flourish to face him.

"I'm going to tell about the gun."

"What are you talking about?"

"The joke's not funny anymore. Mom might be arrested. Damn, Clay. She might be convicted of murdering Ms. DeWitt." Her hands twisted and turned around the strap of her shoulder bag.

"I think you're blowing this whole thing out of proportion, Elizabeth. What in the world has set you off this way?"

"At lunch yesterday, Mom said she was still a person of interest and might be arrested."

"It appears to me your mother is just over-reacting. The police haven't arrested her. If they did, a good lawyer could get her off—even if she did kill that poor woman." Clay crossed to the bureau and pulled out the top drawer. This was turning out better than he'd even planned. Not only was Addison upset, so were her kids. He clamped the cigarette between his lips to keep from laughing. After lighting it, he took a quick drag.

"Clay." Elizabeth drew out the word into a couple of syllables. "You talk like you think she did this."

"Elizabeth, anyone is capable of killing, given the right circumstances." He blew smoke in front of her. Her eyes grew round at the first whiff. "Care for a smoke?" He held out the reefer.

"No, I...Clay, I want to tell them the gun was just a joke." She paced away then back, stopping closer to him.

Clay blew smoke right into her face. She sucked it in. Her breathing increased. Her hands kept up a steady movement up and down the purse strap.

"It's just a joke, Elizabeth. Nobody is getting hurt." He stepped closer to her.

"But..." She swayed toward the cigarette.

"Here you go, Elizabeth, take a couple of puffs. You'll feel better."

"What about Mom?" She inched closer, as if a string drew her.

"What do you really owe her? Has she done anything to patch up things between y'all and your father? More specifically, between you and your father? Don't they both favor your brother?"

Elizabeth's brow furrowed in concern. The expression said he'd made her doubt her mother, which was just what he needed to insure the girl's silence.

"Besides, your mother will be fine, Elizabeth. Afterwards, you'll laugh at how upset you got. Here, this will make you feel better." He held the cig toward her.

"But I—"

Clay slipped the weed between her open lips and she drew in. He allowed himself a satisfied smile.

"That's the way. Sit with me on the sofa. I have more where those came from and won't charge you a penny for them."

Elizabeth sank onto the sofa, all her attention focused on the smoke. She relaxed against the back; her legs outstretched.

"Just one should be okay."

Clay smiled. What every addict across the whole world promised himself and never could deliver.

◆ ◆ ◆

The noon break in the rehearsal came none too soon. Addie only heard a few grumblings about the way she'd cast *Millie*, and for the most part, everyone had been good-spirited about her plans. Even though they'd only been doing a read through of the script, Addie had expended a lot of energy, already making suggestions for ways for the actors to think about, and express, their characters.

She dropped onto the small sofa in her office at Cowtown and propped her feet on the small table. Apple, cheese, and crackers lay there, but she leaned her head back for just a moment and closed her eyes. She'd eat before going back to the rehearsal.

Tap, tap, tap.

"Addie, you've got a visitor."

"What?" She sat up and ran a hand through her hair. "I must have nodded off, Eva. A visitor?"

The secretary pushed open the door farther, and a white western hat preceded Mike Riley into her office. How'd she forget he was coming? Addie struggled into a standing position. With no shoes on, her five feet six inches seemed like nothing to his over six-foot build.

"Sorry to interrupt, Ms. Greer. You did say this would be an okay time to stop by." He twirled his hat between his hands.

"Yes, absolutely. It's been a busy morning. When I sat down, apparently I went out like a light." She grabbed a water bottle and took a couple of large swallows. "Can I get you anything?"

Mike's gaze took in her apple and cheese. "Is that what you're offering for lunch? No, thanks, ma'am." He smiled. "I think I'll pass and wait for something more substantial."

Addie threaded her fingers through her hair. She'd pulled out the scrunchy holding it in place as soon as she'd entered the office. Now she wished the holder still tamed her wild curls.

"Did you get the list for me, Ms. Greer?"

The man was going to think she was an idiot. She didn't seem to be able to put two coherent sentences together when he was around. She scurried to her desk. "Yes. I've included phone numbers to help with making contact." She handed a paper to the detective.

"Thank you." He glanced at the list. "This is everyone?"
She nodded.
He folded the paper and slid it in his inside jacket pocket.

"My partner and I will get on this."

Addie stepped toward him, rested a hand on his arm. "I just—"

He looked down at her.

She yanked her hand away. "I can't believe—"

"I get it. You don't like to think of any of these people bringing a gun into your house and leaving it there. But if you didn't bring it in, Addie, someone else did."

"I didn't." Did he realize he'd called her Addie? It sounded nice coming from him.

"You know, Ms. Greer, I'm inclined to believe that, but the weapon didn't fly through the air on its own. Someone put it in the drawer in your living room. Why would someone do that?" He frowned and twirled his hat faster. "Without proof about who that someone else is, you're my most likely candidate."

He dropped a hand on her shoulder. "I'm sorry."

Did he even realize he'd touched her? Damn her foolishness. She resisted an urge to lean into him for a moment of comfort, but that couldn't be. "Thanks, Detective. You'll let me know what you find?"

"You can count on it."

A knock at the door, and her secretary stuck her head around the door. "Sorry, Addie. Lunch break's over."

"Thanks, Eva. I'll be right there."

"I'll get out of your hair."

He paused. His gaze fixed on her long curls as she tried to corral them back in the band.

"For now." He nodded once and lumbered through the door.

"Addie, you didn't eat." Eva's eyebrows pulled down in concern.

How could her secretary have no comment about the handsome cowboy cop? "No. I slept instead. I'll be fine. I'd better hustle out there. What kind of role model will I be if the director is late?" Addie laughed, grabbed her script and notes, and scooted toward the stage.

◆ ◆ ◆

What a long day. Addie stopped after rehearsal at a restaurant for take-home for her and the kids. The disadvantage of eating out on Thanksgiving was no leftovers. But that was a good thing, too. No leftovers to creep onto the hips. After parceling out the tacos and chips, she and the kids ate in a comfortable quiet. They went to their rooms and she settled down in the living room.

A good bit of work on the blocking lay before her. Because she'd done this show herself, if push came to shove, she could wing it. Not her preference for how to do the job, but it was possible. Her plan for this evening was to complete Act One. Tall order since it was the longer act. Judy Neeson, the choreographer, had a big job ahead of her, which would really take the larger amount of time in this dance-heavy show.

Addie and Judy had done the show together on tour once years ago, with Addie playing the part of Millie and Judy playing

Miss Dorothy. Addie smiled at the memories of those times. Before kids. Before Judson Greer, her thank-God-ex-husband, entered her life. Too bad he'd been such a bastard. Stop. No more wasted time or energy on hating him. He wasn't worth the effort. She grabbed her pencil, lifted the script, and got to work.

CHAPTER TEN

Monday, November 26

"Here's the list of people who'd been in Addison Greer's home." Mike handed a copy of the list of names Addie gave him to his partner.

"Not many on here." Rick flipped the page to see if there were more on the back. "We can either do them together or divvy them up."

"I'll question half; you do the other. Let's get them down here rather than visit on their territory. Somebody put that gun in the Greer house."

"Sounds good. Who do you want?"

"I'll take Harding, Talmadge, and Elizabeth's friend Sonya." Mike didn't make eye contact with his partner, just studied his list. He didn't want Rick digging him about why Mike had asked for Harding. Not that there was any real reason. Yeah, right.

"Good enough. I'll get Tommy Henson and the housekeeper. Touch base with you later." He swiveled around to his desk and picked up the phone.

Mike reached for his desk phone and punched in the number for Talmadge. The rumble of his partner's voice making the first of his calls filtered through the buzz around them. Getting hold of Talmadge proved to be easy and quick, and he agreed to come in during his dinner break. Sonya's mother said she'd bring her daughter in right after school. Harding was tied up until early evening but promised to come in around six-thirty. At this rate, they should have this part of the investigation complete before supper.

"Hey, Mike."

"Yeah, Rick. How're you doing?"

"I got the kid and housekeeper set up. Don't forget to check Facebook, Twitter, and Tumblr, especially on the kids."

"Good idea." Mike wasn't surprised to find Harding wasn't on Facebook or Twitter. Talmadge was on both and Sonya on all three. Talmadge's posts kept up a running commentary on how rehearsals and performances went, with praise for their executive director. Did he feel more than admiration for Addison?

Talmadge sprinkled in political comments regarding certain laws, which in his opinion discriminated against gays, lesbians, and transgenders. He appeared to have a ton of friends, and the discussions became quite lively. Mike didn't pick out any specific motive for the board member's murder.

Did Sonya's mother know what was on her daughter's Facebook page? Kids were so stupid. Between Sonya's three on-line sites, if someone wanted to grab her it'd be easy to pull off. She opened up about her whole life. Where she was, where she was going, who she'd be with? Mike scrolled down some of her pictures, a few more than suggestive. In many of them,

Elizabeth posed with a cigarette or drink in one hand and an arm thrown around her friend. This kind of thing made his gut twist, not just about these kids but also about his niece and nephew.

Mike glanced at his watch. He had time before Sonya and her mother arrived. He slid his cell from his pocket and punched in the number for his sister-in-law. She'd think he was being a fussy old woman, but that didn't matter. If something happened to either of her kids without him double-checking that their parents were aware of the dangers and had personally warned them, he'd never forgive himself.

"Hey, Mike... I was so glad you made it over here for Thanksgiving."

"Lucky I didn't get called in, Cindy. What are you doing right now? You sound like you're running."

"You know me, Mike. Never running, but I am walking—in the neighborhood. We can still talk. What's up?"

"Are Peg and Joe on Facebook?"

"Well, yeah, Mike. So am I. Why?"

Mike rose and shoved his office chair hard against the desk. Damn. Was everyone nuts these days? "Do you know what's on their main pages? Do they tell people where they are? What about their pictures?"

"Hey, there, cowboy. Slow down. Take a deep breath...that's what I'm doing while I lean against a mailbox. What's got into you?"

Where to start? Mike didn't even know.

"Oh, God." Cindy's screech hurt his ears. "Are you

working one of those awful child murder things? You poor dear."

"No, Cindy, that's not it." Mike huffed out his frustrations. She'd told him to take a breath, but that was hard to do, knowing what he did. "I was looking at a teenage girl's social media postings, and it just flew all over me how easy she made it for someone to grab her if they wanted to. I kind of freaked, thinking about Peg and Joe."

"Yes, they're both on several sites, but give us a little credit, Mike. We're up on the whole social media deal—perhaps more than you are. We have warned them both to be cautious about what they put on there. Employees and colleges are checking those out as part of their research on candidates."

"Good, good. Glad you're on top of that, Cindy. Remind them for me, will you? They can really put themselves at risk."

"Sure, Mike. Thanks for your concern. See you soon." She disconnected.

Mike rubbed a hand through his short hair. If he'd made a complete fool of himself, so be it. Peg and Joe were important. Pat and Cindy were good parents. Who was he to tell them what to do? He'd never had a kid. Pictures he didn't like to think of slid behind his eyes of butchered girls. That's why he'd called.

While he waited for the interviewees to arrive, he ran a few other angles on the case eliminating options. It all came back to the gun and Addison Greer.

"Detective Riley?"

He glanced up. "Yeah, Lydia?'

"Sonya Lowry and her mother are here to see you."

Good. Put them in Interview Three, please. I'll be there in a couple of minutes." Mike grabbed up his coffee cup and took a swig. Hell. Cold. That'd have to do. He set off for the interview with a file holding print-outs of some of the pictures from Sonya's Facebook to show Mrs. Lowry.

Mike pushed through the door to the small gray room. "Mrs. Lowry, I'm Detective Mike Riley." He shook her hand. "Sonya." He shook her hand. "Thanks for coming downtown. Can I get you anything? Coffee, soda?"

Both women shook their heads.

"Well, let's get to this then." Mike settled himself in the chair across from them. Sonya's eyes opened wide. She kept glancing around the room and at the glass behind him. She cast quick looks at her mother, but she and her mom never seemed to make eye contact. Mrs. Lowry was well-dressed in a slacks and sweater outfit and boots. Sonya was decked out in an outfit similar to what Elizabeth wore. Mike resisted the urge to say something about her clothes or to jump to any conclusions because of them.

He set up the recorder and went through the required spiel, then got stated. "Sonya, I have some questions about times you've visited at Elizabeth Greer's house. When were you there the last?"

"We've had some school projects we've been working on together, so I'm there pretty often. Sometimes she comes to mine." She shifted in her chair.

"Do you remember specifically when you were at her

house between October ninth and November sixth?"

Sonya's mother studied him then glanced at her daughter.

Sonya reached into a pocket of her long skirt, pulled out her cell, and manipulated some keys. "Sure. I was there Thursday, November fifteenth and Sunday, the eighteenth. We had a big project. We met at my house a couple of times before that. Since Elizabeth got tied up with rehearsals, we don't see each other much unless we have a school project to work on."

"What'd you do while you were there?"

"We worked on our project, like I said"

"And what was that exactly?"

Sonya huffed and glanced toward her mother who patted her hand.

"It's okay, dear. Tell him what you worked on."

"Both times we worked on a huge English project—demonstrating our research and our grammar skills."

"How was it you two worked together?"

"Detective?" Mrs. Lowry asked.

"I'm just getting a handle on their relationship."

"They're friends. Have been since middle school."

Mrs. Lowry seemed to take exception to his questions. Apparently, he hadn't softened his normal investigative tone as much as he thought. Sonya and her mother both exhibited nerves, squirming in the chairs and twisting their hands together.

"I'd like you to answer, Sonya."

The girl looked at her mother then back at Mike. "Mom's

right. We've known each other a long time. For this project, Elizabeth did the research, and I did most of the writing. I'm better at grammar than she is."

Mike opened the folder and shoved across two pictures with Sonya and Elizabeth. "Where were you when these were taken?"

Mrs. Lowry gasped, "Oh, my God, Sonya. What were you thinking to pose like this? Where'd you find these, Detective?"

"On her Facebook page!"

"We'll discuss this when we get home, Sonya. Are you through with us, Detective?"

"Just a couple of more questions. Either time when you were at the Greer's house, did you see anything odd or unusual?"

"Like what? Her gay brother?"

"Sonya." Her mother's voice shrieked with surprise.

"It's no big deal, Mom. I'm used to him, but some people aren't."

Had somebody wanting to get the brother in trouble put the gun in the house? A line to follow another time.

"Sonya, have you ever seen a gun at the Greer house? Do either Jeremy or Elizabeth shoot or talk about guns?

"Guns, Detective?" Again, Mrs. Lowry interrupted. "Is it safe over there? Should I keep Sonya home?"

"Mom. Back off."

The typical teen-age-girl-to-mother tone coated her words. Mike was so glad Peg hadn't been in that mode for long. He and Pat had hated it for Cindy's sake.

"I'm just making inquiries, Mrs. Lowry." Mike kept a sigh from exploding with his exasperation. He stared at Sonya, willing her to answer.

"No, Detective, I've never seen a gun at their house, and neither Jeremy nor Elizabeth has ever talked about guns in front of me."

"You've never taken a gun over there?"

Mrs. Lowry sprang to her feet. "We don't have guns in our family, Detective." She took hold of her daughter's arm to pull her from the chair. "And we don't have to stay here and listen to this."

"Cool it, Mom." Sonya yanked her arm from her mother's grasp. "I've never taken a gun to the Greer house. I've never had a gun to take anywhere."

"Thank you, Sonya." Mike stood. "Mrs. Lowry, I appreciate you coming down. If you remember anything about guns or hear anything, here's my card. Please call." He handed one to each of the women. They took them, and Mrs. Lowry made a quick dash for the door, dragging Sonya behind her. All in all, he believed Sonya. Mom was a piece of work.

Next up was Pete Talmadge, the theatre's stage manager. He blustered in a little after five-thirty.

"I don't have long, Detective. This is the dinner break. What can I do for you?"

The man dwarfed the straight-back chair. Good thing it was metal, otherwise it might break. "Thanks for coming in, Mr. Talmadge. What can you tell me about guns?" Might as well be direct with him.

"Guns? We have some fake ones in our prop room. I've done a little hunting."

"What about a handgun? Do you own one?"

"Yeah, I do. Sig Sauer .22. Got it when I lived in New York, and I have a permit to carry there and here in Texas." He drew his wallet from his hip pocket and flipped through. "Here you go." Talmadge handed over the documentation without Mike asking.

"Thanks." Mike noted the number and expiration date on his pad. The caliber wasn't what had killed DeWitt. Still, the man knew his way around guns.

"How often do you use the .22?"

"About four times a year. Mainly just to keep up some skill level. I'd probably go more often but can't squeeze it in around the theatre schedule. So are you checking everyone out who works at the theatre?"

Mike smiled in a non-committal manner. No need to tell Talmadge that he and Rick were looking only at people who'd been to Addie's house. Mike studied the man across from him. He seemed remarkably calm for someone answering questions at Police Headquarters.

"Have you ever taken one of your guns over to the Greer house?"

"What? I don't have any reason to. If Addie called me in the middle of the night saying she thought she had a prowler then, of course, I'd take my gun."

"Okay, thanks, Mr. Talmadge." So Addie would call him in the middle of the night.

"Listen, Detective." Talmadge leaned across the table as if trying to give weight to his words. "Almost all of us on staff would do anything to help out Addie."

He glanced away as if embarrassed by the slip, but it stood-to-reason Talmadge would call her by her first name. Was there something more to their relationship? Did Pete or someone else on the staff think he could help her fire Bennett by getting rid of DeWitt?

"You said, 'almost all'. Was that a general statement, or did you have someone specific in mind?" Talmadge met his question with silence and a hard stare. Finally, Mike prodded, "Did you?"

"Bennett's been a pain in the butt almost since he came." Talmadge lowered his voice, almost as if he thought someone would overhear what he was saying.

Of course, the interview was being recorded, but...interesting.

"He's got a history of producing great shows and came well recommended. But he has an eye for the ladies and plays fast and loose with the budget."

"You think he might—"

"I'm not saying, Detective, but I don't trust him. After the board fired him, he came back to the theatre when Addie was alone and physically attacked her."

"What?" Mike's heart jumped to his throat. Only his years of training kept him in the chair. Why the hell hadn't she told him about this? "Did she report it to the police?"

"No. She called me, and I raced over there. I wanted her

to report him, but she believed the theatre had enough to do with you guys. Sorry." He cocked his head in Mike's direction. "We alerted the staff. Bennett isn't allowed in the building anymore."

Mike was damn glad Addie had Talmadge for a guard dog. Looked like he could handle himself if a situation became physical. On the other hand, Mike would've preferred she'd called him or 911. Then they'd have a documented record.

"If something like that happens again, you call and report it even if she doesn't want you to. It helps in these cases to have documentation."

"You can count on that."

Mike stood and held out his hand. "Thanks for stopping by, Mr. Talmadge."

"That it then?" Talmadge rose and grasped Mike's hand.

It took all Mike's will power not to engage in a battle with the man, whose grip was more than needed for a polite gesture. Mike gave him his card. "Call me if you think of anything else."

Talmadge nodded once and left.

Mike turned off the recorder. He was no closer to figuring out how the murder weapon got in Addie's home. He glanced at the next name on list. Jonathan Harding. Wealthy oil and gas man. Wife dead for five years. Philanthropist. According to Cindy Riley, Addie was keeping company with him. Hell. He'd be a hard man to compete with.

Not that Mike was competing for the beautiful executive director. She was still a person of interest. If he couldn't move her off that status, they'd never have a chance to go out again. God forbid she actually became a suspect. His insides twisted, sending him in search of coffee. Probably wouldn't help his stomach, but it gave him something to do before facing Harding.

"Hey, Rick. How's it going?" Mike filled a cup with black sludge.

"I don't know how you keep drinking that stuff, man." He put the required quarters in a machine and popped out a soda.

"Like that's not curdling your gizzard." Mike laughed to cover a grimace at the stale coffee taste.

"I've talked with Sue Patterson, the housekeeper. Zip from her. She goes in once a week, spends several hours cleaning, and she's gone." He checked his notes. "Has never seen anything like a weapon in all the years she's cleaned the Greer house. Had nothing but good to say about Ms. Greer and Jeremy, but she's concerned about Elizabeth. Thinks the way she dresses is the girl crying out to be noticed. Didn't have anything good to say for the ex.

"What about Jeremy's friend. What's his name?" Mike leaned against the counter, crossing his right foot over his left ankle.

"Tommy Henson. Seems a good kid. He's planning on college. Plays in the school orchestra and wants to major in music composition." Rick scratched his head. "Is that something you can get a degree in?"

Mike chuckled. "Apparently. If you're talented. Sonya Lowry announced Mike was gay. You think his friend Tommy is?"

"Probably, but it looked like Tommy and his father, who came in with him, have a solid relationship. How would that connect to our murder?"

"Don't know that it would, just good to keep everything on the table."

"You've talked with the daughter's friend?" Rick gulped the last of the soda.

"Yeah. Sonya and Elizabeth have been friends for years. Sounds like they'd do anything for each other. But Sonya's never seen a gun there and says the brother and sister haven't even mentioned one to her.

"Talmadge has a gun and a permit to carry, also says he's hunted. If getting rid of DeWitt would've helped Ms. Greer—he'd be someone I'd want to keep an eye on." Mike wandered toward the sink, emptied his cup, ran water and soap around, and dried it with a paper towel.

"You haven't seen her anymore since the investigation began, right?"

"Just to talk about the case. Mike's hand clenched as he fought an inclination to pop his partner for suggesting he'd act less than in an ethical manner. He was willing to bend some rules but not that one. Imagining seeing her in different circumstances didn't count.

"Hey, Mike." Lydia stuck her head into the break room. You've got a Mr. Harding here to see you. I've put him in Interview Three like the last ones.

"Thanks, Lydia. I'll be right there."

"I'd like to meet this guy. Think I'll tag along." Rick tossed his can in the recycling bin.

"Great. Come on." Mike stopped by his office and left his coffee mug on the desk before he and Rick made their way toward the interrogation rooms.

When they entered, they found Harding pacing the small cubicle.

"Thanks for coming in, Mr. Harding. I'm Detective Mike Riley, and this is my partner, Rick Martinez."

Harding stared at the two men. "I remember who you are. You still trying to pin Shannon DeWitt's murder on Addison?"

"We're not trying to pin the murder on anyone. We're just gathering information." Mike pulled out one of the chairs. "Have a seat, Mr. Harding." Rick moved to lean against one of the walls. Mike walked to the other side of the table and sat. After a moment, Harding settled onto the metal chair.

He folded his hands on the table. "What do you want to know?"

"We understand you've been to the Greer house?"

"That's right. Addison has been gracious enough to accompany me to a number of fundraisers in recent months. I don't know how you treat women, Detective Riley, but I make it a point to pick them up and provide transportation."

"Yes, well, can you give me specific dates?"

Mike noted them on his paper even though the recording was getting everything. "How long did you stay on each of those visits?"

"Addison's very punctual. Not more than five minutes to visit with Jeremy one time and one time just to say hello to her daughter."

"And when you took her home after the fundraiser?"

"Are you asking if I spent the night, Detective?" One of the man's eyebrows rose almost to his hairline, his voice held a hint of humor.

Good thing he wasn't drinking anything. Mike would've choked. He wanted to plow his fist into the older man's jaw for suggesting that. No telling what Rick would make of his behavior if he did, not to mention how out of line he'd be. Mike took a moment to study his notes, making a point not to look at his partner, and then he turned back before answering. "Did you?" He gritted his teeth, preparing for an answer he didn't want to hear.

Harding leaned back in the chair and crossed his arms over his chest. "I saw her safely inside, kissed her cheek, and stepped back on the porch, only returning to the limo after the lock clicked."

Mike's grip on the pencil turned his knuckles white.

"I'm not sure I get the direction of your questioning, Detective."

Mike looked down then up at the man. "You've never seen a gun in the house?"

"No."

"Do you know if Ms. Greer has a gun?"

"I don't know whether she does or not."

"Do you own a gun?" Ricky threw in the question.

Harding focused his attention on Rick. "Yes, Detective. I own several including some rifles." He pulled out his wallet. "I've got a permit to carry." He pushed the card across the table.

Mike leaned forward and noted the expiration date and the number. Interesting. Two men who were obviously supporters of Addie both had access to weapons. If someone threatened her, Mike didn't doubt either would use one to protect her.

"If you'd told me more about what the subject of our meeting was, I could've brought you a list of my guns and their registration numbers. Although a couple of my rifles have been in the family for years and don't have one."

"Appreciate you're offering the information, Mr. Harding. Please email the list to this address." Mike stood, gave Harding his card. "Thank you for coming in."

Harding stood, looked first at Rick then back to Mike. "You're welcome, Detectives." He nodded once, turned, and ambled out. Mike followed him and closed the door.

Rick walked away from the wall, pulled Mike's chair out and straddled it, resting his hands on the back, his preferred way of sitting in a straight back chair.

"He's a cool customer. We'll have to wait to see what caliber his guns are, but I can see him doing this. Getting rid of a board member made an opening for him."

"Would a person kill someone for a seat on a non-profit board? Those aren't paid positions." Mike paced the small area, running the scenario through his head.

"Might not be a motive for some, but for others, maybe." Rick smiled. "Struck me you got a little hot under the collar, partner."

"Oh?" Mike put as much ice in his voice as he could, hoping to shut off the line of questioning.

"Yeah. When Harding asked if you wanted to know if he'd slept with Greer, I thought you'd snap that pencil of yours in half." He stood and pulled it from Mike's hand. "Nah. It's still solid. Watch yourself. You don't want the lieutenant to yank you from this investigation. How would that help your executive director?" Rick danced and spun from the interview room.

Just as well. What could Mike say to him?

True to his word, within thirty minutes, Harding's email with the list of his weapons arrived. Mike printed it and put it in the paper file, as well as saving it to the electronic file. How long before they'd stop using paper at all? In some ways, that would an improvement.

"Cup of joe, Mike?" Rick sauntered up to Mike's desk with a cup in his hand.

"Yup. How bad has it gotten?" Mike slugged it back and fought his gag reflex. "Hell." He strode into the break room. "We'll poison the whole floor with this stuff." He emptied what remained in the pot, ran hot water with a little soap, and scrubbed it out with a sponge.

Rick trailed along behind Mike. "You must be getting weak in your old age, man." He poked Mike in the side. "You used to be able to down this even if it tasted like dirty dishwater."

"Yeah, must've been when I was young and stupid." Mike laughed. The aroma of fresh perking coffee settled his stomach but not so much his worry. He settled in a chair and rocked back on two legs. "Let's talk while the java is brewing."

"Sure, what's on your mind?" His partner turned a chair around and straddled it. "We got nothing from any of the people who entered Ms. Greer's house between October ninth and November sixth."

"Got any other ideas?"

"Yeah." Mike rubbed a hand over his more than five-o'clock shadow. "And I don't like it very much."

CHAPTER ELEVEN

Friday, November 30

After weeks of rehearsal, it was opening night for *The Music Man*. "How're you feeling, Jeremy?" Addie could guess but wanted to hear from her son how things were going.

"I can't eat anything, Mom." He shoved his sandwich and chips away.

Well, this was significant. Jeremy never turned down food.

He ran a hand through his hair then hopped up and dashed for the hall mirror. He'd just finished a shower, used a blow dryer, and gel on his hair to give it that slicked-down look for Professor Harold Hill. So different from his usual sticking-up-all-over casual look.

"You didn't mess it up, Son." She followed him. Met his gaze in the mirror.

He grinned. "It's okay. I worked a long time for just this look."

"The hair is perfect, and I know you're going to do just great." Addie patted his shoulder.

"Dad still coming?" Jeremy drifted into the living room, and nervously made a complete circle.

This was important to him. His father had never attended one of his performances. Addie believed if the man ever saw how good his son was, Jud would accept Jeremy's dream to go to Broadway. She didn't believe Jeremy had come out to his dad yet, an altogether different issue.

"Yes, as far as I know." She hated using the caveat, but too many times, they'd all thought Jud was making the trip from Dallas and "something" always came up.

Jeremy's anxious steps propelled him back to the kitchen where he circled the table.

"But whether he makes it or not, your fan club will be out in force. Pete's coming, said he wouldn't miss this for anything. He thought it was neat you and Elizabeth were both performing. I do, too. It's the first time."

"Yeah, I'm glad. She needs to hustle her buns. I'm about ready to leave. Hey, Elizabeth, what's keeping you?" He hollered so loud Addie almost covered her ears.

"Jonathan Harding called to say he was coming, and he'll want to see you after, like everyone else. Kate told me she and Blair are coming, too. And it's so nice of Mrs. Riley to throw an after-party for all of us."

"Good. Be fun to see them. You know Elizabeth and I won't stay long at the Riley's house?"

"Yes, sweetie."

"Give me three minutes, Jeremy." Elizabeth's muffled voice came from her bedroom.

"Mom?" Jeremy looked at her then away.

"What is it?"

"Are you interested in Mr. Harding?"

"Oh, well..."

"He seems like a nice man, and you wouldn't have to worry about money anymore."

Addie yanked out her ponytail holder and dragged her fingers through her hair to gain time. She then secured it back into place before she put an arm around her son's waist. "Thanks, dear. I appreciate you saying that." Not the time for Mike Riley's face to flash before her. He couldn't be anything to her. He thought she'd murdered Shannon. Damn her stupid hormones for falling off the top of the building every time she saw him.

"So are you?"

"We're more... business associates, I'd say. And yes he is a nice man. I just not interested in him that way."

Jeremy nodded. "Hey, Elizabeth." He shouted for his sister.

Addie laughed and rubbed her ears. "No need to worry about you projecting, I guess."

Jeremy smiled his blue eyes lit with excitement. "Nope. Wonder where I get that?"

"So what are you waiting for?" Elizabeth appeared in the hallway which led to the bedrooms, face scrubbed clean, grasping the handle of a make-up kit. "Let's go."

"You got it, Sis." Jeremy slung an arm around her shoulder, which she didn't shake off, and they headed for the garage.

"Break a leg, you two." Addie waved and fought the

tightness in her throat. God, she wanted them both to do well tonight. Playing Professor Hill, so much of the success of the show rode on Jeremy's shoulders, but she wasn't as worried about him as Elizabeth, who had much less experience in this world of theatre. Put a paintbrush in her hand, and she was amazing.

With some time on her hands before Addie had to get ready, she headed for their wing of the house, certain their bathroom and bedrooms probably had the look of tornado alley. She chuckled. This should be a fun evening.

◆ ◆ ◆

"Now, Mike, I know you can get called in, but if you do, you do. Pat will run you back to our house for your truck. Hopefully, you'll get to see a little of the show, and if we're lucky the whole thing."

Cindy's sweet as molasses tone came through the phone clear as if she were in the room with him. The tone she used when she really wanted something from Pat, the kids, or Mike. Generally it worked. Partly, because they knew she never gave up.

Mike sighed. "But it's a musical, Cindy."

"I know, Mike. Pat's going. He even managed not to be on call. For all the good we know that does us—"

"Yeah, sometimes he has to go in anyway." Mike nodded. His brother, a good man, did a lot of life-saving work. When someone needed him, he went.

Mike loved his sister-in-law. She kept his brother from being a total workaholic. While Mike wasn't a fan of musicals, he was certain if he went, he'd get to see not only the teenager playing the lead part, but his mother, too.

A little chancy, but there'd be lots of others around. He wouldn't talk with her, just look. *That's pitiful, man.* He had to get this case solved—one-way or the other.

"So what's it to be, Mike?" his ever-patient, ever-persistent sister-in-law asked.

Mike sighed. "You got it. Hard to say no to you."

"Yippee!"

Mike's laugh bellowed into the phone. Cindy was such a nut.

"You come to our house, and we'll go together."

"Yes, ma'am."

"Now don't be late."

"Okay, Cindy. I'll be there in plenty of time. Let me go now." Her phone disconnected and Mike fought the little trickle of excitement rushing through his blood. In a few hours, he'd see Addie.

◆ ◆ ◆

Fifteen minutes before show time, Mike shifted in the back seat of his brother's car. Why had he agreed to attend? Oh, right. Cindy, like a dog after a bone, wouldn't give up until he did. An off-duty police officer helped with the traffic as Pat wheeled into the school parking lot. Good judgment on the part of school administration.

"Right there, Pat." Cindy waved her hand at the space she wanted his brother to use. He maneuvered into the spot, and Mike helped Cindy out of the car.

"I'm tickled you both arranged to be here. We're going to have a good time." She linked each of her arms through one of theirs and sailed toward the high school auditorium.

"The school has a reputation for putting on a good show, and everyone loves *The Music Man*. Remember, Pat? We saw a revival in New York one time."

Mike looked across his sister-in-law to his brother, who rolled his eyes and nodded.

"We in for a tough evening?" Mike asked.

"No. The show has its moments. The horns number is cool. But it's a sappy love story."

"Pat Riley." Cindy yanked on her husband's arm. "How can you say that? It's a delightful love story."

Mike met his brother's gaze over Cindy's head.

Pat shrugged his shoulders. "Sorry, man. It's just one evening. We'd both be working if we weren't here."

Mike chuckled and nodded. "That's true." And he might be working here. He could use the opportunity to set up a time for Addie to come down to the department. He wanted to tell her none of the other people who'd come into her house could be connected to the gun, but he didn't intend to have that conversation on the phone. He wanted to see her reaction.

They went through the front doors and into a lobby. Not like any high school auditorium Mike ever remembered seeing.

It was more like a theatre with a box office and flashy pictures of the cast members. A noisy buzz of conversation greeted them along with the unmistakable smell of popcorn.

"Yum. Guess that's for intermission." Cindy presented the tickets to ushers, who handed them their programs and led them to a row with three empty seats on the end. Addie sat on their row, several seats in with Harding just past her. Harding again. Mike ground his teeth. Cindy went in first.

"I'm glad you could come." Addie rose and embraced Cindy. "You know Jonathan Harding, I think."

"Oh, yes. So good to see you again, Jonathan." Cindy quickly reminded the men they'd all met.

"You take this one, Mike." Cindy scooted back into the aisle. She indicated the chair next to Addie. "I want to make a stop in the restroom before the show starts. When I return, I only have to climb over Pat." She trotted up the aisle.

Mike looked at Pat who shrugged his shoulders.

Mike didn't want to sit there. Yet, he did. They settled into their spots. His arm brushed against Addie's, and warmth spread from there to other areas of his anatomy. This wasn't going to work. Mike opened the program and pretended to be engrossed.

"I didn't know you liked musicals, Detective."

"I don't." Hell. "I mean Cindy—"

"Cindy dragged you here?" Addie's soft chuckle indicated acceptance and pleasure.

Mike nodded. "Yeah."

"If you don't want to stay through the whole show, you

won't hurt my feelings. We're glad to have a full house tonight. It helps with making the budget for the show."

"So high school theatre has budget issues, too?"

Again, her sultry chuckle sent chills across the back of his neck.

"Unless a company is lucky to have an angel, Detective, almost all theatre companies have budget issues."

Was Harding the angel for Cowtown Theatre? What perks came with that role? Mike squirmed in his chair, not happy with the direction of his thoughts. Would Addie sleep with someone for the good of the theatre? Would she kill?

"I'm back." Cindy squeezed in past Pat. "I loved the pictures of your kids out in the hallway, Addie. They are so good looking."

"Thanks. I think so, but of course, I'm biased." She smiled her pleasure.

"Oh, I ran into your friend Kate. She said to tell you she'd see you at intermission."

"I'm glad she made it." Addie rolled the program into a tube shape and unrolled it. "I tell you, I'm more nervous than for one of my own shows. I want them to do well tonight. Jeremy's got a load on his shoulders."

"He sounded great the other afternoon when I stopped by to get you, Addie." Harding leaned forward to speak so the others heard. "The boy was practicing the River City song in the den. Pretty impressive. Looking forward to seeing him in the role."

Hell. Mike swallowed the words that nearly flew out of his

mouth. What were you doing there? What are your intentions with Ms. Greer?

Fortunately just then, the houselights dimmed, and a spotlight came up on a person on the stage. Mike missed most of what was said when Addie's hand touched his. Electricity zinged up his arm.

"Detective." She leaned close enough for him to get a heady whiff of some scent, which nearly had him grabbing her and kissing her. *Hold it just a damn minute. That is not happening.*

"What?" Hell, he didn't need to snap at her.

Cindy elbowed him a good one. "Shh."

"Your cell phone. You need to turn it off," Addie said

He nodded, dug at his belt, and switched the cell to vibrate.

"Sorry, not good enough." Addie's soft, sibilant whisper undid all his good resolutions where she was concerned.

"You'll mess up the microphone system if you leave it on."

Mike did as she asked. The orchestra started, but the curtains didn't open. He glanced toward Cindy, but she'd cocked her head toward Pat, saying something. Mike turned to Addie. His expression must've indicated his question.

"It's the overture."

He nodded. Yeah, he vaguely remembered something about that. He didn't know much about orchestras, but to his ear they sounded good.

Again, Addie leaned near "They're all high school

students."

Mike nodded. He guessed that was significant. The lights went down, and the curtain opened to reveal an interesting stage set suggesting a train, with the young men's jiggling bodies providing the movement. As the show progressed, Mike decided his brother was right. The story was lame, but Addie's son Jeremy was doing a great job of pulling off the Harold Hill role. According to Mike's boot tapping out the rhythm, the "Ya' Got Trouble" number was a real winner.

A couple of times, Addie leaned toward Harding. During a scene with townspeople, she also leaned toward Mike.

"That's Elizabeth in the green dress." Addie's breathy words tickled his ear, and he squirmed to find a more comfortable position. His gaze followed Addie's direction.

What a change from the Goth clad girl Mike was used to seeing. The stage make-up contrived to give her a wholesome look.

The first act ended with the female lead singing something corny about a white knight. Women who waited for one of those were mostly doomed to be disappointed. Had Addie never remarried after her divorce because she was expecting her own white knight? He sure as hell hoped she wasn't looking to Harding for that. Oh, he had the money to deal with any of her concerns both personally and for the theatre, but he was a lot older than she. Not that it mattered to Mike one-way or the other. His fingers twisted the program and shoved it into his pocket.

They stood and prepared to file up the aisle. Pat stepped

aside to let Cindy go first. Mike did the same thing for Addie, but before he took a place behind her, Harding stepped in ahead of him. An elbow jab would've slowed the older man down, but Mike resisted.

When Harding rested his hand on Addie's back, as they made their way toward the lobby, a blast of heat shot through Mike's body. He gripped his fingers into fists. It wasn't anything to him what Greer and Harding were up to. He wasn't free to follow up on anything. If anything existed between him and Addie. A big *if.*

"Don't you love it, Mike?" Cindy's excited voice brought him back to the lobby and all the people milling around.

"Sure, Cindy." He turned on his phone. No messages. Good or bad? He slid the phone back in his pocket.

Cindy turned to Addie. "I've been able to civilize Pat, so he's gone with me to New York for a number of shows. Mike's not had anyone to smooth out his cowboy ways."

If he wasn't mistaken, his sister-in-law had just apologized for some lack in him. Addie cut her gaze at him-a questioning look.

"Just horses and murder, Detective?" One eyebrow quirked upward, and her lips twitched.

Mike nodded. "Pretty much, Ms. Greer."

"Oh, Addie, Jeremy's doing a super job." A woman swung Addie into a hug.

"Oh, hey, Kate. I'm so glad you came." She turned to the others. "This is one of my longtime best friends, Kate Thompson. You may recognize her name from real estate signs, and some of you met her at our recent fundraiser." Addie was gracious in making the introductions until she came to him. She paused, as if trying to figure out how to describe him.

"I bet I know who you are." Kate looked him up and down for so long Mike felt like he was a side of beef hanging there for the inspectors. She extended her hand. "Nice to meet you, Detective Riley. I've known Addie since she was a kid. Let me assure you she's no murderer."

Well, hell, how should he respond to that? Before he figured something out and the silence became awkward, Addie grabbed her friend's arm.

"Kate, I'd love to see Blair. Back in a bit, y'all." She hustled Kate through the crowd.

There was an awkward silence for a minute or so. Cindy shifted, cleared her throat, and said, "Well, hard to argue with friendship like that."

Nobody said anything. He kept his head down. No way he'd open his mouth on the subject.

"Sorry about that." Addie rejoined the group.

"Have you seen *Kinky Boots* in New York, Cindy?" Harding totally changed the subject, all the while standing closer to Addie than Mike liked.

"No, but it's on our must see list. We're going in December."

"You are?" Mike glanced at his brother. He didn't remember hearing about the trip.

"Yeah. In a weak moment, I promised to take her."

"Have you been there during the holidays?" Addie's voice

held a touch of excitement and maybe even yearning.

"Oh my, yes." Cindy answered. "Took the kids when they were younger. It is truly something to experience. "You've been, haven't you, Addie?"

"I've been to New York, but never during the holidays. I've seen it on TV and in the movies, of course. It's something I've always wanted to do."

"Maybe that's something we can arrange, Addie." Harding said with a look in his eyes suggesting he'd like to be the one to go along with her. He could certainly afford to pay for the trip.

Mike had some money set aside, but vacations across country weren't regularly on his to do list. The Vermont trips were the exception. He'd gone several times in his efforts to solve the murder of Jill Barlow's husband. Just another example of his stupidity where women were concerned. He glanced at Addison Greer. Hell, if things were only different....

Her smile said she'd like nothing better than a trip to the Big Apple. "I can't personally swing that right now."

"I could put some extra money in the budget to send you. Valid reason is so you can scout for material and talent."

A blush flooded Addie's cheeks. "Well, I don't know, Jonathan."

The lights flashed several times.

"Time to go back in." Cindy slid her arm through one of Addie's. "Maybe you could go when we do. We'd have such fun."

Mike lost Addie's response as the two women moved

ahead. The men followed behind and then everyone filed into the row. He settled into his seat, pulled the crumpled program from his pocket, and glanced at it. Looked like not quite as many numbers in the second act. At least he got to sit next to Addie. She continued to whisper to Harding but occasionally also threw comments his way. Mostly she seemed caught up in the sappy story enacted by her son and a teenage girl with an amazing voice.

"Till There Was You," toward the end of the show, sounded familiar. Did anyone today experience that all-consuming sudden burst of recognition? While the actors took their bows and the audience gave the kids a standing ovation, Addie's soft voice hummed the tune.

It didn't take long for the cast to join the audience members in the lobby, which soon was crowded enough to make Mike to consider it a safety issue. People were jammed together like cows in a slaughterhouse.

"Jeremy, you were wonderful!" Addie hugged her son.

"Thanks, Mom."

"Did you see Kate and Blair?" Addie looked past him.

"Yes, they were the first people to give me a hug. Kate said to tell you she'd talk to you later."

Addie nodded. "Nice of them to choose to come to the show when Blair's here for only a few days." She craned her neck. "Where's Elizabeth?"

Mike looked around but wasn't sure he'd recognize her from the others in their early 1900's costumes.

"Oh, here she is." Addie wiggled an arm between some

people and snagged her daughter, drawing her into their group." Honey, you were so good. I never once saw you break character. Did you have a good time?"

Elizabeth nodded. "Thanks, Mom. You really thought I was okay? Jer was great, of

course." She sent a light punch to his middle. Jeremy grabbed her around the waist.

"Good job, Sis." He kissed her on the cheek. "Those lessons paid off." Elizabeth stomped on his foot. "Ooof."

"What lessons?" Addie looked between her two children. Something was up. Elizabeth's face blanched. "What lessons?" she repeated.

"No big deal. I just took a couple of acting lessons." The muscle in Elizabeth's jaw clenched and released several times. Her whole body pulled into herself.

With only a little imagination, Mike saw her take on her Goth persona. The glare she directed at Jeremy appeared life-threatening. He ran a hand through his hair, messing up the center part he wore for his character.

Addie's gaze passed between her son and daughter, and then she hugged Elizabeth tight. "Good for you. We'll talk later."

"Do you all know how to get to our house for the party?" Cindy was in her element, playing hostess with the mostest. Mike grinned at his brother, who nodded back.

"Thanks for doing this, Mrs. Riley. Elizabeth and I won't stay long. A bunch of the kids are getting together at Billy's Burger Store, and we planned to go."

"It's perfectly okay with me, Jeremy. Y'all won't hurt my

feelings. I'm glad you can come for a while."

"It's lovely of Mrs. Riley to have us all over, but y'all need to have fun with the cast and crew, too," Addie said.

She must've attended plenty of those over the years. "You do throw good parties, Cindy." Mike smiled at his sister-in-law.

◆ ◆ ◆

Pat and Cindy's large house made it easy to accommodate everyone. Addie appreciated her efforts, but she'd have to think of a way to repay their hospitality. Given the difference in their incomes, that might be a challenge. Maybe they'd enjoy pizza and beer at her house, especially if she had homemade fresh pizza. She and the kids used to do that often, but not in recent years.

Cindy had prepared an array of finger foods. Nothing Addie liked better than bite-size tasty morsels of meat and veggies.

"Addie."

The deep voice made her jerk. She'd recognize his accent and tone in a dark alley.

"Hi." Well, that was clever. No one would guess she made her living by dealing with words and how to say them.

"I'd like you to come down to police headquarters Monday."

Addie's hand clenched around her wine glass. Her eyes cast around the room to see if anyone were near enough to hear what he'd said.

"I can be there around two. Will that work for you? And do I need to bring a lawyer?" Her tone was a tad strident, but not bad considering how tied into knots her stomach was at his request.

"No. But I want you to bring Jeremy and Elizabeth."

"What? Why?" Her breathing jacked up at the idea of taking her kids to the police station.

"Just do what I'm requesting, Addie." The steel in his voice sent a shiver up her spine.

"Well, it won't be until three-thirty or so, after they get out of school."

"That will be fine. I'll look for you then. It was a nice evening, Addie. I...well, I didn't exactly enjoy the production, but Jeremy was good with all those words coming out so fast."

She couldn't help but smile at his honesty. "Thank you."

"See you Monday then."

Mike headed over to Cindy, who stood talking with a couple of people. He gave her a hug then grabbed his western hat from the rack standing behind the door and strode through.

Addie exhaled a deep sigh. She really shouldn't like the man one bit. Nor did she need these stirrings of hormones anytime he was near. Damn, what was wrong with her? Riley might actually throw her in jail. Her stomach pitched, and she regretted the shrimp wrapped in bacon she'd inhaled earlier. Maybe she needed to check into getting a lawyer. Not as expensive a one as Jonathan suggested, but someone. She'd give that more thought.

And what about the kids? Why did Mike want to see them? Where did Elizabeth take acting lessons? Questions rolled around in Addie's brain, making her almost dizzy. Addie agreed with Jeremy that the lessons obviously helped. Their father should've made a point to get to school to see them. He'd called and left a message, which was better than nothing. Work had kept him from coming. Yeah, right.

"Addie." Jonathan stepped up next to her. "The show was very well done, and Jeremy was quite...awesome. I believe that's the word everyone uses these days."

"Thanks, Jonathan. Glad you could attend." She took a sip of her wine.

"Has he picked out a school yet? Or is he going straight to New York when he graduates?"

"Oh my. That's very flattering. I certainly count on him going to college first. I went to Oklahoma City University, and he's interested in their musical theatre program. They have a track record for putting their graduates to work."

Jonathan nodded. "If you're ready to leave, I'll follow you home."

"Thanks, but it's not necessary. I drive home late from rehearsals and performances all the time."

"Ask anytime you need anything, Addie. I'm there for the theatre and for you." He leaned in, kissed her on the cheek, then stepped back and walked toward his hostess.

Addie touched her face. Jonathan Harding was a terribly nice man. Handsome. Wealthy. And clearly interested. Too bad not even a smidgen of a spark ignited when she was with him.

Too bad the man she wanted to kiss her cheek and her mouth, and any place else he wanted was the homicide detective who might at any moment arrest her for murder.

CHAPTER TWELVE

Monday, December 3

Addie drummed her fingertips on the steering wheel, waiting for her kids. They'd both insisted they needed a snack before heading down to police headquarters. What was Mike thinking to ask her to bring them?

She opened the car door, climbed out, and went up the steps to the kitchen. "Hey, guys come on."

"I'm coming, Mom." Jeremy took a bite from his apple and walked around her. "I've got shotgun."

Addie shook her head. "Elizabeth."

"Coming."

Elizabeth had returned to wearing her long flowing dark clothes. Addie had enjoyed seeing her make-up-free before the play performance and had hoped it would last. Apparently not. She followed her daughter to the car, got in, and hit the garage door opener.

"So, Mom, why do we have to go down to see the detective?"

Addie glanced at her daughter, answering as she backed out of the garage. "I don't know, sweetie." She navigated the traffic, zipping along past slowpokes. They were already later than she'd told Mike they'd be.

"Well, I don't much like it," Elizabeth said.

Addie met her daughter's gaze in the rearview mirror. "Let's just wait and see." Her calm tone belied the tense hold her fingers had on the steering wheel. "I let the staff at the theatre know I was coming back down here. We all hope Detective Riley has some word for us about who killed Shannon." But why bring the kids then?

She stopped at a light behind a truck. "Would you look at that? He's belching all kinds of black stuff into our air."

Jeremy coughed. "Get around him quick"

"Will do." As soon as the light changed, she swung the steering wheel hard left and gunned the engine.

"Jeez, Mom, you're going to get arrested for reckless driving," Elizabeth squealed.

"Give it a rest." Her brother waved his hand over the seat at her.

They continued to bicker until Addie pulled into a city garage near the Fort Worth Police Headquarters. She pried each finger from the steering wheel. Wished she didn't feel so apprehensive.

"Let's get this over." Addie trudged into the building, the kids following closely behind. They stopped at a reception desk.

"I'm Addison Greer. We're here to see Detective Mike Riley."

◆ ◆ ◆

Clay stopped by the theatre to finish cleaning out his office. He nearly bumped into Roger Garland, Cowtown's accountant, and Judy Neesum, the choreographer, so deep in conversation they didn't notice him at first.

"Are you sure she said she was going down to police headquarters?" Roger asked.

"Yeah. I asked her if she knew why. She said she didn't, unless the police had information about who killed Shannon."

"So, Addie's been called back to Police Headquarters, huh?" Clay stepped between the two.

"I didn't think you were supposed to be here, Clay." Judy crossed her arms over her skinny chest.

"Just stopped by to finish cleaning out my office, but it's a good thing I'm here. What happens if they arrest Addie for the murder?"

"What? You must be nuts!" Judy jumped to Addie's defense.

Roger, as to be expected, was quiet.

"Well, if they arrest her, what happens to the theatre? Who will run things? I'm just saying it's a good thing I came in today. I'd be willing to step in and run Cowtown Theatre."

"You are certifiable, Clay." Judy spun around and stomped off.

Clay's voice stopped her. "We need to call the board and let them know what's happening. They can reinstate me, and we won't miss a beat. Good idea, Roger?" Clay clapped the accountant on the back, squeezing his shoulder.

"Uh, uh...sure, Clay."

Smart guy. He knew who the real deal was.

"Clay, I don't think that's necessary." Judy took two steps back.

"Well, Roger and I do. If you want to keep your job around here, you better get on board." He clapped his hands, and both Roger and Judy jumped. "Let's get calling."

The two staff members literally scurried away. Clay couldn't contain his laughter. This was going to work out just the way he needed.

He leaned back in a chair in the theatre's small boardroom. Showing up when he did, proved to be good timing on his part. Board members actually agreed to come down. They'd called an impromptu meeting to take place in thirty minutes. They left messages for the only two people they hadn't reached, Cindy Riley and Jonathan Harding. Both of them seemed like Addison's buddies, so starting without them was okay with Clay.

"Glad so many of you could make it down here on such short notice." Clay glanced around at the members present. With Jonathan and Cindy not attending, Clay bet he'd push this through.

"It appears that as we talk, Addison is being arrested for the murder of dear Shannon." Gasps and murmurs filled the room.

"The only way we can help her is by making sure the theatre keeps running. We all know how much Addie loves Cowtown. She doesn't need the added concern of what affect her situation will have on all of us."

"What should we do, Clay?" Linda Alexander asked.

"For starters, you can reinstate me, and I'll handle things until Addie gets all this misunderstanding worked out." He nearly chocked on the words, but everyone was eating it up.

"That sounds like a good plan to me." Linda exhaled a long sigh. In her favor, besides being a good lay, she loved the theatre.

Just then, the door opened, and Jonathan Harding walked in. Shit.

"What are you trying to do, Bennett?"

Clay scrambled to sound as positive as he had earlier, but Harding just blew right by him.

"There's no way the police are arresting, Addie. You are entirely premature. Let's all take a couple of deep breaths and calm down." Harding made eye contact with each board member. "If she's arrested, we'll have plenty of time to take necessary steps to keep the shows going."

The board members looked at each other and began to nod. Shit. Always easier to take no action in a situation. After a brief conversation, they voted to wait to see what happened. God damn Harding!

Clay went to his office to finish the task of cleaning out. Maybe he'd get some more dollars from Roger before he left.

♦ ♦ ♦

"Thanks for coming in to see me, Ms. Greer."

Addie gritted her teeth and waltzed past him into the

small gray room. It might've been the same one she'd been in before. "I didn't feel I had a choice."

"Have a seat."

Detective Riley held her chair for her, and she settled into it but kept her back straight. The chair wobbled. Maybe it wasn't the same room. "What's the purpose of this meeting, Detective, and why did you want me to bring my children down here?" He'd asked Jeremy and Elizabeth to wait in another room. Not sure what she made of that.

"One thing at a time, Ms. Greer. The detective sat in the chair facing her, leaning back, one leg crossed casually over the other, as if this were nothing more critical than a social visit. Difficult to mimic his behavior when what she wanted to do was jump down his throat.

First, for raising her interest in him.

Second, for thinking she was capable of murder.

Truth be told, she'd be capable of murder if someone threatened her kids. She inhaled deeply through her nose and let it out slowly at the same time she relaxed the death grip her hands had taken on each other. She'd been a good actress in her day. She ought to be able to "out-cool" the detective. She waited in silence, with only her eyebrows arched to indicate her interest in the outcome of the meeting.

"You were going to tell me why you needed me to come down here, Detective," she said when Riley continued to stare at her.

"The gun we found in your house is the murder weapon."

Her heartbeat accelerated. His words fell like ice picks

hitting her brain. They just could not be true. "That can't be."

"I'm afraid it is. We've interviewed all the people you said had been in your house." He paused.

Addie's heartbeat pounded in her eardrums as the silence drew out. If he didn't speak soon, she'd scream her frustration at him.

"Ms. Greer, none of them has any knowledge about the gun—the one your daughter showed us."

"That brings you back to me then." Her shoulders sagged. One hand traveled on its own to her mouth, and she chewed on a nail—an action she'd been prone to after her husband chose to put his lover in their bed. She thought she'd broken herself of the nasty habit. With effort, she put her hand back in her lap. Looked like it might be time to check into getting a lawyer.

"Well, no, Ms. Greer." The detective rose and proceeded to pace around the table.

Straightening her back, she asked, "Who else is there?"

"We need to talk with Jeremy and Elizabeth."

"What?" Her heart thudded against her breastbone. "My kids don't have anything to do with this."

"I don't know that they do." He sat on the corner of the table nearest her.

"Well, they just can't." She couldn't stop the tremble rumbling through her entire body.

"I just want to talk with each of them. You can be right here." His deep brown eyes warmed a place in her middle. Sheer madness on her part. He was a cop with a cop's job. She and her family didn't mean anything to him. He just wanted to solve his damn case. Her lip trembled against her will. Guilt washed up making her almost sick. *Forgive me, Shannon.*

"We'll work this out, Addie." He rested his hand on her shoulder for only a moment.

"Okay then. What do we do next?"

"I'd like to have Jeremy come in for a little chat first."

She nodded afraid she couldn't force out any words. This was all madness. Her stomach tightened into a knot at the idea of a homicide detective questioning her kids.

"I'll be back." He walked across the room and out through the door.

Try as hard as she might, Addie couldn't stop her crossed leg from swinging, and her index finger kept finding its way to her mouth. A nail no longer extended past the tip.

When the door opened and Mike let Jeremy enter, Addie flew out of her chair straight to her son.

"What's going on, Mom?" Jeremy hugged her.

"I don't exactly know." She hated that she was somehow responsible for involving her kids in this awful mess. Her ex-husband would be all over this, saying she was a bad mother for letting Jeremy go down to the police department.

"We'll continue as soon as you both sit down." Detective Riley extended his hand.

He was being a hard-ass. Did he really think she or her kids knew any more about Shannon's murder? Guess so. If the gun in her home was the murder weapon.

"Jeremy, I told your mother we didn't find anything

incriminating about the people whose names you gave us."

"So what does that mean? Why did we all have to come down here?" Her son's eyebrows crinkled into a frown as his gaze shot between Mike and her. Jeremy's knee jumped under the table. She laid a hand on his arm in hopes of calming him down.

"We have three possibilities." Mike leaned forward and pinned Jeremy with an icy stare. "Your mother brought the gun into your house."

"No." Jeremy said.

Dear God. Mike really believed she had something to do with the murder. Addie's stomach heaved, and for a moment, she feared she'd throw up. She reached deep inside for a calm she didn't feel, patted Jeremy's knee to help ground him and then forced her hands to be still on the table.

"Then you brought the gun in." No mistaking the steel in Mike's voice.

Jeremy jerked as if someone had belted him in the middle with a two-by-four.

"No." Addie said in a tight voice. She propped her elbows on the table and dropped her head forward. This truly was a nightmare. Then she straightened. "How dare you accuse Jeremy." She'd never apologize for the outrage in her voice. How could she have thought she was attracted to this man? He not only considered it possible she'd killed Shannon, but that one of her children might be involved.

"I dare because it's my job to find who murdered Shannon DeWitt. Don't you want to know who took someone's life in your precious theatre?"

She dragged in a sharp breath. The venom in his tone stung.

"Hey, don't talk to my mother that way."

Addie swallowed over the tight ball of hurt, anger, and fear. Somehow, she had to keep it together and get her kids out of here.

The detective thrust back his chair and stormed around the room; the only sound was from his boots hitting on the concrete floor. He came back to face them. Leaned both hands on the table. "I need the truth, Jeremy. Did you put the gun in the living room end table?"

"No. Honest to God, I didn't put it there."

Addie fought the sickness threatening her again.

Mike—Detective Riley—she'd be hard pressed to ever think of him as "Mike" again— pulled up a chair close to her and leaned forward. He shot a glance at Addie then pinned her son with that same fierce stare.

"Then what about Elizabeth?"

The words dropped into the silence like a bomb. Addie sat unmoving. He now suspected that her daughter had something to do with the gun. Jeremy squirmed in the chair next to her. She glanced at him. Did he know something about his sister?

"Jeremy?" Her voice came out sounding pitiful and pleading. Not what she'd intended.

"Mom." He said in two syllables he'd used when he was a small boy. Her heart clutched in her chest.

"Sweetie, if you know something, you need to speak up."

Her son ground his teeth, making the muscle in his jaw jump. His mouth worked as if he was trying to swallow something that didn't taste good.

She slid her hand to his neck and massaged tense muscles. "It's okay, Jer." She used the nickname his sister often used. "What's troubling you?"

"Elizabeth... Elizabeth...." His eyes moved to her and then to the detective, who sat still as an oak tree at midnight.

Jeremy swallowed twice before straightening in his chair. "I'm afraid she's using and has gotten involved with some bad dude."

"Using?" Addie leaned back in the chair as if she could distance herself from the claim. Even though Jeremy had hinted at something like that before, it was still hard to take in his words. They refused to compute.

"Go ahead, Jeremy." Detective Riley's low commanding voice did things to Addie's insides she both loved and hated. How could she have any kind of reaction to him but anger?

Apparently, the man's voice also affected Jeremy. His gaze traveled around the room. His fingers drummed on the table. Finally, he raised his head and met Detective Riley's gaze straight on. "Elizabeth has been sneaking out of school."

Again, Addie felt her muscles contract, pulling away from Jeremy's announcement. It took her a moment to find her voice. "No. That can't be. The school would've called me. If you knew, you should've told me." Her voice rose, and she loathed her lack of control.

"Be quiet, Addie. Let the boy talk." Mike's expression sent a clear message. She nodded.

"One day I followed her." Jeremy shifted his shoulders as if they ached. "She went to Joe's, that little mom and pop store, a block from the school. You can always get a little pot there. She told me to mind my own business."

"You didn't tell anyone what you suspected?" Mike's eyebrows drew together. The lines at the corners of his eyes crinkled with concentration.

Jeremy didn't say anything.

"It's okay, Son." Addie squeezed his hand where it clenched on the table. She looked at Riley. "Jeremy hinted to me there might be some problems. I blew him off. Obviously, I should have listened." Guilt raged through her system threatening to drown her. What kind of a mother was she not to know that about her own daughter?

"Okay, so she's smoked pot. Any other issues concern you about your sister?" Mike must be the calmest person she knew. In no way, did he show any emotion. But then, why should he? No reason for him to feel anything for her or her family.

"Another time, we left the house, and I dropped her off at the open air mall."

"What's so bad about her going there?" Addie asked.

"Tell us the rest, Jeremy," Mike pushed in his determined way.

Her son sat there with his mouth glued together.

"I appreciate your loyalty to your sister, but you need to

tell us the rest of the story. If there's more."

Addie liked how he left the choice open.

Still her son sat there dumb.

Mike got up and came around to sit on the corner of the table nearest her son. "You know, Jeremy, my dad told my brother and me there were three times he expected us to squeal on someone or each other."

Addie's gaze glued onto Mike. Jeremy's did too.

"First, if someone is going to hurt another person. Second, if someone is going to be hurt by another. Third, if you think the person is going to hurt themselves. Now, if what you know falls into one of these categories, I encourage you to speak up."

Jeremy looked down and began in a quiet voice. "Elizabeth didn't stay at the mall."

"Tell us where she went Jeremy."

"I followed her to an apartment."

"Where was this apartment? Did you know whose it was? Did she go there more than once?" Riley's questions shot from his mouth like a machine gun.

"It's a couple blocks from campus, just past the open air mall. I'm sorry, Mom. I should've done more to stop her."

"Was she meeting Sonya?" Addie asked, though for the life of her she couldn't think why the girls would do that. Both parents were equally happy for them to hang out at either home.

"She met a man."

The blood drained from Addie's face. The room spun.

She used a hand on the table for balance. A chill raced through her system. What had her sweet baby girl gotten herself into?

"How do you know she was meeting a man there? Did you see him? What did he look like?" Again, Mike fired AK-47 type questions.

Jeremy cleared his throat, sat a little straighter. "I saw him. He was standing on the top floor balcony of an apartment. He waved to Elizabeth. She rushed up the stairs, and he took her into his apartment."

"Oh, my God." Addie dropped her head into both hands and rubbed her temples where a giant drill pounded into her brain.

"Did you wait for her to come out?" Riley continued the inquisition.

"Hell, no. I went in after her."

"That was gutsy, Jeremy."

Addie raised her head in time to catch Mike squeeze Jeremy's shoulder.

"You could've gotten yourself hurt. What'd you find?" The detective continued to pound away with the questions, even if in a softened tone.

"At first he claimed not to know what I was talking about, but I brushed right past him. Elizabeth was sitting on a sofa, smoking a weed. She says it wasn't but, dude, every high school kid recognizes that smell."

Addie didn't know what bothered her the most.

Her daughter was smoking.

Her daughter was smoking pot.

Her daughter was in the apartment of an older man.

If a ton of bricks had fallen on her, she couldn't have felt worse. Addie had always prided herself on being a good mom. Even though she was by herself and things were tough, she'd have sworn she was doing okay by her kids.

Yeah, Judson Greer was an ass for the way he treated them, especially Elizabeth, but Addie thought she'd done a good job compensating for their loss of a father figure. Obviously not.

"Jeremy, if I got a sketch artist in here can you describe the man?"

"Well, yeah, but I guess it'd be faster if I just told you his name."

Mike rose and went around to the other side of the table. He sat and picked up the small pad and pencil lying there. "Yeah, that would do."

Jeremy glanced at her once then back at Mike.

"It was Clay Bennett."

CHAPTER THIRTEEN

Monday, December 3

Addie's heart threatened to explode with all the revelations she'd heard. Heat flooded her body. She clenched her fingers into tight fists. "What?"

"We need to bring Elizabeth in and see what she has to say about this." Mike rose, patted Jeremy on the shoulder. "You're a good brother." Mike left the small gray room.

Jeremy rose fast, knocking his chair over. "Yeah? Then why do I feel like a piece of shit?"

"Oh, Jeremy, Son. It hurts me to hear you say that." Addie rose, crossed the distance separating them, putting both arms around him. "I think Detective Riley said it right. You've been a good big brother. You tried to tell me. I let you down. I let Elizabeth down. I'm so sorry."

The door opened and Mike and Elizabeth walked into the small drab room. Addie crossed to her and squeezed her hand. Mike pulled the second chair on his side around to the end. "Have a seat, Elizabeth."

"What's going on? Y'all have been in here a long time."

"We have a few questions for you." Mike's voice held no censure, but a determination to get the information he wanted.

Elizabeth settled uncomfortably on the chair, which wasn't conducive to slouching. Now when Addie looked at her daughter, she was amazed at her own blindness. Addie dropped into the chair next to Jeremy. Even with him trying to tell her, she'd refused to see the nervous habits, the blood shot eyes, the over-pale skin, which Addie had attributed to her daughters' Goth make-up. She'd give anything if the attire were the worst of their worries.

"Let's talk about the gun, Elizabeth." Mike checked his notes then nailed her with a look that would've wilted a person considering lying to him.

She fidgeted in her chair. "What do you want to know?"

"How did you come to find it in the drawer again?"

"I've told you. I was looking for scissors, and I opened that drawer and there it was."

"And you didn't report finding a gun to anyone? Not to your brother or your mother?"

"No. Like I told you I thought it was a prop."

Mike continued through a whole series of questions. All of which Elizabeth answered in the negative.

"I can't imagine what Jeremy is talking about. Yes, he took me to the mall, but I met Sonya there, and we shopped. I don't know anything about meeting some man."

Mike let out a long sigh. "Okay, Elizabeth. I guess that's it. Ms. Greer, you can all go now. I'll check the kids' stories with Sonya and Bennett." He rose and walked toward the door.

Addie just sat there, not sure where she'd find the strength to move, but she had to. That's what moms did.

"Come on guys. Let's go home."

The ride was silent. Even when they got to the house, by mutual consent they all went their own ways, as if they'd agreed to a needed cooling off time. Whether she and the kids celebrated their joint birthdays, which was the plan for this evening, was doubtful.

◆ ◆ ◆

Mike downed a couple of aspirin followed by cold coffee that tasted like water from the gutter.

"Sorry I've been out of touch so long. Testifying in court on the Donavan case." Rick leaned against the cabinet in the break room.

"How'd it go?" Mike glanced over his cup at his partner.

"You never know with juries, but I'd say we nailed him." Rick's gaze fell on the pill bottle on the counter. "Tough day, huh?"

"Hell, yeah."

"Did you have trouble with Greer and her kids?"

"Not the most pleasant interview I've ever been involved in. At least one of them is lying, and I can't tell who." His gut told him it wasn't Addie, but maybe that wasn't the part doing the thinking where she was concerned. "Let's do another follow-up chat with Clay Bennett. I need to see this apartment Jeremy talked about. You drive."

"Sure, happy to. On the way you can fill me in on what everyone said."

It didn't take long to reach the apartment. Mike kept picturing the scene through Jeremy's eyes.

"Not a place I'd want my sister walking into. Gang graffiti on a few outside walls." Rick pulled behind another car entering the complex.

"Yeah. Took balls to bust in the way Jeremy said he did. If that's what really happened." After Rick parked, they got out and headed across the lot.

"Pretty frustrating when we can't find any hard evidence and just have this he-said, she-said thing going on." Rick followed Mike up the stairs.

"Well, maybe we'll get some corroboration one-way or the other from Bennett or Elizabeth's friend." Mike pounded on the door with his fist. "Bennett, it's the police. Open up."

Sounds of movement inside told him someone was home. Not the most patient of men, Mike pounded again. "Open up."

"Wouldn't think there'd be a back he could get out through." Rick said.

"More like flushing any stash he has, which wouldn't be bad."

The door swung open. Bennett, dressed in jeans and a sweatshirt, stood there, not particularly welcoming.

"Sorry about the delay. Headphones kept me from hearing you right away."

"We have a few questions for you?" Rick said.

"Is this more about the DeWitt woman's sad demise?"

"In a peripheral way. We'd like to come in." Mike said.

"Oh, of course, where are my manners?" Bennett stepped back and let them in. "Can I get you anything? Coffee, iced tea, beer? Oh, probably not the last, I guess, since you're on duty. Well, grab a seat."

"No thanks." Mike spoke for him and Rick.

"Well, do you mind if I sit?" Clay dropped onto an old leather sofa, both arms stretched along the top, the picture of relaxation.

Either he was innocent of any wrongdoing or he was a hell of a good actor. Mike put his money on the man's acting ability. Might as well hit it straight on. "Tell us what you know about Elizabeth Greer."

One of Bennett's eyebrows rose, his mouth twitched. He seemed genuinely surprised,

"Not a whole lot, not all of it flattering I'm afraid. She's one of Addison Greer's twins. The least successful of them, judging from her dress."

"Have you ever given her marijuana?"

Bennett laughed, a large belly slapping bellow, which nearly threw him off the sofa. He stopped finally and settled back. "You've got to be joking. The daughter of my former boss? Like I'd mess with her anyway. And like I'd admit it if I had. Come on, Detective, get a grip. Is that what she's telling you?"

"Let's just say we've heard rumors," Rick contributed.

"Well, here's the other thing I've heard about little Miss Goth girl. Don't like to tell tales out of school, but..." He leaned forward and clasped his hands in front of him. "Hate to speak ill of her, but I hear she was pretty messed up by her parents' divorce. Her father's a real bastard. I mean who ignores their own kid the way he apparently does?"

Mike leaned against the corner bar separating the kitchen from the living area. Bennett was a genius the way he threw dirt while managing never to get any on himself.

"Is there more?" Mike couldn't wait to get out of here before he choked on the BS.

"Well, some of the ensemble girls who are pretty close to her age, says she's making it with an older guy, or at least so she says. But they also mention that she likes to make up stories, evidently trying to keep up with super brother." Bennett leaned back, draped his arms across the top of the sofa again. "I'm afraid she's unstable."

"She's never visited you here in this apartment?"

"Are you kidding? No. As I said, she's not my type."

Even though he'd done it before in earlier questioning, Mike handed Bennett his card. "If you think of anything else we ought to know, give me a ring."

"Sure will do that, Detectives." He nodded and escorted them through the door.

Mike and Rick jogged down the stairs and crossed the lot. "I think I might gag." Mike climbed into their vehicle and strapped in.

"Yeah, pretty heavy on the BS." Rick started the engine and pulled out. "You know he's still standing on the balcony watching us."

"Let's go talk to Sonya. She should be home from school

by now."

He stared out the window content to let Rick drive. Between this and another case they were working Mike was dragging. Dreams of the lovely executive director didn't help. He woke up every morning with a hard-on and frustrated. They had to get this damn case solved before Addie Greer drove him right out of his mind. Rick pulled the car to a stop in front of Sonya's house. Maybe she'd be the key.

♦ ♦ ♦

Addie paced and drank wine. She'd already had some with their birthday dinner at Luke's. Given the trip to the police station earlier in the afternoon, it had been a sober celebration, mostly eaten in silence. Maybe they should've just skipped it.

Because the kids had another performance, they'd chosen to eat early. "Like old people," Jeremy had teased, the only lighthearted moment in the whole dinner. Now both kids had gone to school. Normally, Addie wouldn't miss a single performance. Tonight she just needed to be alone. Maybe she'd go see some of the show but, damn, she was sick. Down deep in the bone sick.

"Agghhh!" she yelled at the top of her lungs. Thank God, the twins weren't home. She picked up her cell and called her friend Kate because Addie needed to unload. "You have a few minutes?" She refilled her wine glass.

"Sure, don't have to leave for a house showing for another thirty minutes."

"In the evening?"

"Only time the family can come."

"So business is good?"

"Certainly picking up."

The sound of her friend adding ice to her tea glass, which was like an appendage, helped relax the frown forming between Addie's brows. Her index finger rubbed at the lines as if she could erase them.

"I'm worried about Elizabeth." Addie told her friend what she'd just learned at the police station.

"Damn, hon, that's lousy. You didn't have any idea?"

"Jeremy tried to tell me, and I blew him off."

"Mom Guilt loaded on and burying you, huh?"

"You know those commercials with the elephant sitting on the woman's chest? That's just what I feel like."

"Okay." The word dragged out and lilted up at the end. "Listen, to me. Do your rag doll slump."

"What?"

"You know what I'm talking about. How many times have you reminded me to use this technique when I was about to jump off a cliff?"

"Well..."

"Put the phone down and do what you've prescribed to me on more than one occasion."

"Okay."

Addie placed her wine glass on the coffee table and slipped the phone in her pocket. She leaned over at the waist, bent her knees, dropped her head, and let her arms dangle.

After a few moments, her neck and shoulder muscles relaxed, and she drew air deep into her lungs. Slowly she began straightening up, one vertebra on top of the other until her head came up last.

She grabbed up the cell. "You still there?"

"Yup. You feel better?"

"Yes. Thanks for the reminder. Can't believe I didn't think of that. Use it all the time with actors."

"Just a sign of how upset you are. If Elizabeth is really into drugs, especially if it's more than marijuana, there's a great rehab place in east Fort Worth—Country Acres. One of Blair's friends did an outpatient program there that helped her get squared away."

"Good to know. Thanks, Kate."

"Any news on the murder front?"

"The murder weapon was found in our home." Addie felt like she was in some two-bit drama. Her life was so messed up.

"Good Lord. That's not something to joke about."

"I wish I were joking, Kate. Detective Riley told me before he questioned me and the kids this afternoon."

"Ah, hon. Bad times. It will all work out. I have faith. "Remember, Addie, all we can ever do is the best we can do."

"Right."

The doorbell chimed.

"Someone's here. Thanks again, Kate. I'll be in touch." Addie picked up her glass and took a quick swallow. Who would be stopping by now and without calling?

She peeked through one of the long windows on either

side of the door. Detective Riley. What did he want? She glanced in the mirror hanging in the front hall. Her hair, out of its traditional ponytail holder, was down and looked like rats had made a nest there from all the times she'd run her hands through it. The rag doll slump hadn't helped her looks either.

Again, the bell chimed. Not a patient man at all. "Just a minute." She flipped open the top of the old desk sitting in the hallway, where she kept a spare lipstick for just such emergencies. She skimmed the plum color over her lips. Now she'd do. What about her glass of wine? Well, she was a grown up and this had been a hell of a day. In fact, a hell of a couple of months. Let him think what he would.

She swung open the door. "Hi." *Such a terribly clever woman*, she mocked herself.

"You really should keep your door locked." He leaned one arm against the door jam. Closer than was good for Addie's breath, which shortened with each moment he stood there.

"We're a safe neighborhood."

"Nobody's that safe. Can I come in?"

"Certainly. Where are my manners? Mother would have my head."

Mike paused in the process of entering. "What's the matter? I thought you wanted to come in."

"Yeah, I do. I am." Mike walked into the living room. "It's just that you used almost the same words Clay Bennett used when we visited him."

Addie took a swallow of wine and then held the glass up to him.

"No thanks."

"Of course not while you're on duty. And you're always on duty. Duty calls and you're there." What was the matter with her? Too much wine. Bitchy wasn't her style. She set the glass down. "Sorry, Detective. I'm a little distracted." Boy, wasn't she? She could hardly keep her hands off the man.

She was clearly a nut case. All he wanted to do was lock her up for a murder she didn't commit, and she had trouble thinking about anything but what it would feel like for him to hold her in his arms. She dropped onto the sofa, emotionally exhausted.

"Have a seat." She gestured to one of the chairs. He surprised her and sat on the sofa next to her. Damn, that just made the job of keeping her hands off him that much harder.

"How is it you used words so similar to Bennett's?" Impatient and insistent. Like a tiger after a gazelle.

Despite herself, she reached for the glass and took a quick sip of the almost clear liquid. When she set the glass on the table, she swiveled around to face him, one leg drawn up under her.

"Last season, whenever a character in one of the children's shows always said, 'Where are my manners?' The staff fell into the habit of using the question anytime they were a little stressed or the situation could, by the furthest stretch of the imagination, call for the words."

"I see." He nodded.

"Do you?"

He leaned toward her; one arm braced on the back of

the sofa. His eyes mesmerized her. She couldn't draw back. God, she wanted him to kiss her. She wanted to kiss him back. Surely, that was just the wine messing with her.

His gaze dropped to her lips. Her lungs stopped working. His thumb and finger captured her chin. She couldn't have pulled away if her life depended on it.

"I see a beautiful, but very stressed-out woman. I see a woman who frustrates the hell out of me. I see no way for anything to come of whatever is smoldering between us. Not until I can solve this damn case. And I'm scared shitless that in solving the case, I'll drive you away." He ran his thumb over her lip.

His rough touch was nearly her undoing. Desire coiled hot and heavy in her middle and sank lower. Despite his words, he must not have felt anything.

He cleared his throat before speaking. "Sonya corroborated Elizabeth's story about the mall. Bennett said there are rumors that Elizabeth makes up things because she's messed up by your ex."

Damn. What a way to ruin a moment. No wonder the man hadn't married. Double damn, what made her think of that?

She finished off the glass. "Where does that leave us?"

"Can you think of any reason for Jeremy to make up those stories?"

"No. No I can't." She tightened the grip she had on her hands.

"Do you believe him?"

Her head dropped for a moment before she forced herself to meet his gaze. "Hell of a position to be in, Detective. Caught between my children, both of whom I love dearly. It doesn't make sense to believe both of them, does it?"

"No ma'am, it doesn't. I can't imagine what pain you must be suffering. Well, a little, if I put Pat and Cindy in your shoes. It must hurt like hell."

"Pretty much. You don't expect to raise your kids without a little pain finding its way in. That wouldn't be realistic at all, but this is so much worse than anything I could've imagined.

"Even when I had to kick Judson out, and I worried about the effect on the kids." She pleated her skirt between her fingers. "I figured it would be worse on them if I stayed, sending two negative messages I didn't want either of them to get. One, it's okay to cheat on your spouse. Two, as long as someone doesn't physically hit you, you should stay in the marriage."

"This is worse?"

"Way worse. Excruciating. Like a blade is shoved into my chest with every move I make."

Mike leaned forward and enfolded her in his arms, resting his head on top of hers. "I'm sorry for you and for them having to go through all of this. I'm sorry I can't get the God-damned murder solved so we can…"

Addie couldn't remember a recent time she'd felt so safe, so content, so cherished. Then Mike dropped his arms and leaned away from her. Not far, but she shivered at the loss of his warmth. She bit her lip and, in lieu of pockets, thrust her hands behind her to keep from reaching out for more of that comfort.

"Addie, you should think doing a drug test on both your kids."

"If that bastard gave my daughter drugs or touched her in any way, I'll kill him."

"Probably not a good thing to say to a cop."

CHAPTER FOURTEEN

Tuesday, December 4

Again with the pounding. Doesn't anyone know how to knock anymore? Clay rolled out of bed and stumbled toward the door. Whoever it was would just have to take him as is, in pajama bottoms and bare-chested.

"Clay. Clay!"

Crap. Sounded like Elizabeth. He peeked through the safety hole in the door. What the hell did she want? Maybe she cut school again. It was mid-afternoon, but his head still felt like hail beating on a tin roof. Too much partying the night before. He unlocked the door and opened it. Despite the cold wind blowing in, he blocked her entrance.

"Thank God, Clay. I was afraid you'd gone on a trip, since my mother canned you. Listen, I need a smoke."

She brushed past him, a cape sending even more cold air around his shivering body. Guess his state of undress didn't bother her.

"Clay, I told you, I need a smoke." She stood with her hands on her hips, very much as he'd seen her mother do on more than one occasion.

"Yeah, I heard you. The thing is, I don't hand those out

anymore."

"What do you mean?" She charged over to the side table and yanked out the drawer where he usually kept his stash. It was empty.

"Where'd you put them?" She pulled out other drawers. Finally, she stopped, turned, and rushed at him. Her fists thumping his chest.

She was strong, but after a struggle, he corralled her with her back to him and her arms across her chest. She still twisted, but he had the upper hand. "Now you listen to me, little Goth girl. I can't help you anymore."

"But I did what you asked. I put the gun in the drawer at Mom's. And there's been all hell to pay, let me tell you."

She raised her leg. He moved just fast enough that her booted heel missed. "Little hellion. You listen to me. I don't have what you want." Though she might have something he'd enjoy. Her hips were snug against him and the fight aroused him. Before he'd gotten her restrained, he'd caught a couple of handfuls of boobs. She was apparently as well-endowed as her mama.

Maybe he could substitute the weed with sex. It could be almost as addicting. He forced her toward the sofa. He could bend her over; the long skirts made her more accessible than if she wore jeans.

"What are you doing? I just want some weed."

Her screech brought him up short. Maybe he'd better get rid of her. She'd proven to be more trouble than she was worth. Her mom wasn't in jail for murder as he'd planned. And now

Goth girl was objecting to gratuitous sex?

Seems like he ought to get a little after all the trouble she'd been. One more try. "Come on, Elizabeth. I've got something you'll like even more than the Maryjane. Stop fighting and I'll show you. You'll like how it makes you feel."

She grew still. Her muscles must be tiring anyway. Make her more compliant back in the bed.

"What do you have?" She twisted her head to meet his gaze.

Clay loosened his grip a little to see how she'd do. She didn't make a move to hit him or bolt. Maybe he'd get himself a little virgin out of all this shit. He released her a bit more. She turned, trembling before him.

"What do you have?" Her arms stretched out in a show-me gesture.

Well, she was a blind girl for sure, if she didn't notice the bulge in his pajama bottoms. He took her hand in a gentle grasp, so as not to spook her. "Come on. It's back here." He eased her toward his bedroom. She jerked to a stop in the doorway, a frown making creases above her nose.

"You keep your drugs in here?"

"Yeah, a kind of drug." He closed the distance between them. "You'll like this, I promise. He brushed the back of his hand across her tits. Nice, like her mama's. He'd always wanted to get hold of those. These would have to do.

She stepped back. "I'd better go."

"You don't have to rush off." He followed at a deliberate pace. He sure as hell wasn't' going to chase her. If he caught her again, he'd give her enough so she wouldn't want to leave. He reached for her waist to pull her against his raging cock, but she bolted, and he was left holding a piece of material from her skirt.

"Hey, wait a minute. You can't tease like that." But the girl could run and was out the front door before he got there.

Blam. Blam.

Shit, what was that?

He stuck his head around the edge of the open door. "Oh, my God." Elizabeth lay sprawled at the foot of the apartment stairs.

Blam. Blam. Blam.

He ducked inside, slammed the door, and moved away from the windows toward the rear of the apartment. If those gang bangers were at it again, he didn't want to be anywhere near the front.

Should he call the cops? Whether a bullet hit her, or she just fell, she might need a doctor. Besides, he was at risk of those bullets plowing through the walls. He dialed 911.

♦ ♦ ♦

Addie sat in her office at her desk working on blocking a scene from the next show. The door blew open without so much as a knock or by your leave. She'd haul someone's ass over the coals for this. She seldom had the door closed, and when it was shut, everyone knew to leave her the heck alone.

Everyone but Mike Riley, who stormed across the floor

toward her. He didn't remove his white hat.

"Detective?" She rose, hating the feeling of heat rushing to her face. How stupid. She was a grown woman with no reason to let a man—a simple man who looked so good in his western cut jacket, jeans, and boots—have this effect on her.

Yet, he did. Her heart rate kicked up, and her hands tingled with the urge to touch him. To stop the foolishness of reaching for him, she reached for anger instead.

He walked around her desk, his eyes never leaving hers.

"You're finally going to arrest me?"

"No, that's not it. Addie, I've got some bad news."

Her lungs hung in her chest. Cold fear choked her throat. She dragged in a breath to force words out. "Oh, my God. The kids. Are the kids okay?" She grabbed his arms, attempting to pry the news from him.

"Jeremy is fine. Elizabeth has been shot."

Her legs went out from under her. His strong arms wrapped around her and eased her into the chair.

"Is she...?" She couldn't bring herself to say the words.

"No, but she's in critical condition."

"Where is she? I have to go to her."

"That's why I'm here. It'll take you to Harris Hospital downtown."

She grabbed her purse. Mike helped her into her black wool coat, and they made for the door. Some people fell apart in a crisis. Addie didn't have that reaction. As she did with business issues, she locked all her emotions somewhere deep inside her until the worst was over. Cool and collected, she found Pete and concisely told him what was going on.

"Do you need me to go with you?"

"No, thank you. Detective Riley is taking me. You and Judy stay here and keep things on an even keel. I'll be grateful." He nodded. She and Mike ran through the front doors and climbed into the truck he'd parked close to the curb. Illegally, one part of her compartmentalized brain noted.

As she drifted in a black hole of fear, the short fifteen-minute drive seemed to stretch on all day. Mike finally pulled into the hospital garage. Their rapid steps clicking on the concrete floor took them to the emergency room. Mike cut through the red tape, and the staff ushered her back to talk with the doctor treating Elizabeth. Elizabeth, who lay deathly pale, on a bed in the emergency ward, medical people gathered around. Looking at her made Addie's insides hurt.

"I'm Dr. Hancock," said a woman in a white jacket who seemed to be too young to bear the title. "You're Elizabeth's parents?"

"I'm her mother, Addison Greer." Addie couldn't make herself meet Mike's gaze. "This is Detective Riley." Thank God for Detective Riley with his protective arm around her waist. She'd get through this ordeal, as long as Elizabeth was alive.

"You don't mind my speaking in front of him?" the doctor asked.

"No." She forced her gaze to his. "Can you stay? I'll be all right."

"Right here for however long you need me." His hand tightened at her waist.

Addie nodded. He must have listened to her heart rather than her words. She was so not all right.

"How is Elizabeth, Dr. Hancock?" Mike uttered the question she was too afraid to voice.

"She has a gunshot wound to the abdomen. Lost lots of blood. What type are you, Ms. Greer?"

Addie told the doctor, but it wasn't a match. Jeremy didn't match either. "Oh, my God, what about Jeremy? I can't believe I just thought of him." She ran a hand across her forehead.

"It's okay, Addie. I asked Rick to locate him and bring him here."

"Thank you, Mike. I'm sorry, Doctor. Her father's blood matches. He's in Dallas. Let me get hold of him." Addie reached for her phone in the pocket of her coat.

Dr. Hancock's hand stopped her. "We don't have that much time, I'm afraid."

Her words froze something in Addie's middle, and her normally cool, calm crisis manager mode shattered into a thousand pieces.

"It's okay, Doctor. I'm O positive, a universal donor."

Addie threw her arms around Mike and hugged him like she'd never let go.

"Come with me, Detective Riley. Let's get you set up. No time to waste."

As the doctor led Mike away, he said, "I give blood often and have an account we can access if needed."

A nurse showed up and steered Addie back to the

emergency room waiting area. "When they transfer your daughter up to surgery, we'll move you upstairs, so you'll be close."

"Thanks." Addie sank into one of the uncomfortable plastic chairs. Guess she should let Judson know his daughter was about to have surgery. She pulled the phone out and placed the call. It took some time, but she eventually got through to him.

"I have bad news, Jud." She used the same phrase Mike had used in preparing her.

"Jeremy?" he asked.

Naturally, he'd think of his son first.

"No, Elizabeth. She's been shot."

"Shot? What the hell kind of a deal are you running over there anyway? Murder in the theatre, and now Elizabeth is shot. You're sure Jeremy's okay? Who the hell shot her? One of her Goth friends playing with guns?"

"All I know right now is what the police say. She was hit in a shoot-out between rival gang members."

"What was she doing in the middle of gang warfare? You really need to do a better job of supervising her, Addie. Letting her wear that awful black stuff and dye her hair with the red streak. All an embarrassment."

Anger swirled through her system, white hot, almost suffocating. Who was he to question Addie's parenting ability?

Embarrassment was her finding him asleep with that bimbo in their bed and finding out she wasn't the first. Embarrassment was the way he treated his son, hauling him out like a trophy. *At least until Jud finds out Jeremy is gay.* And then there was his treatment of Elizabeth all these years, as if he didn't believe she was his, even though the kids were twins.

"I'll let you know when she's out of surgery." Addie disconnected, slid the phone in her pocket. She kept her coat on against the cold in the waiting room where the door opened and closed as others' lives were shattered. Tears trailed down her cheeks. Tears of anger against the kids' worthless father. Tears of fear for her daughter's life. Tears for herself because she'd never again experience that overwhelming emotion when you lose yourself in another.

"Hey, I'm back. How are you holding up?"

Addie glanced up. Mike, his jacket slung over his elbow, his hat firmly on his head, rolled down his sleeve over the stretchy bandage at the elbow. She swiped at her eyes and hurled herself at him. His arms enveloped her. "Thank you. Thank you." He felt so solid and strong and safe. Things she needed right now. She might not ever be able to get more from him. She could still end up in jail. Right now, all she could think of was Elizabeth and getting her well.

A nurse came toward them. Addie's heart lurched. "Is she okay?"

"They're moving her up to surgery. Let me tell you how you get to that waiting room."

Thank God again for Mike. She wouldn't have remembered the nurse's instructions. He called Rick and told him where to bring Jeremy. They were on their way to the hospital now. When they reached the surgery waiting room,

Mike sat next to her on the small bench, one arm draped across her shoulders and the other holding her hand. He stayed with her, and she was grateful beyond words.

After not too long, Rick entered with Jeremy. They both stopped and stared. Addie made herself move out of Mike's embrace. For that's what it was. If she were directing a scene in a play, she'd have blocked it that way. Odd how her mind stepped outside her body to view what was going on. She rose.

"Thank you for bringing my son, Detective Martinez. Jeremy, she's still in surgery. She's lost a lot of blood, so it's iffy." God, how could she use that word in connection with her beautiful daughter? Her life couldn't be *iffy.* That sounded obscene.

Jeremy walked to her and hugged her, his chin resting on her head. He was almost as tall as Mike. He pushed himself away. "If she needs blood, I can give."

"Sweetie, you and I aren't matches. Your father is, but he was too far away to be useful. Detective Riley is a universal donor, and he gave. He apparently does this often and has some banked if she needs more."

Her almost grown son walked up to Mike and stuck out his hand. "Thank you, Detective."

"Glad to help."

"Uh, Mike, can I borrow you a minute?" Martinez took a couple of steps away.

◆ ◆ ◆

Mike looked at Addie. "I'll be right back." She nodded and smiled at him. "Come on, Rick. I could use a coffee." He didn't want to be gone as long as it would take to go to the cafeteria, so they made their way down the hall to a vending machine, where the coffee was sure to be as bad as theirs at work. Mike hoped Elizabeth would come through the surgery and be fine. But it was surgery. Anything could happen.

After taking a sip, Rick said, "You and Ms. Greer looked pretty chummy back there when Jeremy and I walked in. You banging her?"

Mike took a swing at his partner with his free hand, but Rick easily side stepped. "Shut up, Martinez. Just because you hit every skirt that passes by doesn't mean I do."

"Whoa, man. Sorry. I didn't mean to make you mad. But if the lieutenant saw what I did, she'd yank you from the DeWitt murder so fast you'd be spinning into next year. Not to mention she'd probably put something in your file."

Mike glanced at his half-empty coffee cup, which had sloshed over when he swung at his partner. Couldn't believe he'd done that. He tossed the cup and rolled his shoulders. "To answer your crudely put question, no, we don't have a relationship—of any kind. She's alone, and I feel sorry for her. She's gone through some crappy shit here, and her daughter might die."

"Okay. That's all I needed to know."

"What did you get on the gang shooting?"

"Three dead, two injured. They took 'em to the county hospital."

"Do you know who called it in?"

"Odd. It was our boy, Clay Bennett."

"Hum, interesting. You think Elizabeth was visiting him before the shooting?"

"The officer who interviewed him said he found a scrap of black silk on the floor."

"He conned Bennett into letting him take it. No search warrant so might not be able to use it, but if it matches what Elizabeth was wearing, we'll know."

Mike nodded. "Listen, I want to get back there. I want to talk with Elizabeth as soon as she's able."

"Okay. No hard feelings about the crack? Sometimes, I'm an ass."

"Yeah, sometimes you are, but you're a damned good detective, and most of the time I like having you as my partner."

"I'm heading back to check the scene again."

"Thanks, Rick."

Mike returned to the waiting room. Addie and Jeremy were both pacing the small area. "No word?"

Addie shook her head. Mike wanted so much to go to her and hold her, but with Jeremy there, he restrained the urge. They walked, and he sat and flipped the pages of a magazine, but he couldn't have said what the stories were about if his life depended on it.

"Ms. Greer, I'm Doctor Simms, I did your daughter's surgery."

Addie stood and walked quickly to the doctor.

"How…how is she?" Addie's voice quivered and her chin trembled.

"She's going to pull through. It was tight, but she'll make it."

Addie, nodded, tears slid from her eyes. "Thank you, Dr. Simms. When can we see her?"

"A nurse will take you back to recovery soon."

"Okay." She nodded, and the tears gushed from her eyes.

Jeremy looked like he'd never seen his mother cry. He didn't know what to do.

But Mike did. He moved to her side and enfolded her in his arms, crooning nonsense words to her, swaying with her gently from side to side. To hell with whatever Jeremy thought. Addie needed this. God, Mike needed this.

After a time, the sobs subsided into hiccups. Mike grabbed a tissue from the box on the table. "Here." Amazing woman, she even cracked a small smile.

"I'll probably need more than one of those, and I've ruined your shirt."

"I'll dry."

She hadn't immediately stepped away when she came to herself. She reached up a hand and placed it on his cheek. "Thank you for being here."

Mike covered it with his own. "Any time."

"Ms. Greer."

They both stepped apart. "Yes?" Addie straightened up.

"Would you like to see your daughter?"

"Absolutely. You two be okay here for a bit?"

Mike looked at Jeremy, and they both nodded. Might be a good time to have a little talk with Jeremy.

♦ ♦ ♦

Addie thought she'd prepared herself for how bad Elizabeth might look, but she so hadn't. To see her baby as white as the sheet tucked around her, hooked up to all kinds of tubes, felt like she'd dropped into scene from a TV medical drama. Not real. But this was. She was afraid she'd pass out, so she leaned over, rested her hands on her knees, drew air in, and let it out slowly. She had to get it together for her daughter's sake.

A stirring drew her attention to the bed. Elizabeth's eyelashes batted. Was she waking up? She moaned, tearing another hole through Addie's heart. She crossed to the bed and placed a hand on top of her daughter's. "Elizabeth, it's Mom. You're in the hospital. You were shot, but you're going to be okay."

Elizabeth's gaze took in the room, stopping on Addie. "Wa-ter."

"The nurse said ice chips and only one at a time." Addie got what Elizabeth wanted, or at least what she was allowed to have. It'd be a while before she got fluids in a form other than through the vein in her arm.

"Thanks." The smile didn't quite make it, but that Elizabeth made the effort warmed Addie's heart.

A nurse bustled through the door in the way only nurses can. "Ms. Greer, you can leave for a while. Your girl is going to need lots of sleep."

Addie leaned over and pressed a kiss to Elizabeth's forehead. She'd already drifted off again. "Thank you. What's your name?"

"Tilly. I'll be here until seven then Lupe comes in. She'll handle the night shift, and I'll be back in the morning at seven." She checked dials and made notes on a chart.

"Goodness. Long shifts."

"Yes, ma'am. You go home and get a good night's sleep in your own bed. She's going to be here a while, and you'll need your strength for later."

"Oh, I think I should stay the night."

"No ma'am. You get on home. We'll look after her."

"Okay, if you're sure." Jeremy was old enough to stay by himself, but given everything, she'd have hated him to be alone. She squeezed Elizabeth's hand and then nodded to the nurse. "See you in the morning, Tilly."

Addie was almost back to the waiting room when she thought of Jeremy's musical. She burst through the door to find Jeremy and Mike facing each other as if they were in some sort of contest.

"Honey, your show. I can't believe I forgot."

"It's okay, Mom. I remembered. I called Mrs. Sheffield right after Detective Martinez told me. Matthew, my understudy is going on. He's thrilled. Well, not about the reason I'm not there, but for the opportunity."

"How is she, Addie?"

Her gaze went right to Mike, and her hand reached out for his. She smiled at him, at the strength of him, at his compassion. She hoped when all this was behind, something could develop for them.

"She woke up while I was in there. I gave her an ice chip, too soon for water."

"Are you staying here tonight?" Mike asked.

"No, the nurse strongly recommended against it. Said Elizabeth would need us more down the line. So, we're going to follow her directions."

"I'll take you home whenever you're ready."

"Mom, will they let me back to see her?"

"I bet they will. Let's go check that out." She stopped at the door and faced Mike. "Can you wait?"

"For as long as you need."

"We'll be a minute or two."

And they were. When she walked into the waiting room, Mike was playing with the TV remote, flipping from one sports channel to another.

"We're ready."

"Let's go then. How about we stop and grab some supper?"

"Nice idea."

"No." Jeremy stepped away from her.

Addie looked up at her son, "Why ever not?" Her surprise showed in her tone.

Before he answered, Mike suggested, "We could pick up

pizza."

"How about that, Jeremy? Pizza is a food group for you."

Mike held the truck door for her. She smiled her thanks. Jeremy finally pulled out his phone and connected with the Pizza Barn. He ordered a giant the way they usually did, with everything on it.

"I hope that will be okay with you, Mike."

"I don't have to stay."

"Please do." Her hand stretched across the seat to his.

He took it, rubbed his thumb across the back, and smiled at her causing a fluttering of butterflies in her stomach.

"All right. If you're sure."

She nodded and gave his hand an answering squeeze.

Jeremy remained sullenly silent for the evening, even taking his pizza—almost half the box—to his room.

Addie sipped her Sauvignon Blanc, Mike polished off the last of the pizza. Big man, big appetite. They sat at the kitchen table, nice and homey, but Addie wished they'd move to the sofa. She longed to kiss this man. Maybe with another glass of wine and the right location, she'd gut up and do just that.

He let out a long sigh, and actually rubbed his stomach. "I gotta give your credit on the pizza, Addie. Never ate any from there, but it's downright awesome."

"Glad you liked it. Of course it was a little hard for me to tell." She rose and took her glass and his empty beer bottle to the counter.

"You laughing at me, lady?" He crunched the empty box and put it in the trash.

She refilled her glass. Glancing over her shoulder, she raised a beer bottle toward Mike. He nodded.

"No sir, I'd never do that." She swung around her glass in one hand, his beer in the other.

Mike crossed the room in a couple of quick steps, trapping her with a hand on the counter on each side of her. He leaned toward her. His gaze traveled over her face. From the warmth, she must be turning pink. The herd of butterflies returned to her stomach when his gaze settled on her mouth. Her tongue slipped out to moisten her dry lips before she nibbled on the bottom one. He stepped in closer, his legs straddling hers. Her heartbeat so loud he must be able to hear the sound.

Damn, she had this stupid wine glass and his bottle in her hands. No way to put them down so she could run her hands over his broad shoulders and down his back. She yearned for him to pull her close and press his full length against her.

"Probably shouldn't do this, but I've wanted to since I first saw you in that knockout blue dress at the theatre fundraiser, shining like a sapphire. All sparkly and desirable."

Her heart skittered. He bent his head toward her. She lifted hers, and he brushed a feather-light kiss across her lips. Not nearly enough, and still open space was between them. The emptiness in her cried out for his body. For his touch. For his kiss.

"O-oh," she sighed into the next and longer meeting of their lips. Then his tongue dipped to the corner of her mouth and across her lips to the other side. He nipped along her jaw line and down her neck. Shivers followed everywhere he touched. Tingling started in her head and worked its way down her body. She had to get rid of the damn glass and bottle so she could be an active partner in what was going on.

Ah, good. The bottle smacked the counter. Mike slipped his tongue in her mouth, running it along her teeth and sucking on her tongue in the age-old movement mimicking what she wanted their lower bodies to be doing. He tasted of pizza and beer. A heady mixture.

Then he stepped even closer, and the hard ridge of his arousal pressed against her mound. She gasped. Wine spilled from the glass before she got it safely settled on the counter. With both hands free, she reveled in the sensations caused from running her hands through his thick hair, down his arms, around to his back.

They breathed with each other, deep and long. Addie almost became light-headed. She hiked one leg up on Mike to get closer. He dropped both hands and scooped her skirt up out of the way then boosted her on to the counter. Oh, my God. She wanted him with every ounce of her being. She reached for his zipper and tugged. She was wanton with desire for him.

His hands were everywhere. On her. In her. Her head dropped forward to his neck as she gave in to the waves rolling through her, to the explosions deep in her core. Her sighs muffled by his shoulder.

But still not enough. She wanted to feel him inside. The sound of a paper tearing alerted her he'd gotten a condom. He slid her panties aside and pressed ever so gently into her. She was thankful for his control. It had been a long time, and she was bound to be tight. But, oh God, how she wanted him. She scooted forward, taking him in inch by inch.

"Hey, Mom."

CHAPTER FIFTEEN

Monday, December 4

She froze. Time stopped. Was Jeremy coming into the kitchen? How could she have forgotten her son? Her wounded daughter in the hospital? She pulled back. Mike slipped out on a groan. Their eyes met; her shock matched his.

He stuffed himself, condom, and all, into his pants and zipped up in what must have been a painful operation. Mike lifted her off the counter and helped pull down her skirt. Then he walked awkwardly toward the back door. Addie turned toward the counter and picked up a rag to clean up the mess she'd made with the wine.

"You guys still eating?" Jeremy stuck his head around the door. "You mind if I head over to school to see everyone after the show?"

She threw a glance over her shoulder. "No, sweetie, sounds like a good idea." Please don't let him come give her a hug. No way he'd miss the scent of sex.

"Okay, then. I won't be gone longer than an hour."

The door to the garage slammed, followed by the grind of the garage door lifting. She didn't move until the sound repeated as the door lowered.

"Oh. My. God."

"I'm so sorry, honey. I should've had more control than to put you in that situation." He crossed to her and wrapped his arms around her. She placed her hands on those strong hands that had been doing wonderful things to her. "You weren't doing that all by your lonesome." She patted his arm and twisted to face him. "I'm sorry, too. I don't know what I was thinking."

"You've had a stressful time here and especially today. I shouldn't have taken advantage of the charge that kicks in after a life-threatening experience." He rubbed his hand up her temples and through her hair. "God, you're beautiful."

"I had a wonderful time. Not sure your experience was so great. Do you think we should do something about that?" She closed the gap between them.

His hands covered hers where she rested them on his chest, her fingers moving in a way she hoped would make him unable to say no. Clearly, from the bulge in the front of his pants, a part of him was willing and able.

"What about Jeremy? I don't know about you, but I don't want a repeat of that."

"I'm not suggesting you stay over or even that we use a bed." She pressed against him, thrusting her pelvis against his erection. Good old Pilates. "We were managing quite well—at least it seemed to me—right here in the kitchen.

"Then I'll take you up on that offer, ma'am." He pushed her skirt up and once again boosted her up on the counter. "Now where were we?"

His voice, low and sexy, got her motor running in high gear. So what if he'd suspected her of murder. His hands between her legs were already doing wonderful things. Her heart rate quickened, as she anticipated that soaring sky-high feeling he'd brought her to earlier. This time she'd make sure he got his reward.

His mouth found hers and sent trailing sparklers along her arms and legs. She gripped his head between her hands and again they shared the same air. So intimate. When he pulled back,

she nibbled on his ear.

"Oh."

His moan filled her with joy. Then she whispered. She hated to but she had to know. Whatever he said, she was going through with this. "Mike." Her voice hoarse with passion. "You don't still think I murdered Shannon, do you?"

"I never thought that babe. I just haven't been able to prove it. But I will." He kissed her hard on the mouth and then zeroed in on her core again.

She gasped. Between his tongue and his finger finding her hot spot, she flew apart at the seams. Fourth of July and Christmas all rolled into one. He held her close as she floated down out of heaven.

"Here, we're not finished." She tugged at his zipper and slid it down. Then she pulled him free of his boxers. The condom was still in place. "Now, we're almost where we left off." She guided him to her entrance and scooted forward in a way she hoped he'd find provocative. His penis pushed at the opening, which was now thoroughly relaxed after all the foreplay and two prior orgasms.

He pulled her nearer and slid in.

"Oh, my God. Oh, my God. Mike, move, please move."

"You only have to ask once." He plunged the rest of the way in.

She pulsed around him. Again he withdrew and came right back. They hit their rhythm, and in moments white lights exploded behind her eyelids. Trembles cascaded through her body in one giant wave that went on and on.

"Addie." Mike shouted her name as he climaxed.

She drifted in a haze, maybe even dozed, positioned on the counter and connected to a passionate lover.

"You are one damn-fine woman." He leaned back a little and locked gazes with her. "This can't be the only time."

"Good thing you think that way, bud. I don't do one-night stands."

He slid out of her, disposed of the condom, took a wet towel and gently cleaned her up, all the while, planting a few soft kisses on her face. Damn, if that wasn't mannerly. She had to figure a way to keep him around.

"I'd love to stay and snuggle on the couch, but I think that might lead to another awkward moment when Jeremy returns." Addie smiled at him.

"One of those in a lifetime is enough. Thank you very much." He helped her down from the counter and smoothed her full skirt back into place. Then he kissed her in a way that filled her heart with hope for the two of them.

"Walk me to the door?"

They made the trip walking with arms wrapped around each other. Addie smiled. They were acting like teenagers.

"When can I see you again?" Mike stopped in the front hall, twirling a strand of her hair around and around his finger.

"I don't know." Her shoulders hiked up. "I'll be at the hospital a lot while Elizabeth is there. Then I assume she'll come home for a while before she can go back to school."

"We'll figure something out. I'll stop by the hospital soon to see you both."

"Okay. That'll be nice."

"It won't be enough, but it will have to do until we can figure what else to do." He started through the door.

Addie stopped him with a hand on his arm "Mike, I was serious. I don't do one-night stands. This was special for me. If it wasn't for you...I don't want a return engagement."

He kissed her. "We'll find a way."

◆ ◆ ◆

Friday, December 7

Late in the afternoon, Mike made another stop at the hospital. Addie had to be exhausted. She went to Cowtown Theatre every morning, spent the afternoons here at the hospital with Elizabeth and on play days, attended Jeremy's musical. He didn't see how she did it. Not just the schedule but seeing *The Music Man* so many times. His head pounded at the idea.

As soon as he walked into the room, he slid his arm around Addie's waist. Her smile warmed his insides and made his lips twitch. He wanted to kiss her so bad. But he couldn't pull that off with Jeremy standing there, even though he was focused on his sister. A sister who was making such amazing progress the hospital staff bragged about how well she was doing.

"Hi, Detective," Elizabeth said. Jeremy just nodded his head.

"Good to see you're doing so well, Elizabeth."

"Say, Mom. Do you think you and Music Man here could take off a minute? I'd love it if you'd sneak me in a milkshake."

"Oh, honey, I don't think you should have one of those."

"How about a sorbet?" Jeremy suggested. "No milk—all sugar and fruit."

"Yum. Can y'all be dolls and go get that for me?"

"I can go." Jeremy stood from the side of her bed. "I know Mom wants to stay here as much as possible. I keep telling her she doesn't have to come to the musical on show days."

"One of the hazards of single parenting. Hard to cover two kids at the same time."

"Detective Riley could stay with me while y'all go."

Mike swung his head to meet her gaze, full of pleading if he wasn't mistaken. "Yeah, no problem. Y'all run on. Give you a chance to catch up with each other."

"Actually, Mom, I do need to talk with you about college. I have a couple of application questions—financial ones."

Addie shrugged her shoulders. "You sure you don't mind, Mike?"

"Of course not. Elizabeth and I can compare gun-shot stories."

A short laugh burst from Elizabeth. "Oh, not fair. It hurts to laugh."

"And I hate to tell you it will for a long time. See, we've already started. You two run on."

Addie leaned over the bed and kissed her daughter's forehead. "I'll be back shortly with the sorbet. Jeremy will go on to school to get ready for tonight's performance."

"I'll see you tomorrow, Sis."

"Beak a leg, Jer."

He laughed, "Don't you wish," and headed for the door.

Addie sent Mike a grateful smile. He could live on that for quite a while. But if he didn't get his act together with the DeWitt case, the lieutenant was going to have his hide. He'd see what Elizabeth wanted, and then he had to head back to the office as soon as Addie returned.

"So how're you really feeling? Pretty shitty?"

"You've got that right. I have just one bullet wound, but my whole body aches, and I don't have control of that body. Some nurse is always dragging me out of the bed to make me walk."

"Remember those times. Hurts like hell."

"You've really been here, Detective Riley?"

"Yep. Twice. Neither one fun." He sat on the edge of the bed. "So what's going on, Elizabeth? Looked to me like you maneuvered everyone out but me. And it's okay by me if you want to call me Mike."

"You're pretty clever. Guess that's why you're a detective."

"One of the reasons."

"Why'd you become a police officer in the first place?" Her fingers rolled the edge of the sheet and unrolled it.

"So I could solve murders. Make the bad guys pay. Speak for the victims."

"But why?"

"When I was in college, a buddy was murdered. The detective in charge would not give up until he found the bad guy."

"And he did?"

"Yep."

"Where's he now?"

"He was executed ten years after he committed the crime. Faster process than for many. Maybe because my buddy's dad was a cop. I don't know. Seemed way past time to me. I was impressed with how much comfort John's dad felt when the detective told him they'd gotten the guy."

"You were there?"

"I was there. I was there a lot." Mike picked up her hand. "So what's this about, sugar?"

"Because I've turned eighteen, the doctors don't have to tell Mom or anyone I don't want to know about my condition."

"Yeah, it's called the HIPAA act. Kind of a pain, but well-intentioned. So your Mom doesn't know everything?"

"No. They had to run blood tests on me and..."

"They found something you don't want your mother to know." God, please don't let her have HIV. That would kill Addie.

"Well, I want to tell her myself. You know when you're laid up like this, you have tons of time to do nothing. Nothing but think."

He nodded. Those times always made him question what he was doing. After his parents died, it wasn't quite as big a deal. Mike had seen too many parents lose their kids and knew how that would have torn up his. There was still Pat and Cindy and his niece and nephew. They'd hurt for a time but then go on. Not like a parent losing a child. So against the natural order of things.

"Gather you've been doing a little thinking while you're stuck here."

"Yeah." Her hands continued rolling and unrolling the edge of the sheet. "I'm not real proud of some of the things I've done."

"Not a person alive who doesn't have stuff we'd like to have stay out of the papers." He looked at her. Despite recovering from a gunshot wound, Elizabeth looked a heck of a lot better than when she was in her Goth outfit. Healthier somehow.

"So you have some stuff you'd like to keep out of the papers. What'd your blood work-up show? I'm not asking as a cop, just a friend."

She nodded once. "Marijuana. I knew about that, but

some coke, too. I swear, Mike I never knowingly did that." Her agitation showed itself as her hands moved across the covers, and a tear streaked down her face. She shoved it away.

"How are you holding up?"

"Pretty good. The doctors have been cautious with what they've given me for pain. Since clearly I have a problem that way, they don't want to chance me getting hooked on a prescription."

"What are they telling you?" He didn't know if she'd share, but if you don't ask, you don't ever find out.

"They want me to go to a rehab place when I get out. Just for a time."

"Sounds like a good plan. What's the problem? If it's money, I'm sure your father will pay."

"Well, I'm not all too sure of that, but I've got a bigger problem."

Mike's gut tightened and the hairs on the back of his neck pulled to attention. If he were involved in a stake-out, he'd know for sure some bad stuff was about to hit. What could be harder than having to tell your mother you did drugs and had to go to rehab?

"You want to tell me?" Mike couldn't think of why she'd want to tell him, but she'd asked him to stay for some special reason.

"Yeah." Two more tears slid out—one from each eye. She took his hand in both of hers. "Please don't hate me."

"Ah, sweetie"—he unconsciously used the term Addie sometimes used with her kids. "No one's gonna hate you. Not your mother. Not even your brother. And your father—I gotta say, I think he's a loser, but he can't hate you. If he does, he's not worth the money it takes to heat his house."

More tears. God this must really be shitty.

"I—I hid the gun." Her voice so soft, he barely made out the words.

"What?"

"I hid the gun in Mom's house."

Shit. The poor girl sobbed inconsolably. Mike pulled her into his arms for what solace he could give. Hell. This was going to kill Addie. How do you recover from having your own kid set you up?

Elizabeth's tears slowed. He handed her a tissue. She wiped. Blew. Moaned and wiped some more.

"You want to tell me how that all came about?"

Elizabeth sniffed and snuffled but finally met his gaze. "Clay Bennett gave me the gun."

"Goddamn. Sorry. Go on."

"Yeah, right. He told me it was a stage prop, and he was playing a joke on Mom. She'd get a big laugh out of it when it happened."

"He just asked you to do this?"

"He promised me free weed for a month."

"Did he keep his promise?"

"Only at first then he wanted more money. I didn't have any."

"That's what led to the shoplifting?"

"You heard about that?"

He nodded. "When you realized how finding the gun in her house made your mother look, why didn't you speak up then?"

"Because I was afraid, and I'm a jerk. I really thought Clay liked me. When an older handsome face tells you you're beautiful and special, you believe them and will do anything to continue the relationship."

"All the things your father wasn't giving you." Mike nodded. "Well, there is some good in this."

"There is? How do you see that? My mother is going to hate me for the rest of my life. I'm worthless scum."

"I think I'd say you made some poor choices. We all do that."

"Mom will never be able to forgive me." Tears started again.

"You know, I bet she will. It's part of the definition of being a good mom. And you have a great mom."

Elizabeth nodded. "I know that now. My head was just messed up, and then I made it even worse with drugs."

"But you can recover from all of this, Elizabeth. Let's talk about the good that can come of your experience. Number one, your mom is no longer a suspect in the DeWitt murder. Number two, you've made a giant step toward recovery in accepting your responsibility in all of this. Number three—and I don't know how you're going to feel about this, your brother isn't any too thrilled—I can pursue a relationship with your mother." He stopped. He'd be dead in the water if he had both kids against him, but he had to know.

Elizabeth was silent for what seemed a long time. Mike thought he might pass out. Finally, the beginnings of a smile spread across her face. He'd never noticed before, but she had the same single dimple her mother had.

"I think that sounds wonderful, Mike. Mom's been alone for a long time. Dad treated her shitty."

He nodded. "Yeah, he did. I can promise you without any doubt or hesitation, I'll never hurt her. I also need to be upfront with you. I'm not buying your support with false promises. I know there will be consequences to your actions. We've talked about rehab. But you've withheld evidence, and there may be some charges there."

Her chin trembled. She nodded. "Thanks for being honest with me. I've kind of screwed up my life."

"I'd rather say you've hit a few more bumps in the road at an earlier time than most folks do. If your father had behaved like a real man, maybe things would have turned out differently. But if that was the case, I wouldn't now have a chance at a lifetime with your mother."

"I hope it works out for you and her, Mike. Can I ask you for something else?"

"Sure, if I can do it, I will."

"Will you be here with me when I tell her?"

The trembling chin knocked him in the gut. He'd do anything for this child-woman and her mother. "Sure. Give me a little time. I'm going to get an assistant district attorney to come in and take your statement if you're willing. Tell her everything you told me."

"Will it get Mom off the hook?"

"Not only get your Mom off the hook, we'll be able to nail Clay Bennett. My gut feeling all along has been he's involved, but I didn't have a shred of evidence to let me investigate more. You're it, sweetie." He leaned down and kissed her forehead. "It's going to be rough for a while, but we'll all get through this."

◆ ◆ ◆

Monday, December 10

Three days later, Mike and Rick were on their way to the DA's office. The lieutenant had been relieved they'd finally gotten a break in the DeWitt case.

"Guess you're pretty pleased about this, Partner. You plan to get it on with Ms. Greer?"

Mike noted Rick had cleaned up his language a bit in referring to his relationship with Addie. "Yup."

Rick smiled. "Good for you. About time you settled down."

"Why do you say that? You've never even been close."

"Takes you out of the running. Leaves more options for me." Rick laughed and clapped Mike on the shoulder.

They walked into the office of Assistant DA Margie Holmes. "Guys, I'm worried whether we can make this stick. At this point what you've got is a he-said, she-said, and the 'she' is a dope head." She gestured to the pages lying on her desk in an open folder.

"It's not like that, Margie. She smoked a little weed," Mike said.

"He hooked her up with coke she didn't know about. The amounts in the tox screen support that." Mike nodded at Rick, thanking him for his added words of support.

"I get that. I'm just saying what Bennett's attorney is going to say."

"Give us a chance to get it before a jury. The girl will make a good witness. She's accepted her responsibility in the situation. Let them decide." Mike had to get her to agree.

Finally, Margie nodded. "Well, I gotta say, I was impressed when I met with her. Okay, let's give it a go."

"Do we have a deal with her testifying, we won't press charges for withholding evidence or drug use if she also goes to rehab?"

"We've got a go on that, too."

"Great."

Mike walked with a lighter step, having gotten the ADA on board, but a couple things still nagged at him. One had to do with getting Elizabeth to tell her mother. She had to do that before the arrest happened, and Addie found out about it that way.

"Drop me by my truck will you, Rick? I want to let Elizabeth know where we stand with everything."

"You got it." Rick changed direction.

◆ ◆ ◆

"Nurse, Nurse." It didn't matter to Mike that he was yelling. His heartbeat was about to blow off the top his head. Elizabeth wasn't in her hospital room.

He ran into the hall and grabbed the first person in uniform. "Where's the patient in room 306?"

"She's probably in the restroom. We've been getting her up and about a lot this morning. The last time she managed on her own." The grandmotherly woman almost clucked at him. "Let me check for you."

She knocked on the closed bathroom door. "Elizabeth?" She knocked again. "Elizabeth." Then pushed open the door.

Mike felt like his head would explode while he waited to find out if she were all right.

"She's not in here, Detective."

"Hell."

The woman glanced around. "But listen, someone's probably taken her to run another

test." She picked up the chart from the end of the bed.

Again hope battered for a little light.

"I'm sorry. Nothing is noted here. I'll check at the desk to see if anyone saw her leave. Maybe she's just gone for a walk. We encourage that, you know."

"Yeah." Mike remembered being pushed out to walk the halls during recovery. Probably he was overreacting. He stood outside her door, looking both ways. But the prickly feeling he'd learned to pay attention to scrabbled along his neck and back. Not good.

"Sir." The grandmotherly nurse came back. The desk

nurse said Elizabeth went for a walk about ten minutes ago. Expects her back any time now."

"Was she alone?" He hoped to God she was.

"No, sir. She was with her uncle."

"Shit!"

"I beg your pardon." The grandmother nurse's eyebrows rose in surprise.

"She doesn't have an uncle."

"Oh my."

"Alert your security. We may be looking at a kidnapping." Mike used his cell, contacted Rick and the lieutenant, telling them he thought Clay Bennett had taken Elizabeth. The lieutenant said she'd get a team together.

Mike ran down the stairs and outside, heading for his truck. He put in a call, one he'd so much like not to make. Addie. But she deserved to know her daughter was likely in danger. Not just from Clay, but from him dragging her from the hospital before she was ready.

"Mike."

Addie's pleased tone of surprise sent pleasure zinging through his middle. Then he clenched his hand around his cell. *Gut up, man.*

"Addie, I'm afraid I may have some bad news."

"Is something the matter with Jeremy?" Naturally, she'd think of him first. Her daughter was safe in the hospital, making rapid recovery, totally out of the woods.

"No. Where are you?"

"I'm in my office. You're scaring me, Mike. Tell me what's

wrong."

"I'm afraid Elizabeth has been kidnapped."

"What? That's not anything to joke about, Mike. For heaven's sake. I'm sure—"

"I wouldn't kid about this."

"Who would kidnap her? Why?"

Hell fire. Elizabeth had wanted to tell her mother herself but hadn't yet. He hated to break her confidence but looked like he'd have to.

"Mike, talk to me."

"I think Clay Bennett may have taken her."

"Why would he do that? You must be mistaken. Elizabeth was making a lot of progress, walking down the halls. I'm sure that's all this is."

"Honey, I know this is not something you want to think about, but I'm really worried. I'm coming to get you."

"What? Oh my God."

"What's the matter, Addie?" What were the odd sounds in the background? She said she was in her office. "Addie, what's wrong?"

"Nothing's wrong. I'm hanging up."

Silence.

CHAPTER SIXTEEN

Monday, December 10

Bam. Addie's office door swung in so hard it hit the wall. She jumped from her chair. Blood pounded in her ears so loud she had trouble hearing what Clay Bennett was saying.

Clay Bennett, who'd kicked Addie's office door closed behind him.

Clay Bennett, who held Elizabeth, dressed only in her hospital gown and house shoes, tight in front of him. Her daughter shivered, probably as much from the cold as fear.

"What's going on? Elizabeth, you okay?" Addie struggled to keep her voice from shaking, amazed her legs supported her.

"We're going to make a little trade."

Clay's sing-song tone sent icicles down Addie's back. She'd never heard him sound so...deranged. "Okay, I'll do whatever you want, Clay, just don't hurt Elizabeth." Addie took a step around the end of her desk.

"Mom, stay there. This is all my fault." Elizabeth's voice was little better than a whisper.

"No, sweetie. Nothing is your fault." *Stay calm. Don't send Clay over the edge.* Her disconnect with Mike was so odd, she prayed he'd come and check on her.

"Yes. It is."

"Shut up, bitch. I'm doing the talking." He waved the gun toward Elizabeth.

Please don't let that go off and hit her. She might not be able to survive another gunshot.

Elizabeth strained against the hold Clay had on her and kept talking. "I put the gun in the drawer, Mom."

"What?" Addie literally stepped away from the statement, one hand fisted in her middle. She must have misunderstood. "Is Clay making you say that? Why would you say that?" Her pitch climbed hysterically despite her normal steel control.

"Because it's true." The harshness of her daughter's voice confirmed the truth of the statement.

Tears slid down Addie's face, forming shards of broken glass, which pierced her heart, her stomach, sliced down her arms. Blood must be everywhere. Addie leaned on the desk for support.

"Clay told me he was playing a trick on you." Tears dripped down Elizabeth's face. "I thought it would be funny. I'm sorry. I didn't know it was a murder weapon."

"Murder weapon." Addie gasped at the pain her daughter's words caused. "Oh my God." "I told Mike, that's why he's coming after Clay."

Addie's gaze left her daughter and landed on her former artistic director. The horrible truth screamed for anyone to see.

"Yeah, Addie. I killed DeWitt. She told me she was siding with you to fire me. I couldn't have that. I figured the kid here would help me get rid of the weapon. And she did a great job."

He squeezed Elizabeth tighter around the middle, making her groan.

"Let her go, Clay. She'll be hard to handle. You can take me."

"Funny you should suggest that idea, Addie. That would be a good plan, but I still need to dump Elizabeth so she can't testify."

"Testify?" Addie's brain was mush. She kept repeating what others were saying.

"Yeah. Like your girl here said, they plan to use her to testify. But who's going to believe a dope head against my word it was her mama who did the shooting."

"No!" Elizabeth yelled.

Clay tightened his arm around her middle. Her yelp of pain drove a nail into Addie's heart.

"Now you need to keep quiet. I don't want anyone busting in here."

"Mom, I'm sorry. I should've said something right away when Mike thought you'd put the gun there. The drugs made me stupid."

Drugs. Elizabeth confirmed her drug use. God, could this get any worse? Somewhere Addie dug down deep for the right words. "It's okay, sweetie. It's going to be okay." Addie focused on Clay. "I'll go with you. I'll give you money. I'll help you escape. But only if you leave Elizabeth here."

"Mom, how can you think of doing that for me? I betrayed you."

The agony on her daughter's face was another slice of

jagged glass to her insides. "Elizabeth, look at me." Her daughter's gaze, from eyes that everyone said were so like Addie's, locked on hers.

"I love you. You're my daughter, and there's nothing you can ever do that will change that."

"I love you, Mom. I don't deserve for you to do this."

"Yes, you do. But you can do me a favor."

"Anything."

"When Mike gets here, and he will, be sure to tell him how much I love him."

"He loves you, too, Mom."

Addie's fought the trembling in her chin and brushed at a tear threatening to fall. This was not the time for her to fall apart. Miles to go before she could do that.

"I'll go with you, Clay. I'll get you money and help you escape. You leave Elizabeth here, like I said." She was afraid he might not go along, but finally he nodded.

"How much money can you get me?"

"We'll clean out whatever Roger has on hand here. I can access the cash in my personal bank account."

"Use your cell and show me how much you've got. There's probably not much here."

Addie was glad he wanted to take time to check because every minute they stayed here was one minute closer to Mike arriving. Closer to rescue for Elizabeth. Closer to putting an end to this nightmare.

"Look, Clay. I've got five thousand dollars. I'd just transferred it from savings to use for the kids to get ready for college."

"Huh, I need a shit-load of money. Where can you get more?"

Addie's head pounded with the effort to find a solution. Two popped to her mind. Jonathan Harding and Elizabeth's father. Of the two, she thought she had a better chance with Jonathan. Sad. She'd hate to ask Jud and have him turn her down. A double blow to Elizabeth.

"If you don't have more, this ain't happening. You'll both be dead."

"I think I can get Jonathan Harding to add some to the pot. How much are we talking about?"

"Oh yeah." Clay nodded. "Mr. Harding's got plenty of dough. Maybe he's interested enough in you he'll cough up some. Give him a call. Ask for thirty K. Make it quick. We gotta get out of here."

Addie keyed in Jonathan's cell and prayed he was where he could answer. He did after the second ring.

"Addison, nice to hear from you. I've been meaning to check with you about a fundraiser coming up in two weeks."

"Jonathan, I need a favor."

"Of course, anything."

"I need thirty thousand dollars." Addie's fingers on her cell turned white as she prayed Jonathan would help.

"How soon would you like it?"

She swallowed a huge cotton ball in her throat and blinked her eyes to keep the tears from falling. He didn't even ask why.

"I'm sorry, Jonathan. I need it immediately. Can you transfer it to my bank account?"

"Yes. Give me the account number."

Addie moved behind her desk and pulled her purse from the bottom drawer, rummaged around until she found her checkbook. She read the number. "I can't thank you enough, Jonathan."

"Let me know if everything is okay."

"I will." She disconnected the call.

"Whoa. The big man came through. He must be sweet on you. Walk over here by the door, Addie. That's it."

Addie's heart knocked fast enough to break through her breastbone.

"Elizabeth, thanks for all your help. Going to leave you here."

He let go of her, and as if in slow motion, Elizabeth crumpled toward the floor. At the last minute, Clay bashed her head with his gun.

"You bastard," Addie sprinted to her daughter's side.

♦ ♦ ♦

Mike drove through the busy streets, way above the speed limit. He slowed when his cell rang. "Detective Riley, this is Jonathan Harding."

"I'm kind of busy, Harding, be brief."

"I've taken a disturbing call from Addison."

Mike swallowed the bile that instantly rose to his throat.

His hackles could hardly rise higher. "Talk."

"She asked me to transfer thirty thousand to her bank account. I did."

"Thanks for that info, Harding. I'll let you know how things turn out." Mike disconnected and called the Cowtown Theatre where Pete Talmadge answered the phone. Mike identified himself.

"Is Addison Greer in the building?"

"Yes, do you want to speak to her, Detective?"

"No. Is she in her office?"

"I believe so."

Mike's fingers tensed on the steering wheel. "Have you seen Clay Bennett around?"

"Can't say that I have. Can I do anything for you?"

Mike consciously relaxed his fingers' grip on the wheel. He wasn't certain Bennett was there but couldn't chance being wrong. "Yes. I want you to take anyone who is in the theatre out through one of the back entrances. Can you do that? I need you to act fast. No loud noises or yells. You get what I'm saying?"

"Yeah. We've got some sort of dangerous situation."

"That's right. When you're out, cross the parking lot and shelter behind the next building. I don't want people milling around outside the theatre. And, Talmadge, leave a back door unlocked."

"Got it. It will be the left door when you look at the theatre from the rear."

"Thanks and be safe."

Mike called the lieutenant, explained his suspicions that Bennett had kidnapped Elizabeth and asked his boss to send a SWAT contingent to Cowtown Theatre. Would they get there in time? Would Elizabeth and Addie be all right? His heart beat a thousand times a minute if it beat once.

♦ ♦ ♦

Addie's fingers searched frantically for her daughter's pulse. *Thank you, God.*

"I couldn't leave her awake to call anyone." Bennett grabbed Addie's upper arm in a painful grip and yanked her up against him. "Now do what I say. We're going to walk out of here and get in your car and head for the bank, where you're going to take out my money."

Addie took one last look at Elizabeth before Bennett shoved her through the door ahead of him.

"Not a word to anyone. Got it?"

Addie cut her eyes left and right but didn't see anyone. If Clay didn't notice, she wasn't going to call his attention to the oddity. She tried to keep her breathing regular, but the feeling something was about to jump out at her sent her pulses thrumming.

They walked so fast through the atrium she stumbled. Clay squeezed her arm tighter. "Keep up." They made it to the vestibule. He pushed her through the double glass entrance doors.

"Mr. Bennett," a voice blared from a horn.

He jerked her back inside. "Shit."

"Mr. Bennett, I'm Sergeant Hawkins with SWAT. Let's talk and see if we can work something out here that's good for everyone. I'm going to call on your cell. Please pick up."

Addie's heartbeat faster than hummingbird wings and threatened to give out on her. Bennett's cell rang. He didn't answer at once. "Pick up, Clay. They want to talk with you."

Just before the fourth ring, he answered. "What… Hostages?"

"He's talking about me and Elizabeth." Addie didn't want him to think about the others who might still be in the building.

"I want fifty K in cash delivered here. I want a safe escort and a plane at Meacham Field. You let me take off with the money and Addie… Yeah, we'll be real cool. You check with Jonathan Harding. He'd already agreed to thirty K. He'll never miss twenty more." He disconnected.

"Clay, what makes you think Jonathan will give you more?" The pitch of her voice rose as Addie's normal calm-in-a-crisis-demeanor almost deserted her.

"The old man is sweet on you."

Bennett dragged her farther from the front windows, behind a concrete pillar, but the gathering in the parking lot grew larger as more police vehicles arrived. He pulled her to the floor in front of him. "They won't try anything while I've got you, but let's make a smaller target."

Addie shivered when he pushed the gun against her temple. The only good thing she could see about this was Elizabeth was alive and safer in the office than out here. Where was Mike? Jeremy? Would she ever see any of them again? Time dragged. Clay kept glancing at his watch.

Finally, Clay's cell rang. The SWAT Sergeant or some random call?

"Yeah. You got my money?...A plane from Mr. Harding, you say? He is generous...How long?"

"Two hours won't cut it, Sarge. Tell them to speed it along, or I'll have to give them a little bit of Ms. Greer."

Addie gulped at the fear crawling up her throat. Clay Bennett was a letch, a thief, and a murderer, but he wouldn't torture her, would he?

◆ ◆ ◆

Mike and a SWAT officer moved on silent feet through the back of the theatre. Mike had to check to see if Elizabeth was here and if she was okay.

The SWAT officer, shield up, pushed open the door to Addie's office. Empty. Except for Elizabeth lying on the floor. Mike rushed to her side. Blood seeped from a head wound that might've been caused by the butt of a gun. Damn Bennett for treating her this way.

Elizabeth moaned as she came around. They'd found her before she could come to and wander out into the middle of everything.

"Shh, honey. It's going to be okay."

"Mom?" She tried to look at him, but the way her forehead wrinkled, and her eyes squinted indicated she was in considerable pain.

"She's not here."

"Bennett took her. Save her, Mike, please."

Mike nodded. "I need you to stay in here, Elizabeth. Do you think you can lock the door behind us after we leave?"

She nodded. "Mike, one more thing."

"No time, now, sweetie." He and the SWAT officer helped her stand. She was unsteady, but she was up. Mike grabbed Addie's coat from the rack and helped Elizabeth into it.

"After you lock the door, go behind the desk and get on the floor. Regardless of what you hear on the outside, no matter who calls to you, I want you to stay in this room, until your mother or I come to get you. Got it?"

Her chin trembled, but she nodded. "Don't let him hurt Mom."

"That's the plan, sweetie." Mike leaned down and kissed the top of her head.

"Now lock up after us." He nodded to the SWAT officer. "Let's go." Mike cracked the door, and after checking sight lines, they slipped through into the hallway.

"Wait up." The officer put a finger to his headset. "I'm hearing confirmation Bennett and Ms. Greer are in the vestibule. Bennett is using her as a shield, blocking officers in the parking lot from getting a shot at him. We should be able to, though even if it's through the glass."

Mike's mouth grew dry at the thought of them taking that shot with Addie near. "Let's take a look before we decide." They took cautious steps through the hall, into the theatre, and then into the concourse. They crouched down behind the large desk near the box office. Mike eased up and peered over.

He froze. Hearing the danger Addie was in was bad. Seeing her with a gun to her temple made his gut churn and red-hot anger zip down his arms and legs like an electric charge. Not good. He needed to stay cool to deal with this situation. He gestured for the SWAT officer to look then signaled for them to both retreat into the theatre.

"What's up?"

"Thought we could talk better here. We need a plan."

"Yeah. News is they've just about got the money ready."

"I don't care about the money. Addie is not going anywhere with Bennett."

"You got an idea?"

◆ ◆ ◆

"Shit. This waiting is making me nuts."

"I'm sure it takes them a while to get that amount of money in cash," Addie said. Pain in her leg made her cry out.

"What the hell are you doing?"

"My legs are cramping. I just stretched." She moaned and rubbed her calf. Good thing she'd worn slacks today. A skirt would have really been awkward. She rubbed her forehead. She must be nuts to think that way. A shiver shook her body. Cold air seeped into the glass-enclosed vestibule. The theatre's heat was on a timed thermostat and shut off when they didn't have rehearsals or a show going on.

Maybe she could distract Clay. She had to do something to help. Otherwise, she'd focus on what a bad mother she'd been for Elizabeth to fall into so much trouble, although Jud shared a portion of that blame. Addie kicked herself for not listening to Jeremy. Would Jud pay for their college if Bennett killed her? Or continue to be a bastard? The cramp had lessened. Time for the distraction tactic.

"I don't understand any of this, Clay."

"This what?"

"Why couldn't you just make the shows come in on budget? If you'd done that, we wouldn't be sitting here with a bunch of armed cops out front. And why did you drag my daughter into your schemes?"

"Huh. Elizabeth is no little miss innocent." His smile was more of a leer, making Addie's stomach knot. She didn't want to hear anything he had to say about her daughter. Not that she thought he'd tell the truth, but she just didn't want to hear what he'd say.

"Did you skim money from the theatre? Is that why you kept going over budget?" Bennett raised his eyebrows as if he weren't going to respond. Addie was surprised when he nodded. "What'd you use the money for?"

"What do you think?" His expression said she was stupid. "Drugs. I used it on drugs and gambling debts and a few women."

"When I wanted to fire you, why couldn't you have just found some place else to work? You're talented. That was never in question." She bit her lip. The tile floor was cooling off, too, and the cold was stealing into her bones. Shivers became continuous. Lights glared from the parking lot. Addie couldn't imagine how this was going to work out without both of them getting shot.

She remembered her joy when she found out she was pregnant. Jud seemed happy at first. He'd always said he only wanted one child and wasn't thrilled to learn she was having twins.

Jeremy was the first baby delivered. From Jud's perspective, that was all he needed. From the beginning, he'd ignored Elizabeth. Addie had thought she could make up for the loss of a father. She hadn't, and Elizabeth had paid the price.

Bennett's cell chirped. Addie jerked back from her memories.

Clay listened for a moment, cocked his head to look outside. "I see the car coming now. You got the money?... Excellent!" He disconnected. "Harding must really have a thing for you, Ms. Greer." Clay ran the tip of the gun down her cheek, stopping on her chin.

Addie didn't move or breathe. Was this it then? Despite the money and plane? After what seemed like several hours wait, Clay moved his gun.

"Okay, Addison, Let's go." He yanked her arm, dragging her to stand in front of him and shoved her toward the front door.

Addie stared out into the parking lot. Lights blazed from all the police vehicles. A black SUV pulled to a stop in front of the theatre's main entrance. It would protect them from shots from the SWAT officers. She didn't particularly want Bennett killed, but she damn sure didn't want to go with him. Whatever happened, she resolved not to get on the plane.

She trembled like she had pneumonia. Between fear and the cold, she had trouble putting one foot in front of the other. Clay's arm, wrapped around her neck, made breathing difficult. When they reached the door, he slammed her against the cold glass.

"Bennett."

Addie and Clay jumped. Twisting to look behind them, he loosened his grip on her. She tried to slide toward the ground, but he clamped his arm around her middle and squeezed so tight she had trouble getting a breath.

"Drop the gun. Put your hands up. Step away from Addie." The words, spoken in a low voice, left no doubt, the man expected Bennett to obey.

Dear God. Addie could hardly believe her eyes. Mike stood there. No one had ever looked better to her. He and a SWAT officer, both in vests, had their weapons trained on Clay. He glanced over his shoulder at the police grouped outside the theatre, the black SUV at the curb, and back to Mike.

"Get out of here, Riley, if you don't want something to happen to Addison here. She's my get-out-of-jail-free card. I'm leaving and taking her with me."

No one moved.

"Oh." Clay had rammed the gun into the back of Addie's neck. She trembled with fear that it might just go off and that'd be the end of everything.

"See what I'm talking about?"

While Addie had resolved not to get on the plane with Clay, it was becoming obvious that she had to do something sooner rather than later. She gritted her teeth, gave not another thought to the danger, and went into her ragdoll slump, dropping over from the waist, her knees bent, putting all her weight on Clay's arm around her waist. He couldn't hold her.

Guns fired as she hit the ground. Then all was chaos with shouts and rapid movement. Arms came around her and dragged her away from Bennett where he lay on the ground.

"Addie, Addie, Are you okay?"

She dragged in a deep breath and looked into Mike's face, lined with worry. She nodded. "Yeah, I'm good. You?"

"Fine."

"Where's Elizabeth?" Her voice quivered in fear for her daughter's safety.

"She's in your office."

The SWAT officer knelt by Clay where he lay on the floor. "He's alive," the officer said.

"Can I go to her?" Addie needed Mike's strength to help her get on her own two feet. He nodded, and she staggered through the doors separating the outer vestibule from the inner atrium and scrambled then down the hall to her office. She turned the door handle, but nothing happened. Her fist pounded twice. "Elizabeth, it's me. Can you open the door?"

"Mom?" Elizabeth's voice sounded weaker than since right after her surgery.

"Are you okay?" *Dear God, please let her be okay.*

Nothing had ever sounded better to Addie than the click of the lock and the slight squeak of the door as Elizabeth pulled it open.

"Oh, sweetie." Addie swept Elizabeth into her arms. She might never let her go, and only did when her daughter leaned back. "Am I hurting you?"

"Just a bit, and I needed to see if you were okay." Elizabeth's gaze ran from her mother's head to her feet and back up. Her lips thinned into a straight line and she nodded once. "I didn't get to tell Mike. I'm sorry."

"It's okay. What about you? How's your head? I thought I'd die when Clay hit you." She guided Elizabeth toward the small sofa in her office. "Let's sit here."

"What happened to him?" Elizabeth bowed her head and didn't look at Addie.

"Mike or a SWAT officer shot him. He's alive."

"What's going to happen now?"

Two EMTs rushed into the room. "We need to check you both out and get Miss Greer back to the hospital."

Addie squeezed her daughter's hand. "Guess that's what's going to happen first."

A woman EMT sat where she'd been by her daughter and started taking Elizabeth's vitals. A man did the same thing with Addie. Her brain seemed fuzzy. She couldn't even begin to think where all this was going. How much trouble would Elizabeth be in? Would she be able to finish school and graduate? What about college?

What about Mike and her? Sleeping together was one thing, but could they work out anything long-term?

Her head ached from the thoughts whirling around. The light the EMT shown in her eyes sent pain zigging around like her head was the inside of a pinball machine. She winced. Dear God, how did they begin to put their lives back together?

CHAPTER SEVENTEEN

Monday, December 10

By the time Mike finished up with the details of the arrest and went in search of Addie, she and Elizabeth were gone.

"She rode with her daughter in the ambulance. They were heading back to the hospital," Talmadge said.

"Thanks. You did a good job keeping everyone safe. I'll catch up with her there. She and Elizabeth will both need to give statements about what happened."

"Go easy on her, Detective. She's been through a lot."

"Got that." Mike stalked toward his truck, left his helmet and flak jacket in the trunk in the back, and slapped on his western hat. Now that felt better. He picked up his cell and put in a call to check on Jeremy. He probably had no idea what was going on. Mike would offer pick him up and drive him to the hospital.

"Hey, Jeremy."

"Yeah?"

"It's Detective Riley. Have you talked with your mother in a while?"

"No, why? What's the matter?" His voice lost its initial scornful sound to exude worry.

"Where are you?"

"At the house."

Mike threw the truck into drive and took off. "Good. I want to pick you up and take you to your mother and sister."

"Aren't they still at the hospital?"

"Well, yes, they are now, but there was an incident."

"What the hell are you talking about?"

Mike filled him in on what he knew. "I know you want to see them, but I'm not sure you should be driving. I'll be there in less than ten minutes."

A lot of swallowing came over the line, and Mike figured Jeremy was struggling not to cry. "Okay."

In less time than that, Mike pulled to the curb, and Jeremy, who'd been standing on the front porch, ran down the stairs, yanked open the passenger door, and hopped in. "Let's go." He buckled his seat belt, and Mike sped down the street toward the hospital.

He wanted to talk with both kids about their mother and his desire to share a life with her and with them, but this wasn't the best time. He'd just have to put it on a back burner until they got the situation with Elizabeth squared away.

The silence loomed large between them. Like the proverbial elephant in the room. Only in this case it was in a truck. All the more uncomfortable.

"This is my fault." Jeremy ran the zipper of his jacket up and down.

"What?" Was this a family of martyrs? Everyone claimed the situation was his or her fault. "Why do you say that,

Jeremy? You didn't get your sister shot. That was the gangbangers. You didn't have anything to do with her abduction. That was Bennett."

"Yeah, but I was pretty certain Elizabeth was doing drugs. I should've made Mom listen. And her story about acting lessons? I wanted to believe that. She was so much better than I thought she would be it seemed to make sense. I should've told Mom the first time I saw Elizabeth in that bastard's apartment. Should never have given her a second chance. Or third or fourth, whatever it was." He slammed his fist into his thigh.

Mike really wanted to reach out and comfort the kid but didn't know how the boy would take his action. Finally, he gave in to his instincts and reached across the seat to squeeze Jeremy's shoulder. Just twice. Then dropped his hand back on the steering wheel.

"Second chances are important, Jeremy. Sometimes even third and fourth. We never give up on each other. We keep trying. It's what family does." He paused for a traffic light, lifted his hat for a moment, and ran a hand through his hair. How best to get Jeremy to understand? Mike set his hat firmly on his head and pulled ahead when the light changed.

"My father gave my brother Pat and me several chances to make good on a promise until we finally learned if we gave our word, he wanted it done the first time. If we failed, he always gave us another chance." Mike drove for another block in silence before he pulled into the hospital parking garage.

"Were there consequences when you messed up?"

Jeremy slanted a glance at Mike.

He nodded. "Some of those weren't pleasant, let me tell you. We learned. Pop could've given up on us the first time we screwed up, but he didn't. Your mother isn't going to treat you and Elizabeth any different." He turned off the ignition.

Jeremy nodded. "Thanks."

"Let's go see how the girls are doing." Mike almost pulled a smile from Jeremy with that. They walked together into the hospital and checked with the woman at the volunteer desk, who told them Elizabeth was in her room.

"That's good news, don't you think?" Jeremy asked.

"Sure do."

The door was open partway. Mike raised his hand to tap, but voices from inside leaked out to him and Jeremy.

♦ ♦ ♦

"Mom, I'm so sorry about all of this. I nearly got you killed." Elizabeth's voice trembled and tore at Addie.

"Sweetie, I won't pretend I'm not worried about you—the whole drug thing and hanging with an older man. I'm just so thankful he didn't attack you or rape you." Grateful for the chair because she was not sure her legs would support her; Addie kept her arms wrapped around her middle. Still, a shudder ran through her body at the mere idea of something like that happening to her daughter.

"You bear responsibility for things you did but not for what Clay did. Just as I take responsibility for taking you and

Jeremy away from your father."

"But, Mom, he cheated on you." Her daughter's hands twisted the covers.

"Yes, you're correct, and that wasn't the first time. I kept forgiving him. He'd promise not to do it again. When he brought the woman into our home...well, I couldn't tolerate his behavior another moment."

Addie stood then crossed to the window. "I thought keeping our family together was the best thing for you and Jeremy. Probably did you more harm staying in that environment." She turned back to the young woman lying in the hospital bed. The young woman Addie nearly lost.

"Listen to me, sweetie." She sat on the edge of the bed and took her hand. "You mean everything to me. I love you just the way you are—well, maybe without the drugs. You don't have to be like Jeremy or do plays. If you want to stay at the Fine Arts Academy and keep the focus on art, that's fine. You just need to be the best Elizabeth you can be."

Her daughter groaned a little when she pulled herself up and threw one arm around Addie. "Thanks, Mom. I love you. Before Clay took me off, I'd had one session with a psychologist here. If we can swing it, I want to continue. Getting shot made me realize what a chance I was taking with the drugs. I know you've given me second chances before, but can I have another one?"

Tears spilled from Addie's eyes and trickled down her face. "Absolutely, sweetie. We'll get through this."

A light tap on the door made them pull apart. "It's

Jeremy, Mom. Can we come in?"

"Dear God. Jeremy. I forgot to call him." Addie swiped at the tears and then helped Elizabeth lie back against the pillows. "You ready for visitors?"

"Sure."

Addie rose and got to the door just as it swung inward. Her tall, handsome son rushed her and squeezed her in a giant hug.

"You okay?" His voice held a slight tremble, making him clear his throat.

"Yes, if you don't squeeze the life out of me." She surprised herself when a chuckle bubbled out. That felt good. Jeremy let go and walked to his sister's side. Addie drew in a deep breath. Behind her son stood Mike, his hands turning his white western hat in circles. Her insides began a slow melt.

"Hi." His gaze ran over her, head to toe and back to her face.

"Hi." Her heart swelled with yearning. She barely resisted the urge to fling herself into his arms.

"I stopped by for Jeremy. He hadn't heard what happened." Mike stepped in and closed the door.

"Thank you. How could I have forgotten him?"

"You had a lot on your plate. Cut yourself some slack. You're a good mother."

"Just fair to midlin', I'm afraid. My family is pretty messed up." She glanced back over her shoulder to where her children's heads were close. They seemed to be in a deep discussion.

"What about Clay?"

"Wound to his shoulder. He'll be able to stand trial. I didn't get him. The SWAT officer did. Guess I was too worried about hitting you." He raised his voice. "Has anyone been in to take your statements yet?"

Addie and Elizabeth nodded. Elizabeth bit her lip. "Mike, do you think I'll have to go to jail?" Addie staggered back into Mike. His strong hands caught her arms.

"We had a deal worked out with the ADA. Complete immunity for your testimony against Bennett. His kidnapping of you and taking your mother hostage just makes his case worse and yours stronger."

"Is that offer still on the table?" Addie looked over her shoulder at him. His hands dropped to his side. A shiver ran across her shoulders and down her arms.

"I haven't had a chance to talk with the ADA since we arrested him. I'd expect there will be consequences of some sort. Community service, counseling, probation when you'd have to stay off drugs."

"You can count on it." Elizabeth's mouth turned down at one corner.

"If you have your keys, I'll make arrangements to get your car brought up here to you."

"I don't even have my purse or phone. They're back at the theatre."

"Hey, folks, it's about time for Miss Greer to turn in." The same grandmotherly nurse Addie had seen before bustled in. "You can come back in the morning."

"You sure you'll be okay if I leave, Elizabeth?"

"I don't think Ms. Bunson will let you stay, Mom." Her daughter's gaze flicked to the nurse.

"You get some rest at home, Ms. Greer. We'll keep a close eye on her."

Addie glanced at Jeremy, Elizabeth, and finally Mike.

"Come along with me," he told her. "We'll get your keys and purse from the theatre, and then I'll run you home."

"It's okay, Mom. See you tomorrow sometime."

Addie crossed to the bed, leaned over, and kissed her daughter on the forehead. "You remember what I said." Elizabeth nodded and settled back into the bed.

"Night, Sis." Jeremy turned toward the door.

"Thanks, Mike." Elizabeth's voice seemed stronger now than before.

"You're welcome." He settled his hand on the small of Addie's back and ushered her out. Good sign maybe? Or just good western manners? Had Jeremy noticed the gesture, and if he did, what did he think about Mike?

◆ ◆ ◆

Thursday, December 13

Mike turned his truck around and headed to Addie's house. He'd stopped by Pat and Cindy's and she'd given him the what for. Maybe she was right and if he wanted Addie, which he did, he needed to get on with winning her.

It wasn't late. He hoped...well, he didn't know what he

hoped.

He rang the doorbell. Steps echoed on the wood floor. Would Addie open the door?

"Hi, Jeremy. Can I come in?"

"Sure." He swung wide the door.

Mike stepped into the living room. "I—uh—I wanted to see how Elizabeth was doing."

"She's in the kitchen. We're having a snack. Come in."

Mike removed his hat and carried it one hand.

"Mike, hi." Elizabeth sounded stronger than the last time he'd talked with her and didn't look like she'd been through the trauma of a gunshot and a kidnapping.

"You're looking good, Elizabeth." In fact to Mike's mind, she looked better than she had before all this happened. With her Goth-self left behind, she reminded him more of her mother.

He glanced around, expecting to see Addie. "Your mom not here?"

"No, she's at the theatre. Grab a stool. Can Jeremy get you anything?"

Mike swallowed his disappointment but sat at the island with them. "No, thanks."

"I've got to head back to school in just a bit," Jeremy ate a handful of popcorn. "They put performances on hold during all of this, and now we're rehearsing again, and probably a couple of times during the holidays. We'll perform the week we get back to school."

"That's nice."

"Well, it's a tribute to what a great job Jeremy did. The understudy didn't work out so well." Elizabeth sipped what looked like a milkshake.

"Ah, Sis." Jeremy's embarrassment bloomed in his cheeks.

"Well, it's the truth." She smiled at her brother. "Want some popcorn, Mike?"

"No, thanks. Smells good, though. So how's recovery going?"

"Great. I'm at drug rehab-slash-school from nine to five every day. The physical therapist comes and works with me there. And, of course, lots of counseling. I'm doing really good."

Mike nodded. "I can hear that in your voice. And you look healthy."

"Thanks for speaking for me to the ADA, Mike. She came by the hospital the day after the kidnapping, and the deal was pretty much what you spelled out."

"Glad to hear that worked out." Mike had checked to make sure it had, but he didn't need to tell the kids that. "How much longer will you be doing the rehab?"

"For several more weeks. I'll complete the program sometime in January. I can tell you I don't miss a single counseling session. Want to make sure I've got my head screwed on straight. Not taking any chances of relapsing."

"Well that sounds like you already have your head screwed on straight." Mike spun his hat through his hands. He had to ask. "When do you expect your mom?" Was she meeting Harding some place after work?

"I'm not sure. She's fallen pretty far behind, and she's reworking production schedules. I told her I'd babysit until I had to go to rehearsal."

"Hey, now."

Mike chuckled at Elizabeth's tone. She was indeed making progress. He leaned one elbow on the island, his fingers dancing on the granite.

"Something on your mind, Mike? Spit it out. We're almost family with what we've all been through."

Mike studied Elizabeth. He thought he saw an ally in her, but Jeremy... pretty certain not.

"The thing is I like your mother. I like her a lot." Mike swallowed against a knot in his throat. Elizabeth shot her brother a speculative look. "You two are more important to her than anything, so if you have a problem with my interest, you need to speak up. I'm not saying I'll back off, but—"

"I've got a problem." Jeremy rose and stuffed his hands in the pockets of his jeans pockets.

"Jeremy." Elizabeth spoke in a scolding tone. "Give the man a break."

"What's your problem specifically, Jeremy?" Mike wasn't sure he wanted to hear this, but whatever it was, they'd have to work it through.

"Jonathan Harding is interested."

Mike ground his teeth. He was afraid of that. Apparently, the man had been overt enough in his intentions Jeremy had taken note.

"Do you think your mother loves him?" Mike's heart

stopped while he waited for an answer.

"No." Elizabeth spit the word out fast and hard. Mike dragged in a relieved breath.

"He's got lots of money and could provide for her." Jeremy swung a bar stool right then left with his hands, as if it would help him figure out what to say. "She's had money worries ever since she kicked Dad out. I didn't know at first but realized it later. She'd go without stuff she needed to make sure we had what we wanted."

"Doesn't surprise me. She's a good mother."

"She doesn't like Mr. Harding that way, Jer," Elizabeth insisted.

Mike's breath hitched. But then, what did this young girl know of a woman's heart?

"How can you tell?" Jeremy asked the question Mike wanted to ask.

"There's no sizzle when she looks at him, not like when she looks at Mike."

The sharp glance Jeremy shot at Mike almost made him blush, and he couldn't keep from twisting his hat by the brim.

"Huh." Jeremy shrugged. "You got any money?"

"Jeremy. Jeez. Sorry, Mike."

"It's okay, Elizabeth. He's acting the part of the man of the house. Proud of you, Jeremy. I make okay money as a detective. I don't owe anything on the ranch, and I've made some investments. But I'll never have anywhere near the kind of money Harding has. We won't starve, and we'll probably be able to take a vacation once a year, after we get you two through college. You gotta do it in four years though." He cleared his throat, which had clogged up while he spoke.

"Jeremy." Elizabeth glared at her brother. "Don't you want Mom to be happy?"

"Well, yeah, sure."

"Then give Mike your blessing."

She was a very mature young woman. That's exactly what he'd come here for. Would Jeremy bend?

"Let me think about it."

Mike's stomach knotted. Could he buck Jeremy if he said no? Sure as hell would put Addie in a touchy situation. Of course, he could wait until they went off to college. Could he wait? Nah. Now that he realized he wanted her, he wouldn't be happy until they made their relationship official.

What if Elizabeth was wrong and Addie did feel something for Harding? Then he'd back off. Or maybe not. How could Harding make her happy? As crazy as the kitchen deal was, Mike had made Addie happy.

"...on, Jeremy," Elizabeth said. "It's shitty when you want someone special for yourself, and you don't have that."

The kids had continued with their conversation while Mike had zoned out.

"Give them a break. Mom's been alone a long time. We'll be gone soon, and then she'll really be all alone." Elizabeth was a great advocate. Maybe she'd become a lawyer.

"She's got her work." Jeremy remained a hard case.

"That's not enough, Jer. I got hooked on drugs and that awful man because I wanted love."

"If Dad hadn't been such a jackass, you'd have had that love and a man in your life." Jeremy took his sister's hand.

"You know, Jer, that's one of the things the therapy sessions have made me realize. That's his problem. His loss. I get to choose how I react to that. In the past, I haven't chosen very well, but that's changing."

Mike cleared his throat. "I'm impressed, Elizabeth. Very mature. Your mother would be really proud to hear you say that."

"So what are you going to do about Mom, Mike?" Elizabeth sipped her shake.

Mike stood, looked at her and then Jeremy. "I'm going to see if I can win her and you, Jeremy, over. Thanks, Elizabeth. I'll keep working on my brother here. I bet I can bring him around. Mom's your job."

Laughter exploded from Mike's gut. "Thank you, sweetie. That's a job I look forward to tackling." He took a couple of steps out of the kitchen then turned back. "This may take some time, but I'm very persistent."

"Bye, Mike. Good luck." Elizabeth's words trailed behind him.

"Lock up, Jeremy." He threw over his shoulder.

"Got it."

◆ ◆ ◆

Jeremy walked back to the kitchen. He refilled his popcorn bowl from the pot.

"You sure about this, Elizabeth? He's good enough for Mom?" He slid onto the barstool next to her, shoved the bowl her way.

"Yeah, Jeremy, if you'd seen how Mike was at the theatre when Bennett had Mom. He took time to make sure I was okay, even though he was hell-bent to get to her. And before Bennett dragged her off, she told me to tell Mike that she loved him. Afterwards when she found me in her office, she couldn't say enough about how wonderful he'd been."

"Couldn't it have just been the adrenalin flowing from the abduction?"

"Maybe. But her voice changes when she says anything about him. And couldn't you see it in his eyes just now when he spoke of Mom?"

"Yeah." He nodded. "I just didn't want to, I guess." He got up and refilled his iced tea glass. "More?"

"Sure. Thanks."

Jeremy settled next to his sister. "Mike's right. I have seen myself as the man of the house. That's one of the reasons I felt so bad about letting you get in so much trouble. If I'd been a real man, I'd have stopped it."

Elizabeth's hand clasped his arm. "Hey, bud, you're not responsible for me. You're just responsible for decisions you make. I'm responsible for the ones I make—even when they're not good."

She took a swallow of her tea. Jeremy stuffed a few handfuls of popcorn in his mouth and chomped. "Hard to beat fresh popped corn. I could live on it."

Instead of the funny one-liner she'd usually shoot at him

about popcorn, she squeezed his arm again and straightened in her chair.

You okay, Sis?

"Yeah, I owe you an apology, Jeremy."

"What for?"

"All the times I've made digs about you being gay."

"Oh."

"You have been the man of this house, you know. You've been the best big brother a girl could want."

"Jeez, Elizabeth. Shut up. You're gonna make me cry."

She slugged his arm. "Yeah, right. Like that's hard for you. You've always been able to cry at the drop of a hat."

"Not fair. I can't hit you back."

"Okay, okay, I'll give you a rain-check for when I'm well. Then we'll see who's tough."

"Deal." He stuck out his hand. She grabbed it and pulled him in for a hug.

"Jeremy, please consider giving your blessing to Mike and Mom."

CHAPTER SEVENTEEN

Thursday, December 13

Addie's cell pinged a warning. Easy for her to lose track of time when she got lost in a script. The only way to assure stopping was to set a reminder.

"Hey, lady, thought you wanted to leave by six?" Pete Talmadge stuck his head around the door to her office. "Dinner break. Everyone's heading out."

"My alarm just went off. And I'm packing up." She smiled at his teasing.

"Good." He looked around the space. "How do you feel about working in here?"

"It's okay, Pete. I focus on how it provided a safe place for Elizabeth."

"Probably doesn't hurt Harding had it repainted."

"That was very thoughtful of him." She put the last folder in her bag. "I'm so thankful you and Judy are handling the rehearsals for *Millie*, until I'm sure I've got the kids situated."

"Not a problem. Glad to do it." He helped her into her coat.

She nodded, pulled the office door closed, and locked it with the new key.

"Can I ask you something, Addie?" He walked beside her.

"Sure, Pete. Anything."

"Do you have a romantic thing going with Harding?"

She stopped. "What? Why do you ask?"

"Well, you've been seen with him at lots of social functions this fall. Pictures in the paper in Social Notes. He's done lots to make things better for the theatre, painting your office is only one small example. So I wondered."

"I guess that means others on the staff have wondered." She tipped her head to one side, studying her good friend. He nodded. Addie headed for the front of the building. "No. I don't have any romantic feelings for Jonathan. He's a kind man. He wanted someone to accompany him to some fall socials. I did. He likes what we're doing here at the theatre and likes being a part of what I think we are—a family."

A shiver slid down Addie's spine. It did almost every time she walked through the vestibule. Hopefully, in time she'd get past that. For now, she gritted her teeth and ignored the knot in her stomach.

After they went through the doors, Pete turned the lock, and buttoned his jacket. "Thanks for telling me. I'll still the rumor—"

The loud whoosh of a truck speeding into the parking lot made her gasp. Pete actually shoved her behind him. They'd all changed their behavior since the episode with Clay and the SWAT team. Addie's hand tensed on her bag. Pete's muscles bunched.

She let out a breath she hadn't realized she held as relief

and excitement zinged through her system. She straightened and stepped around Pete. "Thanks, but we're okay. It's Detective Riley." Her heart tripped up to a heady rate. She didn't know how to tamp down her reaction to the man. He was here on business. It would just be business. They'd never even talked about what happened in her kitchen. Heat rushed up her neck and across her cheeks.

"Hey, Detective Riley." Pete stuck out his hand to the lawman in his white hat.

"Talmadge." Mike met his hand, but his gaze swung to Addie.

Would he notice her cheeks? Maybe if he did, he'd think the blustery wind was giving her that rosy look.

"Hello, Addie."

"Hi." She wanted to say more, but that's all she could do. Her lungs failed her again.

"If you haven't eaten supper yet, thought we might grab something."

"No, I haven't, but I want to get home and check on the kids."

"They're fine. I just left them."

"Oh."

"Go enjoy a nice supper, Addie." I'll stop by and check on them. Tell them you'll be along after a while."

"Oh." Damn, where was her brain? Hard to believe she made her living in the theatre. She couldn't thread more than two words together. "Thanks, Pete." She glanced at Mike then dropped her gaze. "I'd enjoy dinner, Mike." Well, maybe four words.

A wide grin spread across his face, and he held open the passenger door for her. He nodded to Pete. "I owe you, man." Pete waved a hand and walked to his SUV. "Addie, I'll bring you back here for your car after supper and then follow you home."

She climbed into Mike's truck, scooping her long coat inside. "That's not necessary." He closed her door and walked around to climb in beside her. "I drive home from here late at night all the time. Not that it will be late after supper tonight, but I mean..."

What a ninny.

Addie's gloved hands played with the straps of her purse, until Mike took hold of one in his. She swallowed a couple of times, so loud, he must hear.

"I've missed you, Addie."

She forced a half smile. "Well, we were pretty caught up in...all that nasty business." She couldn't bring herself to say murder. "Where are we going?"

"Nothing fancy. I know you don't want to be out late."

"Jeremy is back in rehearsals, and I try to get home before he leaves so Elizabeth isn't home alone."

"That must be hard for you."

"Yeah. We rescheduled a lot, so I'm there for rehearsals during the day, and Judy, our choreographer, and Pete handle the evenings when we have a show."

He pulled into the parking lot for Timmy's Hamburgers. "See. Nothing fancy."

"And they have food for both of us. Beef hamburger for

you and one of the best veggie burgers anywhere for me."

"Glad you approve." He rested his hand on the small of her back and ushered her into the small mom and pop diner. They headed to the rear of the restaurant. He helped her off with her coat, laid it on one of the chairs, and got her settled. Then he set his hat on a chair and took a seat across from her with his back to the wall.

"Hey, Mike. You haven't been in for a while." A waitress in jeans and a blue T-shirt with "Timmy's" emblazoned across the front in red letters stopped at their table.

"Been busy, Gladys. Can you bring us a couple of draft beers?"

"Your regular?"

"Yup." He turned to Addie. "I know you'd probably prefer wine.

"Nah. Beer is best with hamburgers." Addie relaxed against the straight-backed chair. "You must come here a lot."

"Love a good burger, fries, and a cold beer."

"Do you always have the fries?" Addie loved the diner's onion rings. Her mouth watered at the thought, but if he weren't having them, she wouldn't either. Not that she wanted to assume, but, God, she hoped she got to kiss the man again.

"Yeah, they're crispy and seasoned just right." He shoved the menu toward her. "I don't need this because most of the time I eat the burger. But I hear the catfish is really good, too."

She smiled. "I'm good with the veggie burger." All this casual chit-chat was making her nuts when she wanted to put him in a lip lock.

Gladys brought their beer and took their orders. Addie sipped but knew she needed to go slow. She hadn't eaten anything since a small salad at lunch, and this would go right to her head. "So you said you stopped by to see the kids?"

"Yeah, to see how Elizabeth was doing, and I wanted to talk with them about something. She's doing great, Addie." He leaned forward. "Do you realize how great she's doing?"

Addie leaned forward, too, one hand clasped around the beer mug, the other flat out on the table, her fingers almost dancing. "Yes. It's amazing. I should've put her in counseling a long time ago, but I thought I could compensate for the loss of her father. My friend Kate reminded me on the phone again today that all we can do is the best we can do."

◆ ◆ ◆

Mike lifted the hand with the dancing fingers. "Sweetie, she's right. We do the best we can with the info we have at any given time. Don't blame yourself. Elizabeth's come through a rough patch, and she's going to be fine."

"She told the counselor she thought she might study psychology. At the very least she's volunteered to help younger students."

Mike rubbed his thumb over the back of her hand. She didn't pull away. Good sign. No sense beating around the bush. He had to clarify a few things. Find out where he stood and what part Harding played in all of this. "I never believed you were guilty, you know?"

"You did a good job disguising that fact, Detective."

"If I'd let my true feelings show, I'd have gotten yanked from the case. As it was, I had to keep reassuring Rick my mind was open."

"I'm grateful you were on the case. Thank you for how you protected Elizabeth, made sure she stayed safe."

Gratitude would never be enough from this woman. "It was hard to do. I pictured you as Bennett's hostage and just wanted to rush to you. You'd never have forgiven me if we'd saved you and lost your daughter."

Her mouth flattened into a straight line. "I don't want to think about that possibility."

"Let me ask you something."

"Sure, anything."

"What's your relationship with Jonathan Harding?"

Addie broke the connection with his hand, leaned back in her chair, and crossed her arms over her chest. Unfortunately, for Mike, the action pushed her breasts higher and his groin stirred.

"He's a board member, a financial supporter for the theatre, a good friend. Why do you ask?" Her fingers tightened on her forearms."

"Here you go, folks. Burger for you, Detective, and Veggie Burger for you, ma'am." The waitress served their orders. "You have everything you need?"

"Thanks, Gladys."

"Could you bring some extra mustard, please?"

"They've put it on already, Addie."

"Sorry, but I've found no one ever puts on enough."

"Sure, ma'am, no problem. Be right back."

They sat in total silence. Mike bit into his burger and followed with a gulp of beer. This wasn't going as smoothly as he'd wanted. Addie nibbled on a French fry she'd drowned in ketchup. Apparently, condiments were important to her. There was so much he didn't know about her.

"Here you go." Gladys set a small container of the yellow spread on the table.

"Thanks."

"No problem. You holler if you need anything else." She walked back to the kitchen.

"I asked why you wanted to know about Jonathan?"

Mike lowered his burger and wiped his hands on one of the paper towels the restaurant set on every table. Another gulp of beer. "I wondered if you were more than friends. You've gone to those high-tone socials that Cindy and Pat attend. And he coughed up fifty K in ransom without batting an eye."

She flattened her hands on the table and leaned toward him. "You think I'd have...we'd have...in the kitchen...if I were romantically involved with someone else? My God, Mike. You don't know me at all." She laid her paper towel on the table. "I'd like to go get my car now." She stood, slid into her coat, and slung her purse over her shoulder.

Mike stood. "I'm sorry, Addie. I've done this wrong. I want us to be exclusive. I just didn't want to lay myself out here if you and Harding...I'm sorry. Forgive me?"

She sank onto the chair. "Exclusive?"

Mike sat. "Like in see each other regularly and no one else. Spend the night together. Wake up in the morning together. Wash clothes together. Eat Thanksgiving dinner together with Pat, Cindy, their kids, and yours." Mike leaned forward. "Help me out here. I'm dying. Am I totally on the wrong wavelength about us?"

Zing. His phone. Damn. "Excuse me." He answered. "Shit...God damn...Her mother is with me. We're close...Thanks, Rick." He rose and threw down a twenty and a ten. "Let's go." He grabbed her arm and headed out.

◆ ◆ ◆

Addie stumbled after him, barely able to keep up. "Tell me. Is it one of the kids? Tell me, Mike." Her heart battered against the walls of her chest. He had the truck going before she buckled her seat belt.

"There was a wreck. They were transferring Bennett from the hospital out to the Mansfield jail. The driver and back-up officer were both killed. Bennett... Bennett escaped."

"Oh, my God. He could go after Elizabeth, and she's alone. Jeremy's gone to rehearsal." Addie pulled her cell from her pocket and punched in her daughter's cell. "Pick up, pick up!" She disconnected and tried again. No response. "Mike. Drive faster. Faster. Maybe I can get hold of Pete, get him to stay." She pressed his number. "Pete, did you go by to see the kids... I see... Okay... Thanks. Talk with you later."

"What'd he say?" Mike worried Talmadge could get hurt

if he were there, but Elizabeth wouldn't be alone.

"He's back at the theatre. He forgot some set plans he wanted to work on. Not close enough now to help. He said Elizabeth was fine when he left."

"We've got officers on the way. We just may be closer. When we get there, Addie, I need you to do something that will be difficult."

"Anything. I'll do anything. Just save my daughter."

He turned onto her street. Addie's eyes searched for her house and any signs something was amiss. "Why aren't you stopping? I don't recognize that car in front of the house."

"Just driving past, Addie. When I pull to the curb, I need you to get—"

"What?" Even though she interrupted him, she was proud of how she kept the hysteria boiling in her gut from spilling into her voice.

"Get in the back and get down on the floorboard. I don't see how he can have gotten hold of a gun, or even if he's here. He shouldn't be. But he shouldn't be on the loose."

"Elizabeth didn't answer her phone."

"If bullets fly, I don't want to have to take time to worry about you." He stopped the truck, took her hand, and pulled her to face him. "We have to hurry. Will you do this for me? For Elizabeth?"

Addie nodded. "Be careful. Get Elizabeth and you out safely."

They both opened their doors at the same time. Addie climbed in the back, and they closed them with no sound.

"Please, God, keep them both safe," she whispered and did what Mike had asked, hunkered down on the floorboard. Her blood pounded in her ears so loud anybody near would be able to hear. What was going on? Other vehicles apparently drove up. More cops? Please let it be more cops to help her daughter and Mike stay safe. To keep from screaming, she started counting. *One-one hundred. Two-one hundred....*

♦ ♦ ♦

Mike shut off his anxiety about Addie and focused all his attention on scoping out the situation. He moved up to the side of the front windows. The drapes were open, and the sheers allowed a hazy view inside. His heart dropped to his feet. He swallowed the bile climbing to the back of his throat.

Elizabeth stood facing Bennett, who had his back to the window. A knife, held in his right hand, hung by his side rather than up in a threatening manner. Tears rushing down Elizabeth's face indicated the gravity of the situation. Could he sneak in and take Bennett by surprise? If the cavalry arrived, that would push them into a hostage situation. Mike didn't want to put Elizabeth or Addie through that a second time.

He moved toward the front door. Kicking it down was an option, but not recommended for stealth. A motion to his left caught his attention. He swung toward the movement his weapon held in both hands close to his body.

"Mike." The whispered word came from the darkness.

"Hell, Addie. I told you to stay put."

"I brought my house keys. I didn't know if they could help."

He grabbed the keys, vacillating back and forth between yelling at her and thanking her. He chose neither.

"When your door opens, does the alarm sound?"

"Only if the security is set. I disengaged the feature that made it beep once when anyone opened the door even when the alarm wasn't on. Drove me nuts when the kids were younger, and they came and went so often."

"She must not have had the alarm set then. Otherwise, Bennett wouldn't have been able to get in."

"Oh, God. He's in there. You saw him?" Her fingers dug into his arm.

Hell. He hadn't meant to tell her that. He nodded. "If the door is locked, I'll use your key. Glad you never reinstated the beeping feature of your alarm. I don't want to wait longer. I need you to get back to the truck."

"Please, Mike, I have to stay. I want to help. What if I call her again? It would be a distraction. You could go in then. Maybe he wouldn't notice the noise of the door opening."

"Okay. You stand back there. Addie, I love you." He kissed her once the lips. Wanted more, but no time now. God give him more time with her later.

She blinked like she was coming out of a trance. "I love you, Mike. Now go save my daughter and be safe."

Mike stepped up on the porch, opened the screen. He signaled to Addie. She punched the button on her phone. He heard Elizabeth's phone ringing through the door. On the next ring, he slid the key in and twisted. The lock clicked. He held his breath. Elizabeth's phone blared again. He pushed open the door and stepped in.

"Drop the knife, Bennett. Elizabeth, go out the back way. You're mom's out front." She didn't wait and scrambled out of the living room, making for the back entrance.

"Drop the knife."

Bennett turned toward the sound of sirens in the distance. Blood soaked the bandage covering the wound he received at the theatre.

"Give it up man. It's all over." The front door opened. Mike shot a quick glance over his shoulder afraid it was Addie. In that moment, Bennett screamed from way low in his gut and charged.

Bennett was almost on him

Mike fired at the same time he felt the nick of the blade on his side. Warm blood gushed. Bennett fell on him, dragging him down. Someone pulled the weight off, kicked the knife away.

"You okay, Partner?"

CHAPTER NINETEEN

Thursday, December 13

Mike gritted his teeth against the pain in his side. Fear sent his heart slamming against his chest. Where was Addie? Elizabeth?

"Mike, talk to me." Worry poured through the tone of Rick's words. "Let's find you a more comfortable position."

"Shit."

"Right. As comfortable as you can be with a slice out of your side. Here, let me take a look...We've got to stop that blood flow until the EMTs arrive to fix you up."

Ripping sounds followed by what felt like Rick punching Mike in the stomach. "Shit."

"Only word you know?" Rick's teasing must've indicated he didn't think Mike was too bad off.

"Did you...see Elizabeth outside...with Addie?" Pain dug into him with each gasp he took to get the words out, but he had to know.

"In each other's arms. This must hurt like a bitch, but I think you'll be fine with some stitches."

Red and blue lights flashed on the walls, and other officers arrived.

"Bennett?" Mike asked.

"Dead." Rick spoke in a satisfied tone. "You did good."

A commotion at the front door drew Mike's attention, though he couldn't twist around enough to see what was going on.

"It's my house. I will go in. Mike. Mike! Oh. My God. Rick, is he okay?"

Apparently, Addie had slipped past the officer posted at the front door. Mike forced his eyes open and hoped he pulled his lips into a semblance of a smile. He didn't want to worry her.

Her soft hands touched his cheeks, ran down his shoulders, as if she were making sure he was all in one piece. Then she jerked those wonderful hands away. "Oh, my God, Mike. You're bleeding. What happened?"

Mike's hands grew damp with her tears. Hell, he didn't want to make Addie feel bad.

"I'm okay, Addie. It's just a little knife nick. Please. Don't cry. How about Elizabeth? Did Bennett hurt her?" He prayed no. She'd been through so much already.

"No, she's okay, a little shaken but okay. I left her with a policewoman. Didn't know what things would be like in here."

At that, she scanned the room. He knew the minute her gaze locked on Bennett. Her whole being stilled. "Dear God."

Mike dug deep for the strength to reach toward her face. "Don't look, Addie." Her gaze focused on him. The muscles in her throat worked. She must be struggling against the horror of what had happened in her house. What he'd done in her house. "I'm sorry, Addie."

"What are you talking about? You saved Elizabeth." She leaned over him and kissed his forehead. "I'll be forever grateful."

Grateful, huh? He hoped she was a hell of a lot more than grateful.

"Ma'am. Ma'am?"

"I'm sorry. What?"

"We need you to move out of our way so we can treat the detective."

"Sure. Sorry." She backed away.

"Rick." His partner squatted down next to Mike. "Get hold of Cindy and see if Addie and her kids can go stay with them. They won't be able to stay here for some time. Ow. Take it easy." He glared at the EMT.

"Don't worry, Partner. I'll make sure they have everything they need."

♦ ♦ ♦

Saturday, December 15

Once again, Addie didn't sleep well, despite the beautiful bedrooms Cindy made available. Cindy and Pat's kids let Elizabeth and Jeremy bunk with them. Having only been on the ground floor, Addie found the house much larger than she'd realized. Rick had helped them collect clothes and toiletries they'd need for several days. People crawled all over her house, and she hadn't said goodbye to Mike. The ambulance had whisked him off to the hospital while she packed.

Jeremy nearly freaked when he returned home from rehearsal to see the chaos. He calmed down when it finally sunk in for him—Elizabeth and his mother weren't hurt, and Bennett was dead.

Addie wanted to keep her kids home from school yesterday. She needed them close, but both had chosen to go to school. Elizabeth didn't want to miss her classes or counseling. No one wanted the experiences to push her into a relapse. Jeremy had to attend rehearsal. He had one this afternoon and two next week. They got out Wednesday, December 19 and didn't go back until Wednesday, January 2. They had no rehearsals the week of Christmas. The show would run Thursday through Saturday their first week back in January.

"Hey, Mom. I'm helping Cindy get lunch ready. You want water or iced tea?" Jeremy stuck his head in the den where Addie sat on the sofa with her legs stretched out on an ottoman, with Elizabeth curled up next to her.

"Not very hungry, but if you're waiting on me, iced tea would be lovely."

"Don't give me that not hungry bit." He eyed his sister. "Elizabeth needs to eat. It's your motherly duty to set a good example for her."

"Yeah, Mom. If you don't eat, I don't know if I will." She winked at her brother.

"Okay, okay. I give up."

Jeremy laughed and left them in the den.

"Mom, how long do you think we'll stay here at Cindy and Pat's?"

"I'm not certain, hon. The police should finish with everything today. Then we have to get the company that cleans up after an incident like this to come in. When I contacted them, they said it would be at least two days before they could get over there. You sound like you're not comfortable here?"

"Don't get me wrong, this is a beautiful home, and Peg and Joe have been really generous with their space, but this isn't our home."

Addie squeezed her daughter's hand. "I'm relieved to hear you say that, Elizabeth. I worried whether you'd be okay going back there even after all the cleaning is done"

"I'm not going to let Bennett take our home from us. That'd be letting him win."

Addie hugged her daughter. "Good. You're strong."

"Do you think you'll want to move, after we leave for college?"

"Well, I don't know, Elizabeth. Where would I move?"

"Maybe a ranch?"

Addie turned to find Cindy had stepped into the den. "Didn't mean to overhear, but have you thought about a ranch?"

Her smile spread from ear to ear. A Cheshire cat smile if Addie had ever seen one. Heat rushed to her cheeks. She ignored the feeling and Cindy's question. "Can I help with lunch?"

"No need. Jeremy is a great right hand man, and we're just having sandwiches in the kitchen. You didn't say anything about my ranch question, Addie."

Addie raised one eyebrow, ignored her hostess, and extended a hand to Elizabeth. They climbed from the comfy couch and walked into the bright modern kitchen with a huge bar in the middle and stools along three sides.

"Thanks, Jeremy. Attention, everyone. We've laid out the fixings, but y'all have to make your own."

Clinks and clanks from silverware hitting dishes and jars filled the air. Everyone focused on fixing his meal. Addie didn't see how she could eat the whole sandwich. Her stomach still roiled at what might have happened to Elizabeth night before last and what did happen to Mike. The action didn't affect her children's appetite. Jeremy had two sandwiches, and Elizabeth one and a half.

While Cindy and the kids kept the bulk of the discussion going, Addie contributed a few ums and nods. The door-opening chime signaled Pat's arrival. He kissed Cindy on the cheek. "Got anything left for a hard-working guy?"

"Sure. Sit down. We've just having sandwiches if that'll do."

"As long as you've got potato chips, I'll be fine." He looked around the table. "How're y'all holding up? Mike wanted to know."

"You talked with him?" Cindy asked.

"Went by to see him. He must've gotten all the stubborn genes in our family. Says he ought to be able to go home. I told him the doctors really did know best, and they wanted him to stay another night."

"Did he agree?" Cindy set a plate with two sandwiches and

the requested chips in front of her husband.

"He's so damned hard-headed, Cindy." He took a giant bite and swished it down with iced tea. "Um, good. I brokered a deal between him and his doctor. He wouldn't go out to the ranch, but he could leave the hospital. He's coming here."

Addie felt the rise of the unwanted heat up her cheeks. She was hopeless where Mike was concerned.

"Good for you, Pat. We'll need to do a little switching around."

"Cindy, the kids and I can go to one of those suite hotels. One is located right near the theatre."

"Thanks for offering, but Mike would not be happy if he thought his coming here forced y'all out. Rick was specific with what Mike's instructions were about takin care of y'all before the ambulance drove away with him."

Pat set his sandwich on the plate and pointed a finger at Addie. "If you do anything to mess up my arrangement with Mike, you'll have to deal with me." Pat's tone of voice and unsmiling face indicated the importance of what he was saying. "I don't won't him out at the ranch by himself yet, and he was hell-bent to get out of the hospital."

"Okay, if you're sure." Addie's cell rang. She glanced at it. "Excuse me." She rose and

moved into the living room. "Hey, Pete."

"How're you holding up, Addie? How's Elizabeth?"

"I'm okay. Elizabeth is really doing well, considering what she went through. We're comfortable here at the Rileys'."

"Good to hear that. I've had a number of calls from staff

and board members wondering where we are with the next performances and patrons. The news in the paper has raised questions about whether we'll open the show on time.

"I don't know if we can, Pete."

"If we don't, despite Harding's funds, we'll take a giant financial hit."

Addie's stomach tightened over her conflicting responsibilities. The show. Her kids. Mike. Her fingers clutched the cell. She straightened her shoulders. "Will you check with the cast and crew? If we hit the rehearsals hard for the next week and a half and take only a couple of days off Christmas week, I think we can pull this off."

"Sure. I bet they'll get on-board. I'll talk with Judy first. Anything else I can do to help?"

Addie paced from one end of the large room to the other. "No. Thanks so much, Pete. I'll stop by the theatre Sunday to make sure we're all ready to go on Monday morning."

"Good girl."

Addie dropped the phone into her pocket as she returned to the kitchen. "Sorry. That was Pete checking on us." Addie rested her hands on Elizabeth's shoulders. "And asking about the show. TV and newspaper coverage is spreading the word about what happened."

Addie picked up her plate and carried it to the sink.

"Jeremy and I'll get this." Elizabeth rose and gathered up plates. "You guys get out of here.

"Like the sound of that. You get this kind of treatment at

home, Addie? You'll have to give me pointers."

"I've got exceptional children." Addie kissed both of them before her cell rang. Her shoulders hiked up with tension. "It's your father." She left them in the kitchen and made for the living room.

"Hello…Hold on a minute, Jud. Don't shout."

"Why shouldn't I shout when I hear you've involved my kids in another dangerous situation, letting some maniac in your crazy business kidnap my daughter?"

Addie could hardly contain her anger. Now he claimed Elizabeth, after years of neglect. Just so he could dig at his ex-wife. She should've called him, but he didn't react well when she called him after the first incident.

"Do you want to know how she is?"

Silence on the other end. "Sure." He shoved the word through a tight jaw. Addie recognized the tone.

"She's doing okay. Her counselor at the rehab center will stop by this afternoon. Jeremy's going to rehearsal. They're doing the show three more times the first week of January. Since you didn't get to see him before, maybe you could come one of those three times."

"Well, I—"

"Jud, if you once saw him in a show, you'd understand him better. He was born to follow this path."

"Maybe. I've got to go. Try to keep our kids out of trouble." The line went dead.

"Arrghh." It was all Addie could do not to pitch the cell across the room. Seeing it crack into a million pieces would help lower her blood pressure, which judging from the throbbing in her temples, must be off the charts. How dare he claim them now as "our" kids? What kind of father had he been even when they were together as a family, much less since the divorce? She pried her fingers off the cell and set it on the coffee table. She dropped onto the sofa and rested her head in her hands. God, she was exhausted.

She jerked at a touch on each shoulder and glanced up.

"You okay?" Jeremy stood on one side.

"Don't let him get to you, Mom." Elizabeth stood on the other.

Addie took a hand of each and drew them down beside her. "I thought I could make up for the loss of your father. I've failed miserably, especially with you, Elizabeth. I'm so sorry."

"Don't beat up on yourself that way, Mom. Yeah, I've made some bad choices, but not because of anything you did. Even in the best of homes, teenage girls and their moms fight. I was just slower to get to it than most. By then I was so mad at Dad and had no way to hit out at him, so I took it out on you."

"Wow, when did my sister get so smart?" Jeremy reached across Addie and took his sister's hand.

"We do a lot of thinking and talking in rehab, and Mom was generous with the second chances she gave me."

"Thanks, sweetie." Addie kissed Elizabeth on the cheek. Warmth filled her soul when her daughter didn't pull away.

"Guys, this is about as much of this touchy-feely stuff as I can stand, and I need to go to rehearsal." Jeremy dropped his mother and sister's hands and rose. "You okay with that?"

"Sure. I need to get back to the theatre tomorrow and rehearsals on Monday, but we'll be off Christmas Day and the next. I'll arrange to be off the Saturday night of *The Music Man.*"

"But, Mom, that's your first Saturday night of *Millie.*"

"Yeah. Judy will handle the pre-show speech."

"Thanks. Maybe if things are still going well for you, Elizabeth, we could get you into rehearsals, and you could perform in those three shows." He looked at her, his eyebrows raised in question.

"I'd like to do that, Jer. I'll talk with the counselor when I see her today."

CHAPTER TWENTY

Saturday, January 5

Mike's fingers drummed a nervous rhythm on his office desk. The last several weeks had rushed by as if on a racehorse at full gallop. He'd been swamped in paperwork, a murder too close to the mayor's residence for anyone's comfort, Christmas celebrations, and late nights, resulting in no time alone with Addie. He'd agreed to go with her to see Jeremy's show tonight in exchange for her coming out to have an early supper at his ranch.

He hoped she liked where he lived. He needed her to like it. His hand fingered the box in his pocket. He hoped she liked what he'd chosen. Was he rushing this? They'd only made love that one wild, crazy time in her kitchen. Yet he couldn't get the taste of her out of his mind, his body, his heart.

"Hey, thought you were taking off early today."

Mike jumped. "Yeah, Rick. Taking Addie out to see the ranch before we go to see Jeremy in *The Music Man.*"

"A musical, right?"

Mike refrained from saying "Duh!" and accepted Rick was about to make fun of him.

Rick shook his head. "What we do for the women we

love. Hope you get lucky." He waved a hand. "See you Monday."

Mike hoped he did too. Not just to get Addie in his bed tonight, but in his life for good.

♦ ♦ ♦

"Follow up visit with the doctor today and he said I'm as good as new." Mike turned down the long road to his ranch.

"That's wonderful. How much farther is it to your house?"

"Not long. I'm ten minutes from the highway."

"It didn't take but fifteen minutes to get to this turnoff. Faster than I'd expected."

"Yeah, I'm twenty-five minutes from downtown Fort Worth." Mike turned into the driveway leading to the long, low ranch house. His stomach gripped. What would she think? It had always been home. When Mike looked at the place, great family memories colored every glance. He shut off the engine. "Here we are." He hopped out and helped Addie climb down from his truck. She stood there a moment, taking it all in.

"It's larger than I expected and has a certain old world charm."

"Come in." Mike ushered her through the front door, which opened right into the oversized living room. The fireplace was stacked with wood. "Let me take your coat." He draped it over the back of the sofa and put his leather jacket on top. "It'll just take a minute to get this fire going." The firewood cracked, popped and the orange-red flame burst, spreading quickly.

"Nice job." Addie smiled at him.

"Let me show you this." He took her arm and steered her around to the large, open kitchen. Filled with every up-to-the-minute gadget, it made her gasp.

She stared then looked at him for a silent minute. "You never told me you'd been married." Addie's face had crinkled into a frown. She nibbled on one nail.

Mike almost laughed. Hard not to miss the sound of jealousy in her voice. He pulled her to him and kissed her. "Cindy."

"Oh. Ohhhh. She has great style." She kissed him back.

Some moments later, with a hard-on pressing against the zipper of his jeans, Mike stepped back. "I want you to see the rest of the place. If I kiss you anymore, you won't get to."

"Well, that might not be all bad."

"You're a tease."

"Only if I don't follow through."

Mike straightened up and made a decision. "Let's take a look at the bedroom first then." His arm around his woman, he led her down the hallway into the large room he'd converted from two smaller ones, adding a large master bath and closet. Would Addie be impressed?

"Oh, my." Addie sighed after he flung open the door. "Oh, Mike, this is lovely. You had help with this?"

"Yeah." He chuckled at her expression of awe. "Can't lie to you. Like the kitchen, Cindy worked with a decorator, and all I had to do was approve."

Addie walked into the center of the room, made a 360-degree turn as she inspected his accomplishment.

Mike drank in the sight of her in his bedroom. Hard to believe she was real. That she was here with him. That he was about to make love to her in his bed. His heartbeat banged against the walls of his chest as he walked toward her. He couldn't wait.

"Oh." Addie jumped.

While she'd been enthralled with the room, he'd moved to within six inches of her. "Didn't mean to startle you, but I like being close to you." His hand snaked out and fingered one of the long dark curls that fell across her breast, tantalizingly near his hand. With his index finger, he outlined her eyebrows, slid down her nose, paused on her lips.

Addie sucked in a breath, and Mike drew her close, lowering his head for another of those heart-stopping kisses. His lips brushed hers. His tongue sought each corner then slid into her mouth. Her hands skimmed through his hair and down his back to his waist. "I want to touch you, but I'm afraid I'll hurt you."

"I'm tough. I can take it. Please, touch my chest and anything you'd like," he whispered into her ear. She melted against him. His erection throbbed to be inside of her. He tore the covers from the bed like he wanted to do with her clothes. A practical side stopped him. They had places to go later. He backed her toward the bed and began his attack on the buttons of the dress running all the way down to the hem. He'd never make it that far. Their hands tangled as she unbuttoned his shirt.

Mike drew in a long sigh. His eyes wandered across a beige lace bra, which clasped Addie's breast the way his hands itched to. She slid the dress off her shoulders and let it pool at her feet. He helped her balance while she stepped out of it. He leaned down, picked up the silky material, and draped it over a large wingback chair. She had to put it back on when they went to the musical.

Hell. The musical. He wanted to stay here for the whole night, for next week, next month. His heart pounded against his chest. Was she going to agree to that?

He yanked his T-shirt over his head. Addie's gaze was followed immediately by her hand almost touching the healing wound.

"Oh, Mike, I'm so sorry. It's my fault Bennett stabbed you."

"No, hon, it was mine. I shouldn't have taken my eyes off him for even a moment. And it's Bennett's fault." He tipped her head up so he could meet her gaze. "You know that. Whether I have feelings for you or not, I'd have been there trying to rescue Elizabeth. It's what cops do."

She glanced away; her eyebrows drawn down.

"If it's too ugly, I can put my T-shirt on again."

"Don't you dare." Addie slithered on to the bed and pulled him along with her.

He resisted long enough to kick off his boots and pull a condom from his pocket. He laid it on the side table and then yanked down his jeans.

♦ ♦ ♦

Mike's body was hot to her touch, and had her motors not already been zooming along at quite a rate, the feel of him pressed against her would have done it. He brought to mind all those male underwear models, only Mike had layers and depths she'd only begun to uncover. Her fingers skipped along all the planes and contours of his face and body.

She discovered more scars. He could tell her about them another time. Now she focused on pleasuring this man. Her fingers traced the length of his penis still covered by his boxers. So long, but she remembered being able to accommodate him. Her hand tightened reflexively at the idea of him pulsing inside of her. Not just her hand pulsed, her insides clenched in anticipation.

Mike unhooked her bra and slid it off. His mouth, suckling her breasts one after the other, heated the fires within her, causing her to arch against his erection. He kissed a path down to her center. Tugged her panties off. His tongue entered her then his fingers slid in and out and all around, driving her nearly to climax. Desire surged through her. She tugged at his boxers and got them off with his help. He pulled the condom from the top of the table. She helped put it on.

His body slid up hers and she opened her legs wider for him.

"Look at me."

She zeroed in on his eyes.

"I love you, Addison Greer." He plunged into to her.

Her legs circled his middle and drew him in more. Her heart exploded with joy, and her core pulsed at a faster and faster rate as he entered and withdrew with growing intensity. His breathing matched hers.

"Oh, Mike, I love you with all my heart." Her climax hit with blinding lights and fireworks, sending her spiraling off into outer space, beautiful with its contrasts of darkness studded with sparks of brilliance.

"Addie!" Mike yelled as he exploded within her, sending tremors through her soul.

Later, after they'd both spiraled down, she lay with her head on his shoulder. Their arms and legs entwined; she couldn't stop smiling. Mike loved her. This was the second time he'd told her. She was over the moon happy. Like a teenager, she wanted to shout to everyone how lucky she was to have this man in her life.

How exactly he'd be in her life, she wasn't sure. Her kids were still at home. She didn't feel comfortable having him sleep at her house when they were there. How often would they get a repeat of this evening?

Evening. Damn. They had to get moving. She couldn't miss Jeremy's musical. And Elizabeth was performing too.

"You're thinking too much. I can hear the wheels turning." Mike's voice, muffled against her hair, set kindling to her desire.

"We've got to get going, Mike."

"I know." He looked at the bedside clock. "Not even time for a quickie." He nuzzled behind her ear. "I like causing those chill bumps."

"Ooh, I like you doing that too, but not now."

He patted her rear. "I know. Let's get going." He shifted her off to the side, hopped up, and pulled his pants on, while she stepped into her undies and pulled up the dress.

She'd gotten all the buttons done and was searching for her shoes when he said, "Oh, I almost forgot." Something in Mike's light but hesitant tone made her spin around toward him. He was kneeling and had a box extended in his right hand.

"Addison Greer, will you marry me?"

Chill bumps ran down her arms and legs. Her hands flew in front of her mouth. "Oh, my," she gasped. Tears filled her eyes. She walked to him and knelt down. "Are you sure?"

"Oh, yeah. We'll have issues, Addie. People do, but I can't think of anyone I'd rather work out those issues with than you."

"Then yes, I'll marry you." Addie said the words, though her lips trembled, and her heart threatened to explode with happiness.

"You haven't even looked in the box."

"I don't need to. Whatever's in there, I'll proudly wear."

◆ ◆ ◆

The first part of the show had gone well as far as Mike could tell. Addie certainly seemed pleased with both her children's performances. It was half-time at the musical. Content to remain in their own world, they hadn't walked out to the theatre vestibule. Voices buzzed around them. He shifted his tall body in the uncomfortable seats and asked a question he dreaded but needed to meet head on. "What about Jeremy and Elizabeth?"

She smiled at him. "I think they'll be okay. Oddly, Elizabeth maybe more than Jeremy. She said something the other day about appreciating the second chances I'd given her."

"So she thinks you deserve another chance, too."

"I sure hope so. Jeremy will go along when he sees how happy you make me."

Mike picked up Addie's left hand, now blazing with his mother's engagement ring, and placed his arm around her shoulder, drawing her close. He whispered in her ear. "I'm glad I've given this musical thing a second chance. I think I can get used to them. As long, Addie, as you promise to come to the rodeo with me."

"It's been a long time since I've attended one of those, Mike. I'm thinking they probably deserve a second chance, too."

The lights dimmed and the conductor struck up the orchestra.

"Looks like the second act is about to start. You ready?" Mike glanced at her. Could she see in his eyes how much he loved her?

"Yes, but even more ready to start *our* second act." Addie kissed the back of his hand and turned her eyes to the stage.

The End

About the Author

As a retired elementary school principal, former school board member, and theatre arts teacher, I live in Texas with my supportive lawyer husband where I write Romance, Suspense, and Second Chances. Experience Required. Our two daughters presented us with three delightful grandchildren who live nearby. Charley, a Chihuahua/Jack Russell Terrier mix adopted us several years ago.

All of my eight books (Seasoned Romances) are about Texas women in their forties and fifties with a theme of second chances. Finding a new life while danger threatens is challenging but makes the win all the more worthwhile. My four-part series is titled The Second Chances Series, because I believe in Happily Ever Afters. My husband picked up a plaque for me on one of our several trips to Maine that states my philosophy exactly. *Everything will be all right in the end. If it's not all right, it's not the end.*

I'm a member of Romance Writers of America, North Texas RWA, Texas Authors, Word By Word Blog and have my own weekly blog and monthly newsletter. My books can be found on all venues. Print books are also available.

Please sign up for my **Newsletter** and **Blog** and check out my **Website** where you can find links to all my books.

Contact me at marsha@marsharwest.com and follow me on these social media sites.

Facebook   Twitter   Word By Word   Pinterest
Instagram

I'd appreciate a review and would love to hear from you.

Marsha

Other Books by Marsha R West

in The Second Chances Series

Act of Trust. Book 2

Act of Betrayal, Book 3

Act of Survival, Book 4

Stand Alone Titles

Vermont Escape

Truth Be Told

The Theatre

Tainted

ACT OF TRUST Second Chances Series, Book 2

Chapter One

6:30 pm, Sunday, August 18

"Who do you know in Maine?"

Kate Thompson raised an eyebrow at her friend, redheaded Devon Moore who'd driven over from Dallas. The two legal size envelopes in her hand snapped as Devon fanned them against each other.

"You haven't opened either one, Kate. This says, James Donavan, Esquire. Griffin Harbor, Maine. Are you keeping secrets, my friend?"

"Oh, foot. I keep forgetting. I got one last week and then that one today." She nibbled at a cuticle on her thumb.

"You realize the esquire means he's a lawyer, right?" Devon said.

"Think I ought to open them, huh?"

"Of course."

Kate exhaled a puff of frustration. It was one thing to deal with a lawyer in a real estate transaction. She picked at the thumb cuticle on her left hand again. Grabbed a tissue to stop the bleeding. Other than with her real estate business, she'd just as soon keep her distance from lawyers. She'd had enough of them when settling her husband's estate. Time to change the subject. "Where do you want to go for dinner?"

"Anything's fine with me. You or Addie pick. You know the places here in Fort Worth better than I do. Too bad Kim couldn't get away from Wichita Falls for a quick visit."

"Yeah. She had some family obligation." She grinned. "You know I'll pick Italian if it's up to me."

Devon handed over an envelope. "Open. You'll have to stop picking then."

Despite all the products from her make-up company that Devon had given her over the years, Kate still picked at her cuticles.

"Okay, okay," she lowered the drop leaf on the hall desk and lifted out an old letter opener that had been her grandfather's. She slid the long silver blade across the edge of the envelope, the ripping sound grating on her ears. Then she pulled out the one-page missive and scanned the words. "Oh, my goodness."

"What's the matter?"

"John's Aunt Liddy died."

"I don't remember he had an aunt. Wait, I think I hear a car." Devon turned toward the front window and separated the edges of the drapes. "It's Addie's pulling into the driveway." A quick honk confirmed her words. "Bring those with you. We'll talk about it at dinner."

Kate didn't know if there was anything to talk about, but she pushed the envelopes inside her purse that was large enough to carry her laptop when she needed to work away from the house or office. Tonight she left the computer at home. The lightness of the bag fit her mood because she and two of her best friends were having dinner together.

Addie drove them to a restaurant that served Italian three nights a week. Their favorite Italian restaurant had closed, but the people who owned it also owned this German spot, so the two restaurants in effect merged.

"Don't you think this is a bit odd?" Devon put her napkin in her lap and looked around at the oompah decorations.

"Yeah, but I want to be supportive of the Adolpho family." Addie said. She sipped her Sauvignon Blanc. Tell me more about this business with the Maine lawyer, Kate."

Kate pulled the letters from her purse, her fingers trembling ever so slightly. She hadn't heard from Aunt Liddy in several years. The woman had stopped sending Christmas cards, and that had been their main way of communicating. Where she lived on the Maine coast, the phones were iffy, and she hadn't taken up the internet habit.

"John's Aunt Liddy must've been in her 90's. She had a nice long life. Right after John and I got engaged, he took me to Griffin Harbor once. I recall it being the back of beyond. I flew from Fort Worth, and he drove from New York to meet me in Boston. Still we had an all-afternoon drive. The house sat on a ridge of land overlooking some waterway. I don't remember which one now, but it ran into the Atlantic. Lovely view, but no other houses around. God-awful remote."

"I'm sorry, Kate." Addie reached across and squeezed Kate's hand, and Kate nodded a thank you.

"Doesn't sound like a place I'd like to be." Devon shuddered.

Kate smiled at her gorgeous redheaded friend. The consummate city girl drew attention anywhere she went. When they were teenagers at camp, Devon was the only one of the four friends to wear make-up. It wasn't her favorite place, but both her parents worked and needed to stash her where she'd be safe. They knew the camp owners from college.

Addie hadn't been wild about the place either. She returned each summer to be with her three friends. The outdoors stuff challenged her, but she loved the skits. Not surprising she'd gone into theatre.

"I don't know, Devon." Addie sipped her clear white wine. "Maine is a beautiful state. I made a quick visit there when I was in New York before marrying the kids' father."

Kate's middle clenched when she thought of the mess Addie had gone through with her first husband. How he'd nearly destroyed their daughter. The new gold band sparkling on the ring finger of Addie's left hand a testament to how people could find a happily ever after.

That was not for Kate though. Or rather, she'd already experienced her happily ever after. The *ever after* part had just been short and ended in grisly abruptness.

"Have you ladies decided what you'd like to have this evening? Do I need to repeat the specials?" The young server smiled at the three women.

Kate shook off the malaise and straightened in her chair. "I'll have the spinach cannelloni and the house salad."

"Do you want separate checks?"

"Please," Devon spoke before the others.

Kate cut her gaze toward her always perfectly put together friend. Frequently they just asked for one check and split it between them, not worrying who paid more than their fair share. In the long-run, they figured it worked out. This was the third time in recent months Devon had asked for separate checks. She hadn't ordered her usual champagne, settling for the Sauvignon Blanc Addie drank. Devon hadn't mentioned having financial problems. Well, she couldn't be. Her cosmetics company was successful and had been from almost the beginning.

The server moved off after promising to bring the salads soon. Apparently, the other two women had ordered while Kate wool-gathered.

"Well, it was nice of the lawyer to let you know about John's aunt." Devon dipped a piece of bread into the seasoned oil in the center of the table draped with a traditional white and red checked cloth.

Kate sighed, took another sip of her Merlot. "Guess I'd better read the rest of the letter." She lifted the most recent envelope from her purse and removed the sheet. Sounds from the other diners and wait staff swirled around the words she read. She dropped the letter on the table and looked at Addie and then Devon. "Aunt Liddy left the old house and surrounding land to me."

"Oh, fun. A cabin in the Maine woods." Devon's eyebrows shot up, and her eyes almost rolled. Her facial expression and tone of voice suggesting this was not something she'd appreciate.

The waiter set their salads before them. This land business could have nothing to do with her. Kate picked up her fork and dug in. "Hmm. Yummy."

"When are you going to go look at it?" Addie doused her salad in pepper, and then she pulled off a piece of bread from the communal loaf in the center of the table. "Maybe one of us could go with you." She glanced at Devon who shrugged.

Kate dropped her fork and coughed on the last bite of tangy tomato. Finally, she found her voice. "I don't have to look at it again. I'm going to sell the property. It's way out in the boonies. The house wasn't in good shape when John and I went there all those years ago. It must be a wreck now. "Let's just enjoy our salads. Tell us how rehearsals are going, Addie." Kate sighed as the discussion moved to Addie's challenges with the current show. No point continuing the discussion about the old house. An old house in Maine.

They'd finished their salads by the time the server approached and placed their orders in front of them. "Can I get you anything else?" He smiled at Devon and Addie as if he wanted to pay tribute to their beauty. Addie a dark brunette and Devon a redhead. When Kim, also brunette, joined them, they'd been known to turn heads. Each was striking in her own way, and Kate always considered herself the lesser of the lights she hung with. Her dishwasher blonde hair and brown eyes faded in comparison to her friends' more dramatic looks.

"Bring more of this yummy bread, would you please?" Devon spoke before the others. He left quickly to do as she requested. "I like this place." She looked around. "Odd though it may be. We can't come too often, though. This yummy bread is going right to my hips." They all laughed.

Kate cut off a small bite of her steaming pasta stuffed

with fresh spinach and three types of cheese, blew on it a couple of times before putting the fork in her mouth. Nothing worse than bubbling cheese scalding the roof of her mouth. Then she wouldn't be able to enjoy any of the meal.

"You know, Kate, you haven't taken any kind of a vacation since you lost your parents. Maybe this would be a good opportunity." Addie paused to sip her wine. "I know you don't like to fly, but I think we could get you a couple of knock out pills. You'd be there before you know it."

"What?" Kate frowned at Addie. Had she gone back to the idea of Kate going to Maine? What in the world was she thinking? Kate's breathing hitched at the mere idea of getting on a plane.

"But if that's just not an option, what about driving up there?" Addie continued as if Kate hadn't spoken. "Take a couple of weeks. Stop along the way. You'd see some beautiful scenery and historic sights."

"Well, I—"

"I think Addie's right, Kate." Devon stopped eating and leaned across the table. "You've worked constantly since you moved back to Fort Worth after John's death. Except for our get-togethers, have you made any big trips?"

"No, but I was busy working, raising Blair, and later taking care of Mom and Dad. Didn't leave much time for fun and games."

"That's our point, hon." Addie squeezed Kate's hand again. "You need a little, to use your phrase, fun and games in your life. At least think about it, okay?"

◆ ◆ ◆

Monday, August 26

Kate dragged herself up the stairs to her house after her brisk morning walk. Her feet and calf muscles burned. Her hand trembled with the effort to unlock the door. She walked through the living room to stop the jangling of the landline in the kitchen. She hurried to pick up.

"Ms. Thompson?"

"Yes?" Kate grabbed a kitchen towel to blot the sweat from her face. August in Texas. Mind-searing heat.

"Ms. Thompson, my name is Jim Donovan."

Kate stuck a glass under the appropriate spouts on her refrigerator, desperate for ice water. The clinking sounds comforting. Why'd that name sound familiar? She took a couple of gulps.

"Ms. Thompson, are you still there?"

The person spoke with a very deep voice and something she'd call a Yankee accent.

"Yes, sorry. Just got in from a walk. Why are you calling?" Kate snapped off a dry leaf from the violet sitting in the window. Past time to water the plants. She leaned against the kitchen counter, giving her trembling legs a break.

"Ms. Thompson, did you get my letters telling you about the death of your aunt Liddy Oliver Thompson?"

Oh, that Jim Donovan. He sounded a bit impatient.

"Yes, I got the letters. Mr. Donovan. I mailed a response. I take it that you haven't received anything from me, yet?" She took another sip of the ice water, her heart rate slowing.

"No, I haven't received your letter. Can you tell me when you'll come up here to claim the property?"

"I'm not going to claim the property, Mr. Donavan. I'm going to sell it to the highest bidder. I can't imagine its worth very much, but I don't need or want to own property in the Maine boonies."

"Your aunt's house sits on a valuable strip of land, Ms. Thompson."

"Can you recommend a good real estate agent? I'm not licensed in Maine or I could handle the process myself."

"Ms. Thompson, I represented Liddy for many years and especially where this property was concerned. She didn't want it to fall into the hands of any developers. Especially one who has a history of concreting over some of the most beautiful land in the state."

His tone indicated what he'd like to do to those developers, and it wasn't pretty. Well, not her problem. "I'm sorry. I'm just not interested. If you can't recommend an agent, I'll find one myself. I really need to let you go now, or I'm going to be late to work. Thanks for calling." Kate hung up the receiver and let out a long breath.

Goodness, but the man was persistent. She'd talk with Pam and Jerry at work. They'd have ideas of someone who could represent her interests. Her interests, which didn't include owning a piece of Maine.

◆ ◆ ◆

"Damned Texan." Jim Donovan resisted the urge to throw his cell across the room. "I thought they were big on land down there."

A quick knock was followed by Tom Jenson, Jim's best friend and owner of The Lobster Pot restaurant, sticking his head around the door before he stepped into the room that Jim used as a home office when he was in Griffin Harbor.

"Is that a sack of muffins from the Center Café I see in your hand?"

"Ahya." A big smile spread across the man's weather wrinkled face.

"Well, get in here then. I'll trade you a cup of coffee." Jim rose and strode to the sideboard where he kept a pot on all day long. "Did you bring one of those carrot cake muffins?"

"Of course." Tom pulled out a napkin and laid the cake-like pastry on it. "So what has you so bent out of shape? As I came through the door your voice sounded like you'd like to beat someone over the head." He slouched into the chair in front of the desk.

"Liddy Thompson's niece wants to sell the family land." Jim set a cup of coffee in front of his friend then ran a hand through his hair overdue for a cut. He hated to take the time.

"Not to the Conservancy, I take it. That's lousy. Hard to find a prettier view than Liddy's. What have you done to convince the niece to change her mind?"

"Sent two letters. Didn't hear anything, so I called."

"And?"

"Says she's selling. Said it was too far out in," Jim finger quoted, "the 'boonies' is the word I believe she used."

"Well, it's not in town, but it's not out in the wilds either. Sounds like she doesn't know what she's talking about." Tom sipped his coffee.

"The woman asked if I could recommend a real estate agent." Jim slumped into the chair next to Tom and proceeded to crumble the muffin into pieces. "As if I'd do anything to help her sell. Liddy loved the land. I've got to find a way to get through to the niece."

Tom glanced at his watch before swallowing the first half of his muffin. "Well, I gotta get outa here. Need to check on the catch of the day. I'm sure you'll think of something. You usually get what you want."

"Not always." He hadn't been able to stop his ex from giving the chunk of Donavan land she'd received in the divorce to the developer she'd had an affair with. The developer who plowed up the trees and made a parking lot for his condo units. Jim's stomach churned at how he'd let down his family. Oh, they still had considerable property but nothing with the incredible timber that jerk had destroyed.

He glanced at Tom. "You ever miss those early morning trips checking your lobster traps?"

"What?" Tom swallowed the last of the coffee, washing down the muffin. "Nah. Why would I miss such back-breaking hard work, freezing my balls off?" He headed toward the door then paused and looked over his shoulder. "Sometimes. Crazy, huh? See yah."

Had his high school buddy found some solace in running

his family's restaurant? After the injury he'd received in the bar fight with a lobsterman from another town—well, he had to be glad he was able to get around as well as he did.

Jim dusted the crumbs from his fingers into a napkin and threw it into the trash. Now he had to figure out what to do about Katherine Thompson. Tom seemed to think Jim could come up with something. He damn sure wasn't letting the woman sell Liddy's land, at least not without a hell of a fight.

◆ ◆ ◆

Monday, September 2

Blair Thompson's cell chirped the distinctive sound she'd selected for her mother, who concerned Blair more than she liked to let on. One of the reasons she'd set up the separate sound. She didn't want to take a chance on missing a call from her.

"Hey, Mom."

"Happy Labor Day, Blair." Her mother's soft Texas twang came through in a nice reminder of what she'd once considered home. Though Blair had lived most of her life in Fort Worth, she'd been born in New York, and now she thought of the Big Apple more as home than she did Fort Worth. Best not to share that with her mother who had never gotten past the tragic events of 9/11.

"How are you celebrating? Lying around reading a good book?" Her mother shared Blair's love of reading and couldn't think of a better way to spend a holiday.

"No. While everyone at work has the day off, I don't think many of us are taking it. There's a lot still to do before the memorial service on the eleventh, and we're also continuing to push on preparations for the opening of the museum."

Blair paused, giving her mother a chance to deal with the emotions her words would dredge up. Generally, she tried to avoid talking about her job. Awkward, but less painful for her mother. "What are you doing today, Mom?"

"I'm working, too. We're having specials for Labor Day. I've got two open houses. I wasn't sure I could convince the owners to lower their prices, but they agreed. We sure weren't having any luck with what they wanted."

Her voice had squeaked just a bit at the beginning but grew stronger as she talked about work, which she loved. "I'm going to Addie and Mike's for a cookout later on."

"That will be fun. I love her husband's small ranch. I'll probably just grab a hot dog from one of the street vendors and then crash early with that book you mentioned."

Laughter twinkled through the airways. Everyone said what a contagious laugh her mother had, though everyone also said they didn't hear it enough.

"I want you to think about coming up for the memorial service. It would mean a lot to me for you to be here."

Silence greeted Blair's request. Not surprising. The trip they made when she'd been seventeen nearly destroyed her mother. She'd returned to visiting her counselor for a time afterwards.

"I'll think about it, Blair."

"Thanks." That was better than usual when her mother out and out refused. Blair sighed. She'd lost her father, and her mother lost her husband on that dreadful day all those years ago. Everyone had to deal with that loss as best as each could and in her own way. "Good luck with your houses and eat some barbecue for me."

"Thanks, sweetie. You can count on that."

Blair disconnected and prayed again for something or someone to blast her mother out of the cocoon of work in which she'd wrapped herself.

Blurb for Act of Trust, Book 2, The Second Chances Series

A widow since 9/11 and a mother of grown daughter, Kate Thompson wants to keep her and her daughter safe, but the inheritance of land in Maine pushes her out of her comfort zone in Texas and into the arms of a Maine lawyer and environmentalist. Jim Donovan wants to protect Aunt Liddy's land and keep it from falling into the hands of the developers, but first he has to convince Kate Thompson she should hold on to the family land when she doesn't even want to go look at it. However, he's unprepared for the attraction each feels for the other but denies exists.

Will they be able to settle the land deal before anyone else is killed or they break each other's hearts?

Thanks for reading, and I hope you'll come along to meet all four of the friends: Addie, Kate, Devon, and Kim. Marsha

www.ingramcontent.com/pod-product-compliance
Lightning Source LLC
Chambersburg PA
CBHW062008170626
46813CB00001B/80